Guns of Seneca 6

Bernard Schaffer

CONTENTS

1. Cowboys

On the night Jem Clayton came into the world, his mother grabbed Royce Halladay by the collar and said, "You better get this thing out of me."

Doctor Halladay lowered his hands and made ready to catch. "All that is required is for you to push, my dear."

One great heave and a few choice words brought Jem sliding into existence. The way his father told it, Jem didn't even cry when Doc Halladay slapped him on the backside. He just looked at the doctor real mean and asked Sam if he could borrow a pistol.

Sheriff Sam Clayton told that story with a steady smile and voice, but always went quiet when it was finished. Claire, Jem's little sister, always wanted him to go on, but no matter how much she begged, Sam wouldn't budge. It was like he needed to go into himself a little and look at the moons above, or stare deep into the mountains of Coramide Canyon. It was like he could see things from the past that could not bear to be looked away from or they might go away and never come back.

Sam always said Jem had been born exactly one minute after midnight. On his twelfth birthday, Jem rolled over and picked up a brass watch from his nightstand. He held it up to the pale light and said, "There it is."

Rumbling in the meadow made Jem forget the watch and sit up. Hooves trampled through their front yard and someone barked, "Go get him."

A fist hammered their front door. The hallway light came on and Jem watched Sam storm past his bedroom door, saying, "There had better be one hell of a good goddamn reason for all this racket."

"It's a raid, sir. Savages."

Jem leapt to his feet and ran to the living room, nearly colliding with Sam in the hallway. Sam pushed Jem out of the way and continued back to his room. "I'm coming with you," Jem said.

"Like hell you are. Get back in bed. I don't have time to tell you twice." Sam spun the dials on his safe's thick metal door and yanked it open. He grabbed his gun belt and strapped it around his waist then removed both six-shot Colt Defenders from the shelf and fixed them into the holsters on either hip. Sam scanned the rifles in his cabinet and selected a military-grade anti-personnel rifle. "I said to get back in bed."

"I've got a rifle too! I want to help."

Sam hurried into his boots. "Get back in your room, now!"

There was a distant burst of gunfire and Sam held up his hand for silence. Something screeched like a wounded animal. "Son of a bitch, Frank," Sam shouted. "How'd they make it through the perimeter?"

"No idea, Sheriff. But it sounds like we need to move fast."

Something tugged on the corner of Jem's shirt that sent him leaping a foot into the air. Claire looked up at her brother and said, "What's happening?"

"Nothing. Get back to bed."

Senior Deputy Tom Masters had Sam's destrier ready in the meadow. "It's bad, Sam. They're crawling all over."

"How close?"

"All over."

Sam turned to Frank Banner, the deputy standing at his door, and said, "Stay here and guard the house. Don't let anything happen to these children, you hear me?"

Frank opened his mouth to speak, but stopped when he caught the look on Sam's face. He watched the two older men gallop through the tall grass and disappear from view, then took his hat off and wiped his brow. Frank Banner was the youngest part-time deputy on Sam's force, and he was normally assigned to patrol the perimeter and covering the desk overnight. The pay wasn't enough to buy two beers with, but Frank wore his brass star on his lapel all over town like it was woman-bait. He looked at Jem and said, "Guess that makes two of us left out of the fight, Jem. Where's that gun of yours?"

"In my room."

"Ever shot anything with it before?"

"A few leapers. One at fifty yards."

"Is it charged and loaded?"

"What the hell do you think?"

Frank cocked an eyebrow at the boy and smirked. "Well? Go get it. I reckon two guns are better than one."

Jem darted into his room and fumbled with the lock on the chest at the foot of his bed. He was so excited he could barely open the lid to remove the weapon. He racked the rifle and tried to breathe.

Claire was clutching a stuffed animal to her chest, sitting in bed, when Jem stopped in her doorway, holding his rifle. "Listen, I'm going to be out here with Mr. Frank, and you need to stay quiet." Claire ducked her head under the blankets and whimpered when he reached over to turn off the hallway light.

"Shut the rest out too," Frank whispered. "Make it nice and dark in here."

Jem went to the kitchen and snuffed out the small lantern. He ducked low and hurried back into the living room to squat beside Frank near the front door. Nothing moved in the darkness outside.

"Hand over that big, bad leaper-slayer," Frank said. He took the rifle from Jem and held it up in the dim light, grunting in disbelief at the site assembly. "Christ almighty, boy. Who put a tagger on this thing?"

"I did."

"Where'd you get one of these?"

"I used all the money I ever saved, plus a year doing chores for Old Man Willow and Doctor Halladay. My dad loaned me the rest and I've been working it off."

Frank reached into his pocket for a small tool and began fiddling with the rifle's settings. "I'm taking the safety binders off the sites, but just for tonight, all right? Listen to me, now. This weapon is hot. Don't you touch the trigger unless you plan to shoot at something and don't shoot at nothing unless you're fixing to kill it. Understand?"

"I understand," Jem said. He took the rifle back and glued his trigger finger against the side of the barrel. "Like that?"

"Exactly." Frank clenched his mouth and shook his head. "Goddamn savages. It's one thing to go after our storehouses, but this is over the line. Blood's gonna spill before this is finished."

"All the kids at school were talking about how the mining company took over more of their territory and they swore a blood oath against us. You got any cut, Frank?"

"Boy, your daddy would skin me alive if I gave you any. You don't chew sweetweed, do you?"

Jem squinted just like Sam would and said, "All the damn time."

Frank chuckled and looked back into the yard. "First off, nothing on this planet is their territory. It's ours, and we allow them to squat on it. They should be grateful for the space we do give them so they can run around killing each other and worshipping the moons, or whatever the hell it is they do."

Torchlight flickered in the distance, leaving long trails of smoke. One of the torches flew through the air, spinning end over end toward the roof of a home. Flames spread across the roof and screams filled the valley. The blaze revealed Sam charging toward the front of the house with his rifle raised. He fired several times into the darkness, and was gone.

Claire hollered out, "Jem! What's happening?"

Frank ducked and lifted his rifle. "Go tell that girl to shut up or she'll get us all killed. Stay low."

Jem crawled down the hallway and stuck his head in Claire's room, cringing at the sight of her empty bed. "Claire? Where are you?"

"I'm down here."

He pulled up the blanket covering the side of the bed, "Girl, you scared the hell out of me."

"Shhh!" Claire hissed at him. "You'll get us killed, dummy."

"No, you're gonna get us killed with all your squawking. You have to shut up."

"I am shutted up! It's you making all the noise."

Jem looked back and saw Frank moving toward the front door. He covered his mouth with the side of his hand and said, "Frank! Don't go out there. It ain't safe."

"I think we got 'em on the run," Frank said. "The gunshots are getting farther away."

"Frank? Frank? Damn." The Deputy vanished onto the porch, and Jem lifted his rifle.

"Are we alone now, Jem?"

"No, course not. He just went outside to wait for Daddy. Everything's going to be ok."

"That's what you said when Mama got sick. That didn't turn out ok, now did it?"

Something crashed against the porch and Claire squeaked in fright. She covered her face with the blanket. Jem told her to hush and said, "Maybe it's just a bassaricus. Frank probably caught it going through the trash."

"We're gonna die," Claire moaned.

"No we aren't. Stay still and I'll go look." Jem's hands shook so badly that the rifle bounced from the door to the ceiling and he walked right into a table in the hallway. He flipped a switch on the site assembly and it hummed, glowing bright green. A mechanical voice said, *"Auto-Targeting Activated."*

"Frank?" Jem called. There was no response.

Boards creaked under his bare feet as he leaned to open the door and crept onto the porch. He searched the meadow but saw nothing, and as he moved to first steps, he tweaked a loose piece of wood.

A bare-chested savage stood up at the bottom of the steps. He was dark skinned and slick with sweat and blood, standing over Frank's crumpled body. Frank was writhing at his feet, fingering the top of his head that was now just a ghoulish crown of pale bone. The Beothuk had a dripping knife in one hand and a chunk of Frank's scalp in the other. He screamed at Jem, and the front of the boy's pants turned wet.

"Go on," Jem whispered, backing away as the savage came up the steps. "Get out of here. I mean it. I'll shoot."

The Beothuk sneered at the rifle in the boy's hands and flipped the knife in his hands, catching it by the tip, readying to throw.

"Target acquired."

A soft puff of air escaped from the gun's barrel that sent a blue dart into the center of the Beothuk's chest. He looked down at the dart curiously and a gunshot cracked the air that blew a hole in the savage's chest. Jem watched in horror as he staggered backwards and toppled down the porch's steps.

A destrier came crashing through the meadow so fast that Jem only had time to raise his rifle and fire blindly in its direction. Sam Clayton swung his hands in the air and said, "Cease fire! Cease fire! Son of a bitch, Frank, you almost shot me." The Sheriff's voice pinched as he came in front of the two bodies scattered on the ground.

Jem stood motionless on the porch, staring at his father, his mouth working back and forth with nothing coming out of it.

Sam's face twisted in horror and Jem shouted out, "He killed Frank. He was gonna kill Claire! I had to do it, Pa, I'm sorry. I didn't mean to kill him. I swear it. It just happened."

Sam jumped down from the destrier and grabbed Jem into his arms, kissing the boy over and over on top of the head and saying, "Good boy. Good boy."

2. Gunfighters

He hadn't practiced medicine since acquiring a nasty ailment that ended his career in Seneca 6 forever. His wracking cough had a way of erupting out whenever he leaned over a patient's mouth. Blood mixed with saliva, horked into the unsuspecting face of a man saying "Ahh," or a woman asking him to inspect a suspicious lump, had a way of determining the finality of their patronage. Even Doctor Royce Halladay's most loyal patients found other doctors. Ones who didn't fold up like a chair and clutch their stomachs like their guts were about to uncoil.

One morning Halladay got up to go into the office and stopped walking at the kitchen door. He took off his hat and sat on the porch rocking chair, watching the grass sway in the wind for hours until his wife, Katey, came out. "Why aren't you at work?" she said.

"My office has turned into a graveyard, and I am doing my utmost to avoid them at present."

In time, sitting on the porch no longer contented him, but the addition of small tin cups of whiskey helped. "It helps soothe my throat," he told Katey. It was not long before he'd assembled a pyramid of empty bottles on the porch.

In the beginning of the summer, Sam Clayton came to visit. The sheriff tied his destrier to the post below the Halladay's porch and drew a rifle from his saddle bag. "It was my understanding that you were working late, Sheriff, and that is why my wife needed to watch your children."

"I was," Sam said. He came up the porch and sat down. "When I got home, I saw something that needed to be addressed, so I came to do that."

Halladay eyed the rifle. "A euthanasia. Come to put me out of my misery, then?"

Sam turned and fixed Halladay with a hard stare. "Your wife is looking skinny, Doc. Too skinny. You ain't got money for food, have you?"

"I am trying to not take offense at that, Sam. It is not working."

"I'll offend all day if that's what it takes." Sam held out the rifle and said, "Hell, it's nothing fancy. My boy's got better sites on his gun, but it will put meat on your table if you use it correctly. You ever shoot anything before?"

"No."

"Get up, put that cup down, and let me show you how this is done." Sam demonstrated how to hold the weapon and aim down the sites at his target. He was in the middle of explaining the mechanics of the weapon when a flock of birds kicked up from the grass and Halladay blasted one of them from the sky.

The Sheriff watched the dead bird drop and said, "Okay, that was beginner's luck, but don't think the rest will be so easy."

Halladay fired five more times in quick succession, littering the ground with feathers and carcasses. The two men stood in silence for a moment and Halladay said, "Please, go through the part about the front sites again, Sam."

The sheriff tipped back his hat and smiled. "Weren't no need to play me for a fool, Doc. Nice to see you still have your sense of humor."

Halladay handed the weapon to him. "You have my assurance that I have never even touched a gun before."

"Well it's the damnedest thing I've ever seen." Sam removed his Colt Defender and aimed the weapon at one of the metal fence-posts lining the property. "Pistols are trickier than long guns." Sam squeezed the trigger and the fence post vibrated and clanged dully. He gave Halladay a satisfied smile and handed him the gun. "Give it a try. Just look at the front site and do your best."

The doctor raised the handgun, took a second to adjust his grip and closed one eye. "Aim down the barrel? Like so?" He squeezed the trigger and a fence post two lengths further down from the one Sam shot rang like a bell. "What a shame. I missed the one I was aiming for and accidentally hit one twice as far as yours." Halladay twirled the gun in the palm of his hand to present it to the Sheriff.

Sam looked down at the gun, then back at the doctor. "You're a damn liar, Royce Halladay."

"I owe it all to the quality of your instruction, sir. When can you come by for another lesson?"

"Very funny. Now go to hell."

"No doubt, I will do that quite soon." Halladay stopped smiling and said, "Thank you for the rifle. You are a good friend."

"Don't mention it. Katey's like a second mom to the kids. We'd be lost without her."

Halladay watched the Sheriff get back on his destrier and ride off to check the security perimeter. "Me too," he said.

By mid-summer, Katey became well-practiced at cooking conejos. She held the creatures by their ears and slit their furry length with one hand then scooped out the innards and tossed them into the waste processor. Necessity had brought out ingenuity in her. Sometimes she stewed the conejo with vegetables from the garden, or fried them until the skin crackled in her husband's mouth when he bit it.

Halladay admired his wife as she bent to check the stove, thinking that she would have little difficulty finding a suitor after he died. He expected she would spend a year or two mourning out of respect, but he harbored no expectation of her running out the rest of her life pining for him. At some point he meant to tell her that; to let her know he wanted her to find someone after he coughed up his last bit of lung. To have a long, happy life. It just never seemed an appropriate time to talk about it, and Katey got upset when he tried.

"Darling, it smells like a Presidential kitchen in here," he said, sipping the last drop of whiskey from his cup. "I am often astonished at the miracles you produce from such simple means, but tonight you have outdone yourself."

Katey smiled and swept her hand through her hair. "I suspect you are trying to lure me into some state of compromise with all that fancy talk, mister."

"I would have to be robbed of far more faculties than my ability to breathe in order to not have designs on relieving you of your clothing." He reached out to pinch her bottom. Katey laughed and swatted his hand away before lifting a sizzling tray from the oven.

She tasted the meat and frowned. "It needs something more."

"I could sneak onto the Johnson's farm and steal away with whatever you desire. That would be proper compensation for the way that rascal takes such longing glances at your backside. However, I cannot fault the man for his obviously excellent taste in women."

Katey laughed, then said, "You stay right here and rest. I know just what I need."

He unscrewed the cap on a bottle of whiskey and filled his cup up once more. "It is getting dark. Do not wander off far."

Katey Halladay went down the back stairs of the house and passed by her modest garden, seeing nothing that caught her interest. She headed through the thicket that separated their property from the tall electronic fence surrounding the entire mining colony. Katey passed the blackened corpse of a dead leaper that had gotten too close to the Perimeter's lethal current. The towers powering the Perimeter were set at quarter-mile intervals and crackled with so much energy that it filled the air and made all the hair on her arms stand up.

She saw Deputy Tilt Junger and his younger brother, Walt, standing in front of the nearest tower, both of them too focused on its key-grid to notice her approach. Tilt was a senior deputy assigned to maintain the fence and patrol the outer perimeter. Walt Junger had just joined the force. "Hey there," she called out. "Trouble with the tower again? Any chance you can make it less noisy? Between Royce's coughing and that damn thing, I can't get any peace."

Both men turned to face her as the security gate slid open and a party of Beothuk warriors came through. Katey screamed in terror and Walt shouted, "Get home, Mrs. Halladay!"

Tilt Junger shoved Walt out of the way and charged toward Katey. "Stop right there, woman!"

Katey dropped her basket and ran, screaming for her husband.

"Shut your mouth!" Tilt shouted, ripping a long skinning knife from his belt while he ran.

Walt watched his brother disappear around the bend and said, "Let her go, Tilt!" There was no response. The last of the Beothuk came through the gate and assembled into formation.

Their leader wore cords around his neck adorned with feathers and long, curving fangs. His chest was criss-crossed with scars that covered his lean, muscular torso. The others ducked into the tall grass, but the leader stood straight, surveying the settlement. Katey Halladay screamed in the distance and the savage looked at two of his men, who took off after her, into the thicket.

"Uh, excuse me," Walt said. He held out his hand, "I believe my brother made an agreement with you boys regarding payment."

The Beothuk looked at Walt, and the young Deputy put his other hand closer to his gun. Finally, the leader removed a small sack from his belt and dropped it into Walt's palm.

Walt untied the drawstring and shook out several small rocks into his hand. They were the size of marbles and glittered in the sunlight. It was enough severian to keep the entire Junger family wealthy for generations.

The savage leader watched Walt tie up the bag, then muttered something and spat on the ground at Walt's feet. Walt looked down at the gob of spit next to his boot and shrugged, then turned and headed after Tilt to show him the bag that contained their entire future.

"Got you!" Tilt shouted, swinging wildly with the blade and catching Katey Halladay across the neck. Blood squirted out of her and she collapsed at the edge of her garden, staring at the back of her house.

Katey squirmed in the dirt, making wet, gurgling sounds while Tilt bent over with his hands on his knees, trying to catch his breath. "It's your own fault. I told you to stop. I'd have just tied you up until we was finished or something but you wouldn't shut up."

She dug long gullies in the dirt with her boots, squirming as the last of her life leaked out of her. Tilt brushed her hair out of her face and said, "Just try and be still now, Mrs. Halladay. It'll all be over soon."

Two savages ran up behind them and stopped at the sight of Katey. One of them said something in their twisted, guttural language that Tilt took to be some sort of insult. "You rust-colored sons of bitches got something to say about this?" They stared back at him with cold, blank expressions. "She'd have alerted the whole damn colony you were here. Action had to be taken."

A bullet caved in one of the Beothuk's face's. The report of Doctor Halladay's rifle echoed from the back porch, and he shot at them again. Blood and tissue from the Beothuk warriors sprayed Tilt, who raised his hands to shield himself. A bullet stamped Tilt's kneecap, blowing it to fragments and knocking him backwards in the dirt. Halladay stopped firing and ran to Katey's side.

"Son of a bitch!" Tilt shouted, struggling to prop himself up on his elbows. The pain in his leg was like a hot knife stuck under the bones of his knee. He turned to look at the others and saw that they were dead. Tilt slid backwards on his rear, trying to make it into the thicket while Halladay was bent over Katey's corpse.

A gunshot struck Tilt in the right hand, shattering his fingers. Tilt screamed, "Wait a second! Wait!"

Halladay picked up Tilt's skinning knife from the ground. It was still wet with Katey's blood. He went toward Tilt, who moaned and tried backing away. Halladay stabbed the knife halfway into Tilt's thigh and said, "You move another inch and I will make you a eunuch."

Tilt flopped on the ground like a fish and gasped, "Stop! For God's sake, Doc, I'm a lawman. I need a doctor, and if you help me, I'll make it worth your while." He pointed at the bodies of the dead savages, "It wasn't me that killed your wife. Try and have a little perspective here!"

Halladay turned to look at the Beothuk just as Tilt reached for the handle of his gun. He nearly had it unholstered when

Halladay touched the tip of the knife to Tilt's adam's apple. "You most certainly do need a doctor, Mr. Junger," Halladay said. "I believe I am just the man to perform the particular surgical procedures you require. Let's see if you can try and stay still now."

3. Legends

By morning, the dead were tallied and packed onto wagons for transport to the Willow Funeral Home. Old Man Willow directed the drivers to the side of his house to wait until he could figure out where to put them all. The barn at the rear of the property was already full.

Anna Willow looked at the crowd gathered in her front yard through the kitchen window while she made breakfast for Jem and Claire Clayton. The Sheriff left them there when he dropped off the body of Frank Banner.

Jem sat on the front porch watching the wagons arrive. Anna tapped on the window screen with her fingernails and said, "Why don't you come inside, Jem? These biscuits are almost done."

Jem shook his head from side to side, seeing that another wagon was coming. People in the crowd gasped as it rolled past, and some of them covered their faces and sobbed. When Jem saw Mrs. Katey Halladay sprawled out in the rear carriage he started to tremble. Anna dropped her things and went outside to grab Jem by the shoulders. "All right, honey. It's all right. Let's go," she said. She pulled him inside and shut the door. Little Claire was sitting on the floor, sorting through a pile of dolls that Anna had pulled out of the closet. "Into the kitchen, both of you. It's time to eat."

At noon, Sheriff Sam Clayton came down the road toward the Willow home in a wagon of his own. He guided the destrier through the crowd, giving people a chance to get out of his way.

"Who you got there, Sheriff?" someone called out. "We already counted everyone up."

"It's those God damn savages!" another shouted.

"Those sons of bitches don't belong here, Sheriff!"

"We're gonna string them up by the fence to show the savages what happens when they come onto our land."

Billy Jack Elliot pushed his way past the other onlookers and stood in front of the Sheriff's destrier, forcing Sam to yank the reins. Elliot wrapped his hand around the destrier's bridle and said, "You ain't gonna bring them savages into this place of mourning, Sam."

Sam looked down at Elliot and said, "Old Man Willow can only make so many caskets, Billy. Get your hands off my animal."

Old Man Willow came out of the house with his hands raised like a preacher's, "Everybody settle down! This is my property and I'll decide what happens." The funeral director was only ten years older than Sam, but was bald as a bowling ball and the sun had turned his skin the texture of leather. Erazamus Willow patted his rotund belly and fingered the buttons on his vest as he looked over the crowd. He went down the steps toward Sam's cart and looked in the rear at the savages stacked on top of one another in the back. "Not too sure about this, Sam," Willow said, holding his hand over his eyes as he looked up. "Seems to me those bodies aren't fit to lay with the ones we have in the barn already."

The crowd murmured in agreement.

"I understand your feelings," Sam said. "That's why I'm going to wait until all our people are properly situated before I ask you to attend to this lot."

"Please tell me why in the world we'd extend them that courtesy, Sam?"

"Because I intend to return them to their people, and it would be unseemly to bring them back all bloody and bullet-ridden."

The entire crowd roared and several husky miners ran forward to grab the ankles of the dead savages and yank them from the cart. Sam vaulted over the back of the cart and landed with his Colt Defenders aimed square in the faces of the closest men to him. "Hands off. We clear?"

Billy Jack Elliot came around the side of the cart toward Sam, with several men following. "You can't take us all, Sheriff."

The front door of the Willow house crashed open and Jem Clayton came through, shouting, "Any of you two-bit yellow-belly rock breakers so much as takes a step toward my daddy and I'll kill every damn one of you!"

Sam looked up at his son and said, "Get your ass back inside, Jem."

Billy Jack Elliot lunged at Sam's guns. Sam turned aside in time and cracked the butt end of one of his pistols across Elliot's face and dropped him to his knees. Elliot hunched over and clutched his nose with blood squeezing between his fingers. He spat two teeth into the red clay and moaned.

Sam looked down at Elliot and sighed. He reached into his pocket for a handkerchief and pressed it against Elliot's face. "Hold that tight to your face, Billy. Keep your head tilted back."

Two men came forward and took hold of Elliot, helping him through the crowd. Sam shook his head and said, "Now can everybody else just go home for a little while? There's been enough bloodshed today and for right now, I think we all need to be with our families."

The crowd began to disperse and Jem came down from the porch to wrap his arms around his father's waist. "I need you to get back in there and shut the door, Jem. Lock it and don't let anyone in."

"But it's over. They're all leaving," Jem said. "It's over."

"Listen to me when I tell you, nothing is ever over."

Old Man Willow looked up on the porch and lifted his glasses. Anna Willow was standing there with one of his hunting rifles at the ready. "What, exactly, did you intend to do with that, young lady?"

Anna's eyes were fixed on Sam and her fingers were white against the gun's stock. "I wouldn't have let anybody harm you, Sheriff," she said.

Old Man Willow patted Jem on the shoulder. "Go on inside, boy. Let your father be for a moment. I won't let anything happen to him."

Jem sulked as he went up the porch steps, holding the door for Anna but she did not move. Old Man Willow said, "That means you too, missy. The Sheriff don't need any admirers right now."

Anna's face flushed as she raced into the house and slammed the door shut behind her. Old Man Willow chuckled, "I reckon she's sweet on you, Sam. Has been ever since that trouble with Zeke."

"She'll develop better taste in men when she grows up, I'm sure."

"Her mother didn't, thank God," Willow said. "I was able to fool that woman into thinking I was the only man worth marrying on this miserable rock. Ever since she passed on, it's like all the goodness went out of the world with her. But still, I have learned to respect her memory without feeling like I'm haunted by it."

"We having a discussion about one thing while talking about another, Erazamus?" Sam said.

"Loneliness makes a man do strange things, Sheriff."

"Like?"

"Like going off into Beothuk country with the bodies of a bunch of their fallen sons. If I didn't know better, I'd say that's the behavior of a man that wants to come see me again, but on a more professional basis, if you understand my meaning."

Sam Clayton fished a pouch from his pocket and pinched off an inch of sweetweed. He tucked it into his lower lip and sucked on it until he had a mouthful of juice to spit into the dirt. He chewed for a moment then spat again. Finally, he said, "Nope."

Old Man Willow sighed, "I should have known better than try to wear you down, Sam. Meet me around the back with these fellers and we'll get them down into the cooler. Then you can go on and get cleaned up for supper. Anna will burn the house down trying to fix it and still keep an eye on you if I leave you out here. Come on. I'll get the gate."

That evening, Sam sat on the Willow's front porch bouncing Claire on his knee. His rifle was propped against the handrail, within reach. He told her a story about princesses and castles as the sun lowered over the horizon and painted the landscape in hues of red and gold. He kissed her forehead. "You know, you're *my* princess, right? You always will be." He lifted up her chin and gave her a kiss on the lips, tickling her with the scruff on his chin until she squirmed and tried to get away.

Sam set Claire down on the porch and sent her inside. He saw Jem standing in the doorway. He held out his hand and waved for the boy to join him. "You look like a man with something on his mind, son."

Jem shrugged and looked down at the porch's floorboards. "I keep seeing it."

"Which part?"

"The look on that savage's face when my gun went off."

Sam nodded silently and rocked back in the chair. "Someday when you're an attorney out on some big Metropolis-Class planet, you'll look back on all this with amazement, I bet. All this fighting and killing over what? A barren bunch of land with the misfortune of having some of the rarest stones in the galaxy buried underneath it."

"What if I said I'm not going anywhere? Maybe I'll be a Sheriff just like you."

"Just like me?" Sam said.

"That's right."

He smiled and pulled Jem close to him, lifting the boy onto his lap. He grunted and said, "Won't be long before you're too big to sit on my lap."

Jem put his head on his father's shoulder and didn't speak. Sam played with the boy's hair and said, "Why are you moping? I won't be gone long."

"Okay. That's good."

Sam put his head against his son's shoulder and said, "I don't know why I'm about to tell you this, but here goes. That security gate was opened from inside. I checked it after we chased the Beothuk back through it."

Jem's eyes widened. "Why would somebody who lives here want to see the place attacked?"

"Probably the two most dangerous qualities a man can possess, son. Stupidity and greed. Put them together and it's bad news, every time. I need you to keep your eyes on the place while I'm gone. Tell me what you hear."

"When you get back, I'm going to help you figure out who did it and we can put them in jail."

"That sounds like a plan," Sam said. He kissed the top of Jem's head and told him it was time for bed. Jem helped him collect his gear and set it by the entrance so Sam could get dressed at first light and ride out.

"Goodnight, Pa," Jem said.

Sam put his hand on the boy's shoulder and stopped him from going up the stairs, "When I get back, we'll ride out to the canyon together and get a few leapers. We'll camp out and cook 'em over a pit. Claire can stay with these folks. Just you an' me."

"You promise?"

"I said it, didn't I?"

"Yeah."

"That's better than a promise."

Several hours later, Jem Clayton heard his father downstairs strapping on his guns and riding gear. He listened to Sam's spurs jingle on the floorboards and the slow creak of the front door open and shut. Jem went down the stairs to peer through the window, watching as Sam climbed onto the back of his massive destrier.

In the years that followed, Jem relived those last moments of his father riding away. He sometimes convinced himself that Sam stopped and waved at him before departing.

In reality, Sam Clayton thought his children were both asleep inside the Willow's house, and he didn't want to disturb them. He rode his mount around the back of the house to hitch the cart containing the dead bodies of the Beothuk warriors.

Clayton rode across Seneca 6 toward the Halladay property. Royce Halladay had not been seen since the raid. Sam stopped at the rear door and knocked several times but there was no answer. He quit the house and got back on his mount to leave the settlement through the same gate that the Beothuk savages had snuck in.

He looked back in the direction of his own home and thought, there is nothing in the world that can keep me from coming back here.

He was wrong.

Sam Clayton was murdered in the wasteland beyond the confines of Seneca 6 just two days later.

4. Outlaws

The distance between the Seneca 5 and Seneca 6 mining colonies was approximately 400 miles, separated by a wasteland filled with burned out shuttle hulls that leaked radiation and tall energy mills that stretched so high into the atmosphere their tips appeared to spear the low, hovering moons. The well-heeled traveled by shuttle, making short hops from colony to colony aboard small-passenger craft that were stocked with fine beverages and enough shielding to prevent the outer hull from melting in the atmosphere's intense heat.

Regular folks travelled by land, which sometimes meant renting space on rickety locomotives still powered by compression engines. They made good time but ran the risk of sucking up too much dust and muck into their manifolds and dying in the middle of nowhere. There were numerous stories about passengers setting up flares and waiting for weeks to be found. Not all of them always were.

Most preferred the planet's best source of transportation, the destrier.

Massive, fast moving, four-legged beasts covered in thick, coarse fur that kept them insulated from the heat. They retained water like camels and responded to direction and training easily.

Entrepreneurs invested in large wagons and two destriers and rented out seats to passengers. There were bandits and Beothuk in the wasteland, and bad things happened to the unprepared.

Mrs. Wilma Alcott and her son Jesse rode aboard a carriage bound for an observation outpost forty miles into the wasteland, where her husband worked collecting energy cells from abandoned vehicles. A handsomely-dressed merchant sat across from her clutching his suitcase on his lap. Ralph Brenner, the wagon's owner and driver, sat inside a fortified chamber at the perch, overlooking two sturdy destriers fitted with bridles and thick metal shafts.

Wilma looked out at the wasteland through shatter-proof windows that were covered in red dust and grime. Two masked riders came leaping over the sand dunes, heading directly for the front of the wagon. Wilma opened her mouth to shout to Brenner, but one of the riders lifted a pistol and fired at the nearest destrier pulling the wagon.

The animal collapsed into the dirt and they spun sideways, nearly flipping over as the carriage skidded across the ground. Wilma slammed into her son and they both hit the carriage door. The merchant rolled onto the floor, clutching his case, screaming louder than Wilma did.

They slid to a stop and Wilma covered her son's mouth, pleading with him to not make a sound. The carriage door opened and a man wearing a black cloth over his nose and mouth looked in. Only his eyes were visible under the brim of his dark hat and he looked over the passengers with his gun in his hand, his finger off the trigger. "Everyone all right in here?"

"No we are most certainly not!" The merchant struggled to get up from the floor without letting go of his case with either hand.

The bandit nodded and said, "Well, why don't you all step outside and we'll assess the damages."

"I absolutely refuse," the merchant said. He had the case held to his chest like it was a shield.

"That a fact? All right, then. Ma'am, you and the boy come on out then so he and I can discuss this in private." The masked man held his hand out and helped her down from the wagon.

When he reached for Jesse, the boy slapped his hand away. "You touch my mother and I'll kill you. I heard about men like you. I ain't afraid."

The bandit looked at him and chuckled lightly under his mask. "Fair enough, killer. You and your mama go stand over there by my associate. Make it quick now, and there won't be any more trouble."

Jesse put his arms around his mother's waist. The bandit leaned close to her ear and said, "I am not the type to allow harm to come to a woman, or do anything else untoward to them either. You and the boy stay quiet and we'll be on our way."

"Thank you, Jim," she whispered.

"What's that again?"

"I've read about you," Wilma said. "They call you 'Gentleman Jim' in the papers."

The bandit looked over at where Ralph Brenner was kneeling in the dirt with his hands behind his head. "Not everybody calls me that," he said. The second bandit was holding a rifle to Brenner's forehead. His mask was nothing more than a dirty vegetable sack with lopsided eyeholes.

Gentleman Jim walked back to the carriage and frowned at the merchant, who still refused to come out. "You need to step outside, friend. Otherwise, I'll be forced to adapt my methods."

"That woman has an ounce of pure severian hidden on her person," the merchant whispered. "I watched her hide it there when you stopped the carriage. I'll come out, and I'll even tell you where it is if you swear not to harm me or take this case."

The bandit glanced at Wilma and back at the merchant. "I like your style. It's a deal."

The merchant stepped down, still clutching the case close to him. "It's stuffed between her bosoms. I'm sure if you take her back inside the wagon and search her, you'll find it. You'll need to get her out of that corset though. I can keep the boy distracted while you do whatever… you need…to do."

The bandit led the merchant over to the others. Wilma and Jesse were kneeling next to Ralph Brenner and had their hands behind their heads. The other bandit marched in front of them, moving the barrel of his rifle from one forehead to the next. Gentleman Jim smacked Bob across the back of the head and said, "What did I tell you about putting your finger on the trigger?"

Bob yanked on his sack, adjusting it so he could see properly. He removed his finger from the trigger and put it against the frame.

"You bastards didn't have to cripple the nag," Ralph Brenner said. He scowled at the whimpering destrier, lying on the ground with its injured leg tucked under its belly.

Gentleman Jim said, "That was just an impact round I hit it with. There might be a light fracture but it will survive. I recommend you bind the leg up real tight once we leave and take it nice and easy back to the settlement."

"You and your recommendations can go to hell."

Bob stuck the barrel of his rifle into Brenner's cheek and pushed him backward into the dirt with it. He cocked the hammer and said, "Say one more thing an' I'll put your brains all over the ground, understand?"

Gentleman Jim cleared his throat. "You two men take everything out of your pockets and put it on the ground in front of you. Now take off your jewelry and your watches. That's good."

The merchant played along with the charade. He looked over at Wilma and assessed the swell of her bodice, hoping its contents would be enough to distract the robbers while he made a run for it.

Gentleman Jim looked over at Bob and said, "What did I tell you about those raggedy threads of yours?"

"What do you mean?"

"This distinguished lady recognized me from the papers. Now that we're becoming famous I think it's only right that we take the time to attire ourselves appropriately. You come out here and deal with respectable businessmen like these fine folks looking like whatever the cat dragged in. It's no wonder they don't listen." Gentleman Jim squatted down to stare face to face with the merchant. "For instance, this man knows how to dress. I admire your choice in fashion, sir."

The merchant smiled and said, "Thank you."

The bandit smiled back. "In fact, why don't you stand up here next to me and take them off."

"What?"

"Put your little case down on the ground, stand up here, and take off all your clothes."

After much hand-wringing and one serious threat to shoot off any dangling appendages, the merchant stripped naked. Gentleman Jim told him, "You can put your boots back on. Seneca 5 is twenty miles in that direction. Start walking."

"I'm taking my case."

The bandit fired three shots at the man's feet and the merchant took off running. Gentleman Jim cocked his head at Bob and said, "Go look at that nag and see what needs to be done. Wrap her leg up tight for these fine folks. I believe they've had a rough day."

The bandit helped Brenner to his feet and pointed in the merchant's direction, "Listen, if you want, you can pick him up on your way back. We'll leave his clothes with you. I'm warning you, though. He was ready to send up this woman for sacrifice like a prize goose just to save himself. I'd prefer if you kept him up front where you can keep an eye on him."

Brenner yanked his arm away from the bandit and said something under his breath. He walked over to yell at Bob for splinting the destrier's leg improperly. Gentleman Jim waited until he was alone with the woman and her son to open up the merchant's wallet and remove all of the bills inside. He counted them out and handed half to Wilma. He licked his thumb and took out a few more that he folded up and put into Jesse's shirt pocket. "This stays between me and you all, ok? If you tell the papers about this part, it might make my next customer think I'm soft, and I'd hate like hell to have to hurt somebody to prove otherwise."

"What's in the case?" Jesse asked. Wilma scolded him to be quiet, but the masked man looked down at the boy's eager face and asked him if he really wanted to know.

Jesse nodded, and Gentleman Jim bent on one knee to look him in the eye. "There's a four-ounce severian bounty on my head. Ain't no way whatever's in this case could be worth as much as the risk I took getting it. Most times, cases like these are worth a lot more to the person that owns them than the one who takes them. I've taken a hundred of these from men like him, and they cried and whined every time, but when I popped them cases open there was nothing but dirty pictures or secret plans, or something stupid like that. This case won't be any different. Sometimes, you have to sell it back to them just to make a profit."

"But if you do that enough, you can pay off that bounty and be free," Jesse said.

"I could pay off that bounty right now if I wanted to and still be rich. I got plenty of money."

"So why do you keep doing it?"

The bandit winked at the boy and said, "A man's gotta have a hobby, son."

Bob was Gentleman Jim's eighth assistant, and his magic number was up. Each time the outlaw took on a new helper, he picked a number at random. The man would work exactly that number of jobs with him, and no more. It kept him from developing a personal affinity for anyone.

Two assistants had been sent on their way before their time came. They were simple, decent men who'd fallen on hard times and become desperate. They couldn't be trusted, when push came to shove, to be cut-throat enough. Both of them woke up in the desert next to an empty bedroll with a thousand dollars stuffed in their pockets.

One assistant was killed and left underneath the scorched frame of a spaceship out in the wasteland. Gentleman Jim had caught the man forcing himself on a female passenger and slit his throat.

Bob made it to the allotted amount of robberies and it was time to drink. "I'm thirsty," Gentleman Jim said. He sided up to the bar at the Dalewood Saloon in Seneca 5 and ordered two whiskeys. He held his glass up to Bob and said, "To our continued career, fame and good fortune."

Bob swallowed his whiskey in one drink. He wiped his mouth and grinned stupidly, "Today sure was fun."

Gentleman Jim nodded and ordered another round. "I've got an important assignment for you. I need you to go to this address in Seneca 4. It's a little hideout I've got. Stash our weapons and masks and wait. A buyer wants to come look at that merchant's case. He's willing to pay a fortune for it."

Bob put his hand on the outlaw's elbow and said, "I swear to God you can trust me."

"I know I can. Let's drink to trust."

Gentleman Jim finished the next drink and let his head hang. He grabbed Bob around the shoulder and pulled him close, slurring when he said, "I never told nobody this, but my real name is Dirk Tirrell. I grew up off-planet and came here to join the mining union. The sons of bitches wouldn't take me, so I got into this business. Now you know more about me than any other person, alive or dead, so make sure you keep it quiet, ok? I trust you, Bob. Let's drink."

Bob left with that information tucked away as carefully as the merchant's worthless documents and photographs inside the case. The authorities caught up with him before he made it halfway to Seneca 4. They seized the briefcase and Bob immediately offered up a story that he thought was worth a reward, if not leniency. The lawmen listened intently to Bob tell of Dirk Tirrell, the infamous masked bandit known as "Gentleman Jim." They started laughing before he even finished telling them the part about the mining union.

"Boy, we've got four different associates of that bastard doing hard time at the penal colony, and each of them has given us a different name for him. You'll see the judge in the morning and then the group of you can compare notes."

The Dalewood Saloon of Seneca 5 was slow. The rotation of fresh poker players was neither to Dr. Royce Halladay's liking nor profit. He watched the same stack of money circle around the table several times, and out of sheer boredom, kept playing even when it passed to him.

He ordered three whiskeys and drank them all in quick succession. The alcohol left him grabbing his throat and grimacing.

He coughed into his sleeve until blood dripped down his mustache. Halladay excused himself and stood from the table. He moved into a corner where he could indulge the cough and spit without fear of splattering blood on anyone. Even when bent over, he kept an eye aimed at the table, letting them know that he was watching both his cards and his stack of money.

Halladay righted himself and returned. "Pardon me, gentlemen, I seem to be a bit under the weather this evening." He sat and took up his cards, looking from them to the faces of the other players. He took their measure as they squirmed under his scrutiny, all of them trying to conceal their opinions of the cards in their own hands. "The hour is growing late, and the time has come to put the children to bed. I'm all in," Halladay said, then pushed his stack of chips into the center of the table.

Each of the other players considered their cards more carefully. One by one, they folded. The turn passed to a young Henry McCarty, seated across the table from Halladay. McCarty tucked his thin lower lip beneath a massive row of buckteeth and smiled, looking like a gopher. He spit a mouthful of black sweetweed juice on the floor and shoved in the rest of his chips. "I'll call you, blood spitter."

Doctor Halladay laid his cards down with the flourish of a magician revealing his greatest trick. McCarty let out a whoop of delight when he turned over a better hand that erased Halladay's magic. "Damn," Halladay said, then coughed.

"Not so much to say now, do you?" McCarty embraced the pile of coins, bills, and chips and dragged them into his lap.

Halladay congratulated McCarty and excused himself from the table. He decided he disliked McCarty, but the level of dislike had not reached the point of wanting to lay in wait for the man in an alley and murder him. However, the night was young. Halladay decided to leave that option open depending on McCarty's behavior.

There was a man at the bar with his head down under the brim of his hat, reading a folded newspaper. Halladay leaned next to him and tapped the bar, trying to raise the barmaid's attention. He looked over and tried to see what the man was reading and said, "My, my, a literate fellow in this den of iniquity." There was no response, not even a nod of the head. Halladay decided he needed to meet this man. "That must be a story of deep personal interest to keep your attention from the delights of these buxom barmaids. Unless, of course, you prefer the more masculine type."

"What the hell did you say, friend?" The man looked up from his paper at Halladay and his eyes widened. "Doc?"

Halladay grinned, his eyes turning into serpentine slits. "Jem Clayton. How is your father these days?"

Jem's hand dropped to cover the article he'd been reading and he pulled the paper closer. "Hello, Doc. He's dead."

"Of course, of course. Forgive me for being so rude," Halladay said. "Let us have a drink in his honor. Barmaid? Your finest whiskey."

"That's really not necessary. I wasn't staying."

The barmaid set down two glasses in front of them and Halladay grabbed one. Jem's hand remained covering the article.

"To Sam Clayton. My dearest friend," Halladay said, lifting his glass.

Jem sighed and took the shot glass. He lifted it to his lips and drank, not noticing that Halladay glanced down to read the newspaper article that quoted the passenger of a wagon named Mrs. Wilma Alcott. *"Gentleman Jim was handsome, I can tell you that much. His eyes were blue as the oceans of the Luatica system, and even though he was obviously a dangerous man on serious business, he was kind and charming. He really is a gentleman, you know."*

Halladay studied Jem carefully before saying, "You know, I haven't set eyes on you since you were a little boy, but it is simply remarkable how much you look like him. You have the same blue eyes. Nearly as blue as the oceans of the Luatica system."

Jem folded up the newspaper and stuffed it into his pocket. "Shouldn't you be dead by now? You were too sick to practice medicine over twenty years ago yet here you are."

Halladay drew his fingers along his mustache and down the length of his goatee. "It must be my dogged commitment to living a healthy lifestyle. So tell me, young Clayton, what brings you all the way out to the Filthy 5?"

Jem swirled his glass and watched his beer move in circles. "It isn't Seneca 6. My father died, Doc. I left. That's the end."

"And what of little Claire?" Halladay said. Jem did not answer. Instead, he downed his beer and looked into the empty glass. Halladay shook his head and laughed, "I see. Thus, it all begins to clarify."

"What does?"

Doctor Halladay ordered two drinks, smiling lasciviously at the barmaid that brought them. He set one of the whiskeys in front of Jem and lifted his own glass. "To chivalry."

Henry McCarty stood up from the poker table as Halladay set down his drink. McCarty leered at Halladay with bucktoothed contempt and pocketed his winnings.

"All finished for the evening, Henry?" Halladay said. "I was just about to sit back down and destroy your dignity."

McCarty went to push his chair back in but missed and nearly fell into the lap for another player. "Get your hands off me," McCarty said as he staggered to his feet. Halladay did not move as he watched the young man approach. "You got somethin' to say? I'm taking your money, and his money, and this piece of trash's money if I want to, too."

"Did I dawdle too long for you, Henry? I apologize if I kept you waiting. Let's say we have a drink and sit back down at the table to straighten this out like gentlemen."

"You ain't gonna live long enough to spend it anyhow, blood spitter. Better for someone who ain't got to worry about dropping dead as soon as he sets foot outside this rat trap to enjoy it."

"I quite agree," Halladay said. He set his empty glass on the bar. "You know, destiny is a peculiar thing, is it not, Henry? My friend and I were just discussing fate, and her fickle habit of intersecting with each of us in ways we are barely equipped to fathom."

The barmaid went to refill Halladay's drink, but he waved her away. McCarty cursed at Halladay and headed for the door, heavy feet operating independently of the rest of him. Halladay watched him turn down the dark labyrinth of alleyways that led back toward the miner's camp. "Like the rest of us, poor Mr. McCarty fails to realize that when his hour is at hand, it is already too late. That is where I have the distinct advantage, you see? My reason for living died twenty years ago. It is ironic that I've been dying of the same disease for two decades and the people dearest to me were cut down in the prime of their existences." Halladay fixed his hat and lifted his jacket's collar to conceal his face. "Now, if you will excuse me, I must go and inform our dear Henry of some rather bad news concerning his immediate future."

5. The Veteran

At 62 years old, Marshal Jimmy McParlan was the oldest active field agent in the PNDA, the Interplanetary Shipping Federation's law enforcement agency. He'd spent his adult life protecting convoys and arresting pirates. He swore he'd be the first Marshal to die of old age on the job, if only to keep both of his greedy ex-wives from collecting one cent of his retirement.

The Agency was good to him though. They put him on easier assignments that allowed him to wind out his days in far-off stations where little needed to be done.

He didn't mind letting the younger agents have the busier sectors. His days of running and gunning were over with. There was a desk drawer full of medals, a body full of synthetic parts and a cybernetic replacement eye on the left side of his face to prove it.

McParlan worked at the Antioch Shipping Station, a small stop over for long-distance haulers to refuel and enjoy all the seedy wonders of a self-contained world. It was a place where no one stuck around long enough to remember anyone else, and had little fear of being held accountable for whatever happened in the meantime. Except for the uniformed Customs Code Enforcement Units that inspected the ships and cargo, the PNDA was the only semblance of law enforcement on Antioch.

McParlan gave less than half of a damn what the Customs geeks did. Those boys seemed to get a kick out of handing out season-ending fines to truckers like they were getting a percentage of the total as a bonus in their pay. He preferred the company of the working stiff haulers to the clean-cut, straight-edged officers, and whenever he got the chance to tip off the haulers about an upcoming inspection, he did.

That morning, McParlan sat at his desk and sipped coffee from a chipped mug that read *Number One Dad.* The print was faded on the mug's surface from twenty years worth of washing. He kicked his feet up on his desk and picked up the small computer tablet to flip through the PNDA's daily activity reports in his sector. At the tablet's activation, the reports synced with the computer inside his artificial eye.

The engineers who periodically made adjustments to the device told him that some of the younger agents were voluntarily having their natural eyes replaced with cybernetic ones. The new units functioned the same as his, but were implants instead of the large mechanical looking box bolted into his skull. McParlan's eye was just a prototype when they gave it to him, and the casing stuck out of his head an inch like a telescopic monocle. His only regret was that he was ruined from wearing a good pair of sunglasses.

His coffee was finished and he got bored of sitting at his desk. He slid the tablet into a holster on his belt and touched a button on his eye's frame. The red feed went dark for a moment, then flickered and started to scan the things he looked at.

McParlan walked into the shipping yard. It was full that day, with large freighters capable of hauling mountains of stone and tiny one-man courier vessels barely able to break through the station's gravitational barrier. McParlan looked them over as he passed, admiring their colorful names. He passed ships with "Hell of a Heap" and "Fat Sally" emblazoned on their sides. Some were decorated with paintings of pinup models.

The registration numbers of each vessel he passed printed out instantly within the red spectrum of his mechanical eye, listing the class, weight, and owner information of each vehicle. Many of them were in violation of some damn code or another. There was a loud buzzing in his eye's case and the word ALERT flashed onto the screen.

"Come on, not again. Damn loose wires," McParlan sighed. He tapped his finger on the unit impatiently. The casing vibrated in his skull, distorting his vision. He tried to focus as information flooded his screen. He stopped moving when he saw:

PRIORITY TARGET ALERT PRIORITY TARGET ALERT PRIORITY TARGET.

"Alert acknowledged," McParlan said.

The next message read PROCEED WITH CAUTION. ARREST IMMEDIATELY. McParlan ducked between two cruisers and removed the tablet from his belt. The mugshot of a slope-browed, simian looking man appeared on the screen.

ELIJAH HARPE—member of the Harpe Gang—wanted for seventeen counts of Rape and Torture. Fifty-three counts of Felony Hijacking. Two hundred and thirty-three incidents of assault by firearm. Four hundred counts of Murder.

Another image flashed of Elijah Harpe standing next to a taller, thinner man labeled as William "Little Willy" Harpe.

McParlan searched for the most recent incident and found a video of Elijah Harpe dragging a woman into a Medical Transport. The woman was screaming and fighting with him but he had his arm around her neck in a chokehold. Laser blasts ricocheted off the hull of the Transport. and Harpe was firing back as he shoved the woman into the ship and shut the door behind him. McParlan punched up a still image of Harpe's face and studied it. He moved the camera over to the terrified looking woman. The feed read: *Wendy Diaz, medical technician. Thirty-three years old, mother of two.*

McParlan scrolled through Custom's list of vehicle registrations that had docked on Antioch and found the same Medical Transport vessel from the video. "What the hell?" he whispered. "How did that make it through?"

He went out into the rows of vehicles in the yard and found it parked between two long-distance haulers. People walked past the transport without noticing the fresh laser marks across its side. McParlan unholstered his Balrog 6K pistol and pointed it at the glass window as he stood on his toes to look inside.

The cockpit was empty. He went to the ship's side door and typed a special emergency inspection code into the panel, stepping back with his weapon raised as the door whooshed open.

McParlan closed his good eye as he went inside, letting the cybernetic one scan the darkness in infra-red. There was dried blood on the floor in trails that led from the cargo area to a small ladder that rose up into the passenger compartments.

McParlan lifted the tablet close to his lips and kept his gun trained on the dark passenger area. "Field Marshal 717-A to Control," he whispered.

"Control. Verify your status, 717-A."

"I'm aboard that vehicle. Confirm directive."

"That vehicle is associated with an Alpha Level 1 wanted subject. Control authorizes the capture or termination of subject."

"How the hell did that ship get clearance to land on Antioch? Customs should have flagged it immediately before it docked," McParlan said.

There was a long stream of static in response from the tablet, and McParlan shook it violently. "Of all the goddamn times to go on the fritz. Control? Can you read me?"

The tablet's lights blinked as the unit went into reset mode. Disgusted, McParlan clipped it back to his belt and climbed the ladder. He lifted his gun over the top rung and inched upward, ready to blast a hole in anything waiting for him. McParlan reached over the ledge and felt a mop of wet hair. When he pulled his hand away and looked at it, it was covered in blood.

The Marshal cursed when he saw Wendy Diaz lying on the floor, her face turned toward him. He tried turning her head but the broken bones in her neck crunched together. He removed the tablet again, seeing that the lights were steady green. "Control, confirm one victim. Prepare to receive scan."

He waved the tablet over the woman's body, recording her injuries. Her wrists were still bound. There were deep cuts in her skin under the ropes that showed through to the bone. "Had fun with her all alone out in space, didn't you, Elijah?" McParlan whispered. "Gonna make you pay for that."

The tablet crackled. There was a stream of static when it said, "717-A, be advised we are unable to maintain a steady signal with your unit at this time."

"Only the best equipment for Field operatives, Control. Thank our superiors for that," McParlan said.

"Negative," Control responded. "There is interference coming from your location that is jamming our equipment."

The screen went blank. McParlan put the tablet away and searched for a blanket to cover the body of Wendy Diaz.

The Marshal checked the supply stores and bath houses, thinking Harpe would be seeking refreshment after a long journey. He checked the gambling halls and bars, and whore houses, thinking that Harpe had ravaged Mrs. Diaz for weeks in the vast emptiness of space, but still not been satiated.

Finally, only one place remained on the station, and McParlan cursed himself for a fool even for considering that Elijah Harpe had ventured into the Antioch Chapel for Travelling Souls. McParlan threw the doors wide and strolled in, lazily scanning the empty pews without even bothering to keep his gun ready. He saw a man kneeling in prayer at the base of the altar with his head bent low toward the ground.

McParlan's cybernetic eye adjusted as he approached, trying to obtain enough visual data to make a positive identification. McParlan came close enough to stand behind the man and listen to him mutter, "Protect thy servants of your will, Oh Lord. Strike them down where they stand." The man had a pistol on the ground in front of him.

McParlan undid his Balrog and quietly slid it from his holster. He leveled the gun at the man's head and said, "Pardon me, mister. You seen the preacher?"

Elijah Harpe turned and looked back at McParlan. His cheeks were smeared with tears and he smiled at the sight of the Balrog pointed at him. Harpe closed his eyes and sighed with relief. "I knew he would send you," Harpe said. "I knew he wouldn't force me to send myself to him in sin."

McParlan cocked back the hammer on his gun. "Don't you move, boy. I am placing you under arrest for multiple counts of every crime known to mankind. If you don't put your hands behind your back and come peaceably you're a dead man. Please don't put your hands behind your back."

Harpe lifted his hands to the sky. "I come to you my Lord, prepare my seat beside your throne."

"I swear to God, Harpe, I will blow your head into pieces all over this floor if you don't put your hands behind your back."

"You would murder the Lamb of God, but when you come before the Lord, I will still speak on your behalf."

McParlan cracked him across the back of the head with his gun and watched him slump to the ground. Blood leaked from the back of Harpe's head and across his ears. McParlan pulled out a pair of restraints and slapped them onto Harpe's wrists, then stood up and caught his breath. He used the tip of his boot to turn Harpe over onto his back. "Can you hear me, Elijah?"

Harpe groaned and murmured, "You idiot. You were supposed to kill me! My table was prepared in the House of the Lord."

"Yeah well, I'm famous for ruining people's travel plans. Sit up." McParlan yanked Harpe upright. "I'm going to tell you about your situation, although I'm tempted as hell to let you find out for yourself. You are handcuffed with a brand new piece of technology pre-set to respond to either my command or your actions. You ain't never seen anything like these before. If you struggle, squirm, run, or otherwise attempt to take undue action, they will administer an electrical shock that will feel like somebody shoved a Tesla Coil up your behind. If you attempt to say anything louder than the volume I am speaking to you in now, they will release a sonic disruption wave that is designed to displace your balance and vision. I had to experience that particular sensation in order to be issued those puppies, and let me tell you, it's all a fancy way to say that if you yell, it'll feel like two steel fists are boring their way into your ear holes and reaching into your tiny little twisted brain. You understand me?"

"You are interfering with the Lord's plan, and I will not listen to you."

"I'm taking you to court so you can stand trial and hopefully they will roll your diseased ass out the nearest space dock and let you float off into the darkness."

Harpe said nothing else, and McParlan pulled him up to his feet. He shoved the prisoner down the aisle, when the chapel's front door opened and a uniformed Customs officer rushed in with his weapon drawn. "It's ok! Calm down," McParlan called out, holding up his badge. "I got him. Took you boys long enough to realize his vehicle was docked in your parking area. What's the matter? Your technology as reliable as the PNDA's?"

The officer lowered his weapon but did not holster it. He moved forward cautiously, looking from McParlan to Harpe and then back again. "I'm taking the prisoner from here, Marshal."

McParlan put his hand on Harpe's shoulder. "Come again?"

"Hand him over, sir. Let's do this nice and easy." The officer's weapon came up again, leveled at McParlan. His eyes turned red and started to water. "Please, sir."

Elijah Harpe rolled his eyes and said, "Just shoot him already."

Information about the officer scrolled across McParlan's eye. "It's Vale, right? You've been here three years. This is your first assignment."

"Stop scanning me with that damn eye!" Vale shouted. His weapon shook in his hand but his finger was wrapped around the trigger.

"This had to be some sort of misunderstanding. Tell you what, let's call your sergeant down here and see if we can't work things out."

"I can't do that."

"Then how about I call my Headquarters?" McParlan reached around his back for his tablet. His eye identified a blinking red device on Vale's shoulder strap that was not part of the standard Customs uniform. "That's a jamming device, isn't it?" McParlan said. "Tell me, son, what's this piece of garbage holding over you?"

Vale's hands shook. "Just let him go! Please, don't make me do this. Give him over to me and we can say he escaped. We can say any damn thing you want. I don't want to kill you."

Elijah Harpe shouted, "Shoot him!"

"I warned you," McParlan said. The Peerless binders released a sonic-disruption wave that pierced Harpe's eardrums and sent him to his knees howling in pain.

Vale looked down at Harpe in confusion and McParlan lifted his Balrog. A jet of flame spat from the mouth of the gun into the center of the young officer's forehead. McParlan pulled Harpe to his feet and shoved him past Vale's body.

"My goodness, Marshal. I cannot believe you just murdered a hard-working , fellow officer of the law, in such cold blood. Very disheartening, sir. Don't he look young just laying there? Like a sweet little angel that you sent to heaven."

"Shut your filthy mouth before I put a bullet in you too, you son of a bitch. You turned that boy and he was dead the second he got in cahoots with you." McParlan shoved Harpe at the chapel door. Harpe's hands were still bound behind his back, and his face made a satisfying thump against the wood before the door swung open.

McParlan looked around the shipyard, inventorying the things that he knew. He knew he'd killed a uniformed customs officer on a space station inhabited by a hundred of his fellow officers. He knew his nearest PNDA backup was three days away. If this were a standard arrest, McParlan would escort the prisoner back to his office and notify Customs, who would agree to house the prisoner until a PNDA wagon came by. A heavily-armed uniformed Customs Officer was standing in the center of the shipyard, looking over the ships. McParlan saw the same blinking device on that officer's shoulder, and pulled Harpe back into the shadows. "Time for Plan B," he whispered.

McParlan found a small, beat-up messenger craft whose landing gear consisted of three good struts and one that buckled. He held Harpe by the elbow and banged on the port-side door.

A pimply-faced youth pulled the door open and stared at the gold badge in McParlan's hand. The distinct odor of illegal mohaderat gas escaped from within. "Uh, wow, hello, sir. Can I help you?"

McParlan scanned the ship's registration plate and said, "This ship is registered to Franklin Carlisle. Are you him?"

"Maybe, but this isn't my stuff. I just found it."

McParlan pushed Carlisle back inside the ship. "I don't have time for games, boy. I'm commandeering this vessel, and we need to leave immediately."

McParlan's cybernetic eye clicked and whirred uncontrollably, unable to focus on anything until he tightened the casing into his skull. He waited for the red lens to stabilize. The image was fuzzy and crackled with interference from the onboard computers.

The ship jerked to one side, and McParlan crashed into the opposite wall of the narrow corridor. "Goddamn it, Carlisle. Can you fly this bucket of junk or not?"

Franklin Carlisle looked back at him from the cockpit and said, "I thought someone was on us."

"There hasn't been anyone on the radar for half a parsec, you idiot. That gas you've been sniffing is making you paranoid. That's why it's illegal," McParlan shouted. He reached the storage compartment's door and opened it. Elijah Harpe was chained to a pylon with his hands behind his back. "You got any food, Marshal?"

"We should be back at Headquarters by morning as long as we can keep up this speed. Guess you should've eaten before you did all that praying, huh?"

Harpe's face twisted like a balled-up fist, "I wasn't supposed to be alive at all, heathen. My Lord is calling me to him. Ain't nothing left for me here."

"I beg to differ," McParlan said. "There's a date with the death chamber for you."

Harpe shrugged. "We'll see what Little Willy has to say about that. Chances are, he's gonna put a spike in your wheel before you get me anywhere close to that compound." Harpe leaned forward, "When he gets here, we're gonna have us a real good time, Marshal. Believe that."

The ship shook again, and McParlan placed his hand against the wall to brace himself. "Well, I love a good time, Elijah. Let me ask you a question, why did you boys attack that medical supply ship?"

"We were gonna give some much-needed relief to the poor and unfortunate, Marshal. The folks your kind don't give a squirt about."

"That's real, real noble, Elijah. But I don't believe a lick of it. We both know there's no medical supply ships with the kind of firepower that they turned on you when you took that girl. What was really on board?"

Harpe just smiled and shook his head. "You think that little boy you got flying this heap will hold up, Marshal? You already killed one youth today. How many more got to die?"

"You killed that boy," McParlan said. "Not me."

Harpe shrugged, "Don't matter. Hey, you got a wife? How about daughters? Some real pretty ones, I bet."

"Nope," McParlan replied. "It's just me and you, Elijah."

Harpe smiled. "We gonna see about that. Me and my brother, we got all sorts of friends in all sort of places, Marshal. They can tell us just about anything about anyone. We're gonna find her. And when I do, phew, it's gonna be slow and sexy. Tell you what. You drop me off at the nearest base and we'll forget all about this."

McParlan opened his mouth to respond but his voice was drowned out by roaring engines and grinding mechanical parts. The ship dropped suddenly and McParlan slammed the door shut on Harpe. He turned toward the cockpit and shouted, "Are we hit?"

Carlisle was standing up, yanking on the steering column as far as it would go. "I told you this ship wasn't equipped to maintain high speeds. The computers are fried and I can't get it to recalibrate manually!"

McParlan hurried down the hall and strapped himself into the co-pilot's chair. He grabbed the emergency controls and punched keys on the grid but the board was dark. The engines started screeching. "Where's the backup system?"

"I don't have a backup system, Marshal! I told you I couldn't do this. I begged you to find somebody else, but no, you just had to have this ship."

"Just point this bucket of shit at the nearest solid object and throw us toward it!"

The ship lurched sideways and began to spiral.

6. Hellbillies

"Where's my brother?"

Hank Raddiger backed away from the small black box sitting at Little Willy Harpe's feet. The box rattled, and Hank swallowed hard. "He took off with that lady who was piloting the Medical Transport. The one with the real pretty hair."

Little Willy smirked . "Damn, Elijah. Always was a ladies' man. How about you, Hank? You a ladies' man?"

"Naw," Hank snorted.

Little Willy looked down at the box and ran his hand over its smooth lid affectionately. "You will be. They'll come running to you like dogs to the heel of their master, if that's what you want."

"Who wouldn't?"

Willy grinned. "The pleasures of the spirit dwarf the pleasures of the flesh, my friend. Do you know what's in this box?"

Hank shook his head no, and Little Willy tapped his fingers on its shining surface. "Guess."

"I know it ain't medical supplies," Hank said. He picked at the dried blood stuck under his fingernails. "I know them soldiers hidden in that ship was armed to the teeth, and they fought like the dickens to protect it."

"That they did," Willy smiled. He licked the file-sharpened tips of his teeth, playing with strings of meat that dangled from them. There was a small finger bone on the ground within his reach. He picked it up and stuck its tip into his mouth, digging out the loose strands. "You get enough to eat?"

"I sure did," Hank said. He rubbed his stomach and said, "Stuffed."

Willy shook his head. "I been watching you, Hank. You still don't fully indulge in the spoils of war."

Hank dropped his gaze to the ground. "A few were still squirming when you started biting into them. I cooked up a little of what I found lying around, like you said. You told me I could start off slow."

"Yes, I recall," Willy said. He tossed the finger bone into a pile of scattered ribs, femurs, and pelvises. All of them had been stripped of meat and thoroughly cleaned. Willy got down on his hands and knees and pressed the side of his face against the box. He smiled as he rubbed himself on it like a cat. He whispered and cooed and pressed his lips against the lid, leaving it smeared.

"Well, we gonna open it, or should I keep guessing?"

"Not yet," Willy whispered. He got to his feet and tucked the box under his arm. "I reckon I'm still hungry."

They stepped out of the ship onto the moon's surface, avoiding the bodies of soldiers and members of their own gang littering the ground. Only an hour earlier, all of those men had been engaged in fierce combat. Only Little Willy Harpe and Hank Raddiger remained. Willy scratched himself and looked around at the scattered bodies, peering through the swirls of black soot and smoke. "What a godawful mess. See any that's moving?"

"Nope."

"Anybody hear me?" Willy called out. "Fighting's all over. Got what we came for. Friend or foe, I can get you some assistance."

Most of the soldiers were obviously dead, with large black holes blown through them by the Harpe's ship's heavy artillery cannons. Willy looked among his own men for survivors. "Grat? Emmet? Any of you still amongst the living?"

Willy grinned when he saw a hand rise in the distance followed by a low moan. "There's one," he said, slapping Hank on the stomach. "Hope you got some room left. Dinner is served."

That evening, Hank was told to build a fire and haul whatever was left of the bodies into it. He stripped off their clothes and kept any valuables. He exchanged his boots for a pair worn by one of the younger officers. They were military-issued and looked brand new. Hank pocketed necklaces and wedding rings, and whooped with joy when he found one carved from ten-percent severian.

"Those trinkets won't amount to much compared to what's in this box, Hank," Willy said. He leaned back against their ship with the box resting on his chest.

Hank wiped his brow. "Way I see it, all the Dalton's got out of this is being dead. Your brother skated off with a hump for the night. All I'm left with is whatever I can scrounge up from these folks. You got yourself that box, and you seem mighty pleased with it, so whatever it is, I hope this all was worth it."

"Actually, I think you're right. It's time we opened the box." Willy stood up and stripped off his shirt and pants, standing naked in the light of the fire. His torso was criss-crossed with scars and burns. He lifted the lid and gas hissed out, evaporating in the cool air of the moon and stirring the thing inside. The box began to rattle violently.

Hank could not see inside the opened lid, but he saw Willy's eyes widen as he reached down. Something black slithered up Willy's arm and cinched around it, yanking him closer to the box. Willy grunted, trying to pull away but could not escape the black tentacle. More black appendages reached up and coiled around Willy's chest and face.

A thing emerged from the box with a pulsating membrane at its center. It was a black gelatinous starfish with tentacles like an octopus that left sucker marks on Little Willy's skin as he struggled to pull them off of him. He screamed for help and dropped to his knees. "Get it off of me, Hank! Help me!"

Hank scrambled for one of the weapons lying on the ground. He found a rifle that looked functional and as he lifted it to fire, he saw Little Willy collapse on the ground. The creature burrowed into Willy's left armpit like it was trying to dig a hole. Its tentacles were stuck to Willy's jaw and torso.

Hank pushed the barrel of the rifle against the membrane. He could see through its thin grey flesh. Underneath the thing's body were dozens of spooling veins that aimed toward Willy's heart. They grew dark every time they slurped on Willy's blood. Hank tried to pry the creature away with the gun barrel, but could not budge it. "I'm sorry, friend," Hank said. He switched the weapon on and the loud battery pack's hum made Willy's eyes open.

"What are you doing?" Willy said. He sat up and pushed the rifle away.

"You told me to get rid of it," Hank said, taking a step back.

Little Willy caressed the tentacle stretched across his chest. "Put that thing down before you hurt yourself."

"You feeling all right?" Hank said.

"Of course." He put one large hand on Hank's shoulder, "But now I need to ask you a question of my own."

Hank squirmed at being so close to the creature. "What's that?"

Willy closed his eyes and breathed deeply. "Are you ready?"

"For what?"

"To fly!"

Hank stared at him for a moment. "Like, with a ship, you mean?"

"No, you damn fool." Willy closed his eyes again and took another breath. The creature's head swelled beneath his arm. "There it is," Willy whispered. "I can feel you now. Listen to me, Hank. Can you see yourself flying around this moon, through the night air, swooping up and down like a bird? I want you to climb up onto that rock above us and see if you can fly."

Hank did not move, and Willy pointed at the rock fifty feet above them. "Yeah, right," Hank said, when suddenly he felt the wind rushing at his face and was overcome with the sensation that he was falling. The ground rushed toward him but somehow he knew he could pull himself out of the fall and soar into the air just by sticking out his arms. Hank shook his head to clear the image from his mind.

"Hell no, I can't see myself flying. Crashing and killing myself is more like it."

Little Willy cursed and shoved Hank toward the ship. "Just get on board. We're leaving for Antioch to meet up with Elijah."

Hank shrugged and gathered up their belongings. As he made his way toward the ship, he watched Willy kneel down by the fire and stroke the creature, whispering to it like a lover.

7. The Widow

Dr. Anna Willow had never been married, yet she dressed and acted like a dowager. In her youth, she never accepted suitors and if anyone suggested an eligible bachelor, Anna politely excused herself from the conversation. Her explanation was that with all her studies, there was no time for such silliness. Now, the only offers of companionship came from lecherous old men and the distant relatives of patients who were described as her "perfect match" despite being passed over by all the women on their own planet.

At thirty-six, her looks were still enough to draw glances from men in the town, but she flicked them away like bugs. Anna's black hair, now streaked with silver, was always pulled back in a severe knot. Not once had anyone seen her put so much as a ribbon in it. Her long dress was buttoned from her waist to high up along her neck and its dark fabric was smeared with dust from the mines. She walked along Pioneer Way into the town's business district and male passersby greeted her with the tip of their hat.

The sign on Anna's office door was old and still read *DR. ROYCE HALLADAY'S FAMILY PRACTICE*. Anna told the curious that it was about keeping the traditions of their town alive. She looked away when they mentioned how much better the town had been back then, when Sam Clayton was alive.

A framed photograph of the former sheriff hung in Anna's waiting room. It was the only public memorial of him within Seneca 6.

When Clayton had not returned from his journey to Beothuk country, Walt Junger formed a search party to go find him. Walt's older brother Tilt's mutilated body was found next to Katey Halladay's and his heroism in trying to save her was the stuff of legend. What the savages did to him was not discussed by anyone but Anna heard her father say there was not enough left to reconstruct. They threw Tilt's remains into a sack and put the sack inside a coffin. Billy Jack Elliot, who expressed great regret at his behavior toward Sam, and said he desperately wanted to make amends, joined Walt's search party. And so did Anna's father, Erazamus Willow.

The search party returned four days after setting out. The townsfolk gathered in the street to hear the news. Jem Clayton stood on the steps of his father's office and watched the men enter from the security gate with lowered heads.

"Well, we found him," Walt Junger said. "He's dead."

There were gasps in the crowd and everyone turned to look at Jem, who remained motionless. Anna put her hand on his shoulder and squeezed it. "Where's the body?" she said. "Why didn't you bring it back?"

"It's at the bottom of a ravine," Billy Jack Elliot said. "There's no way to get to it. Them savages massacred him and the animals had at him after that."

Men in the crowd started to call out for revenge. Walt Junger told them to settle down, but Anna shouted over him, "Why didn't you bring him back home? He deserves a decent burial."

"I told you!" Elliot shouted back. "It's not possible."

"I want to see him, then," she said.

Elliot's face turned bright red but then he let out a laugh. "Why am I answering to a little girl with a crush on a dead man here?"

Walt Junger tapped Old Man Willow on the arm and said, "Tell her."

Old Man Willow looked at his daughter without speaking. Jem Clayton was staring at Willow with hard, unblinking eyes, and Walt Junger leaned close to Old Man Willow and whispered something. Willow's eyes watered and he said, "It's true, Anna. Everything they said. That's the end of it."

"I think all of you are goddamn liars." Anna grabbed Jem's hand and tried to pull him from the steps, but he let go of her. He remained standing, staring at the searchers until they moved away from the crowd and went off to talk amongst themselves.

Jem Clayton's eyes became hollow after that day, and even as people took him and his sister in out of charity, the boy refused to settle into any new home. He left in the night and wandered into the wasteland where he built blazing fires from sagebrush and sat staring into the flames.

The last time Anna saw Jem, he was returning to the settlement at daybreak, half-naked, covered in dirt and ash, grinning like an idiot. He tipped his head as he passed her, "Good morning, Miss Anna."

"What has gotten into you this morning, Jem Clayton?"

"Had a vision."

"Of what?" she said.

"Of myself. I'm gonna be the baddest man that's ever lived."

"Nobody as skinny as you can be a bad man," Anna said, stifling a laugh. "Come to my house and I'll put some food on for you. You look starved."

"Can't," he said as he continued walking. "No time."

He was headed toward his father's house. Anna put her hands on her hips and said, "No time because of what? Where exactly do think you are running off to?"

Jem stopped and looked back at her. His blue eyes blazed in the early morning sun and to Anna, he looked so much like his father that she had to look away. "You've been real good to us, Anna. Take care of Claire for me."

He turned and left even as Anna called out for him to wait. It was the last time anyone saw him.

That was over twenty years ago.

Anna pulled the framed photograph of Sam Clayton away from the wall and removed the small brass key from the base of the frame. She went to the closet at the end of her office and moved several boxes and laboratory coats out of her way to reveal a locked wooden box sitting on the floor.

The box had not been touched since the day her father delivered it to her office and said, "Keep this, but promise me you won't ever look inside of it."

"What is it?" she said.

"It's for Jem Clayton, if he ever decides to come back."

Anna set the box down. "And what if he doesn't?"

"He will." Old Man Willow touched the framed picture of Sam Clayton reverently. By then, her father's eyes were spoiled by cataracts that looked like saucers of milk inside his pupils and he had to squint to see his old friend's face. "Just make sure that boy's ready for it."

"Ready for what?"

Willow sighed, then turned around and took his daughter's hand in his. His hands shook and his skin was purple and splotchy with liver spots. "Every man has a destiny, Anna, and not all of them are good ones. Jem Clayton's destiny is inside that box. Swear to me you won't ever open it. Please."

"Fine, I swear it." She tried to ask him more questions, but her father started coughing until he wheezed. He touched his lips and saw blood on his fingertips. Just a few days after that, Old Man Willow passed from the world.

She bent down to look at the box and tapped the key on the lid. She hardly ever looked at it, and the urge to open it rarely emerged. Anna believed that as long as she didn't open the box, the boy who once told her he was going off to become the baddest man that ever lived would someday return.

The Sheriff of Seneca 6 moved through the town like a monarch visiting his subjects. He played the beneficent regent, handing out candy to children and small coins to destitute women. He dropped a coin into the palm of one old woman and she grabbed onto his sleeve, staining his expensive shirt with her grimy fingers. "Sheriff, why don't you go after the real criminals in this town?"

"What criminals would that be, my dear?" he said, trying to pluck her hand from his arm.

"The damn money lenders," she said. She pointed at the Savings and Loan storefront, "They don't tell you about their fees and penalties till after you miss a payment."

"I think it's only fair they should expect to be paid what is their due in a timely fashion. Don't you agree?"

"But their payments are due the last Thursday of the month, and the unions don't pay out until that Friday. There's no money left by then. And if you don't pay, they put so much interest on top of the payment, you can't never get out of it. Can't you do something?"

He smiled at her and tipped his hat. "I will go and discuss the matter with the mayor straight away. Maybe he can help you. How does that sound?"

"Oh, thank you," she said. The Sheriff hitched his belt up over the lower fold of his belly, hoping the belt would girdle some of the bulk. He walked across the road toward the mayor's office, knocking on the sign that read "HONORABLE WILLIAM J. ELLIOT, TOWN MAYOR and JUDGE."

No one answered the door. The Sheriff took off his hat and wiped the sweat from his forehead with his shirt sleeve. He tried peeking through the office window but the blinds were drawn tight.

"Sheriff Junger?" a thin, worn out man said, looking up the steps.

Walt Junger turned and fixed his hat back to his head. "Yes?"

The man looked to see if anyone was watching him, then whispered, "You still giving out money for information related to specified activities?"

Junger took one step down the rail and fixed his hand on his gunbelt. "That depends on the information *and* the activity."

"I know you and the mayor got a special interest in a few things around here. In particular, the 'Proud Lady.'" The man cocked his head toward the well-maintained saloon down the street with thick swinging oak doors.

Junger considered the man for a moment and said, "Let's just say I'm interested in *every* establishment around here, but there are some I'm willing to pay more for than others."

"And the 'Proud Lady,' sir?"

"That's one of them."

"There's a bartender named Phil Claren giving out free drinks to his buddies for extra tips, and then he shorts the register at night."

"And how do you know this?" Junger asked.

"I went with someone who knows Phil and he said, 'Watch this.' My buddy put a tenner on the bar, and Claren put it into his pocket and we were drinking for an hour straight on that."

Junger's face darkened and he fished in his pocket. He thanked the man and handed him three bills, then reconsidered it and took one back. "This is for the drinks you stole. You're lucky that's all I'm taking and not some skin off your hide."

Less than ten minutes later, Sheriff Junger sat down on the edge of a bed above the Proud Lady, tapping a sleeping Phillip

Claren on the cheek. He curled his nose at the stench of stale alcohol in the room. "Wake up, Phil."

"Sheriff?" Claren said, swiping his eyes. "The hell you doing here?"

Junger put his hat over his knee and tapped the brim with his finger. "Got a problem, Phil. Seems you've been mishandling your responsibilities downstairs. The register is short, and you've been passing out free liquor to those no-good bums you call friends." Claren rubbed his nose on his sleeve and tried to sit up, but the Sheriff laid his hand on Claren's chest and shook his head. "This ain't a you-sit-up kind of conversation, Phil."

"What kind of conversation is it, Sheriff?"

Junger removed a small hammer from his pocket that he twirled by the handle. "Now, I realize it is kind of a common practice to skim a little from most of the bars in this town. Hell, the owners factor it into their liquor sales, and turn a blind eye, figuring that if it keeps you little maggots scurrying around trying to steal a coin here or there, you won't ever get around to taking something important. But the owners of the Proud Lady are a little different, Phil. They take personal offense if so much as a thumbtack is stolen."

"I had no idea you and the owners were so close, Sheriff. I promise on my mother that will never happen again. I will be like your personal guard in there. If anybody tries anything I'll come straight to you."

"That's good, Phil. That's real good." Junger lifted the hammer up and inspected its quarter-sized steel head. "However, I've found that people often require what's called a visual aid. So before I go, I need to ask you a question. Do you have a preferred hand?"

"What do you mean?"

"I mean, someday when you manage to scare yourself up a woman and she's lying next to you in this bed, and you're stroking her body from end to end, running it all across her curves and divides, what hand do you see yourself doing that with?"

"Both?" Claren squeaked.

Junger showed him the hammer and said, "Pick a hand, stupid."

Claren moaned, "Please, I'm begging you, Sheriff. Don't. I'll never do it again, I swear!"

Junger shrugged and picked the hand for him.

8. Fathers

Jem Clayton awoke between both Alvarez sisters. One was nestled in the crook of his left arm and the other stretched out along his right. Their bodies pressed close to his, and legs wrapped around him like serpents trying to shuffle up a pole. Neither woman stirred as he untangled himself from them. Jem buttoned his shirt and slid on his pants, watching the sisters slide closer to intertwine themselves with one another. "I'm starting to wonder if you two are even related at all."

His boots were next to the bed and his coat sat folded neatly on the dresser. In the sister's hospitable arranging of his belongings, they'd doubtlessly checked for compartments containing hidden valuables. Jem Clayton turned the heel of both boots and found them still packed tight with severian. He smirked, knowing that if his hiding place could withstand the scrutiny of women as scandalous as the Alvarez sisters, no road agent had a prayer of finding it.

Jem strapped on his belt and tied both holsters to his thighs. He drew both Colt Defeaters and checked their battery levels, cartridges, and action. They were pristine. He withdrew and re-sheathed the knife hidden in the center of his back, and then the ones stored inside either boot. Finally, he removed the small Mantis two-shot revolver from his coat pocket and tucked it into his shirt, just behind the buttons.

One of the sisters looked at him from the bed. He put on his hat and unfolded several bills from his wallet, then laid them on the dresser underneath a makeup case. The woman reached toward him and brushed her fingers against his waist, "Why are you leaving so soon, Mr. Howard?"

"I ran into an old friend last night. That means it's time to move."

Her fingers traveled lower. "Will you come back soon?"

"Eventually," he said. She pouted and stuck out her lower lip before attempting to raise his interest enough to coerce him back into bed. He swept her hand away. "I left you girls a little something to remember me by while I'm gone."

He left the room and wound down the stairs toward the saloon which was already full at such an early hour. The sun roared through the cracked shuttered windows and Jem found himself tilting the brim of his hat to keep his eyes shaded. His gut was sour from the drinks he'd downed the night before. Everything was cloudy.

A street vendor on the corner sold greasy eggs and meat on a roll. Jem ordered two and walked over to a lamp post with a hanging sign that read: *CARRIAGE TRANSPORT.* Underneath that sign was a smaller, hand-written one that said: *DESTINATION TRADESVILLE.* The wind rose and kicked dust across his sandwich. Jem crushed his hat onto his head to keep it from blowing away and tossed the rest of his food into an alley.

Jem could have easily afforded to travel by air. It was safer and faster, but it carried the scrutiny of Customs Officers, or even worse, the PNDA. Jem preferred travel of the less intrusive variety.

Two men approached the staging area. The older one extended his hand to Jem and said, "Hello, friend. Name's Harlan Wells. This is my son, Adam." Harlan was bent slightly at the shoulders and his glasses were thicker than the bottom of a shot glass.

Adam wore the expression of a bemused child. His hair was cut short and uneven and he rocked back and forth at the waist. He stared at the carriages passing in the street with a wide grin and clapped his hands excitedly. A destrier flew past them so fast it made their jackets ripple, and Adam shouted.

"Fast, ain't they?" Harlan said, patting his son on the back. "Just make sure you don't lean too close to the street. Danger. Understand?"

Adam nodded, staring down at his hands while flicking his fingers back and forth.

"Nice to meet you, Mr. Wells," Jem said. "I'm Thomas Howard." He saw Harlan looking down at the guns on his belt and said, "Aw, they're just for show, really. I heard some bad things about travelling in these parts. Doubt I'd hit the rear end of a barn if I tried."

"I'm just glad to see somebody brought along a little protection. I heard there's bandits crawling all over the place out there."

"That's hogwash. Ain't no bandits," a man said as he came up behind them. He was scrawny with a long, curling mustache that twitched when he spoke. "It's the damn sky flyers trying to scare everyone from affordable transportation. It's perfectly safe out there.

I'm Charlie Boles and you all will be ridin' with me today. You ready?" They said that they were, and Boles cocked his thumb over his shoulder at the carriage waiting down the street.

The group moved toward the coach and Boles said, "Even if we do run into trouble, I've made modifications to my rig to keep your possessions protected. There's a hideaway lock box in the back for valuables. Anybody carrying anything they want to secure just in case there's trouble?"

"I thought you said there weren't any bandits," Harlan said.

"Can't hurt to be too careful."

Harlan put his bag into the box. Jem held up his hands, "I travel light."

"Weapons too," Boles said. "It's standard procedure."

"None that I ever heard of," Jem said.

"Suit yourself," Boles said. "There's other coaches for hire."

Jem saw a young, nervous boy sitting in the forward carry, holding the destrier's reins. The kid had a scattergun at his side that looked bigger than he did. Boles saw Jem looking and said, "That's just my boy, Charlie Junior. He rides shotgun with me just in case there's any trouble. That's why you don't need those hand cannons, Mr. Howard. We can take care of any problems that arise, but I don't want one of my passengers shooting us in the butt by accident."

Harlan held the door open for Adam and told him to get on. Jem said, "Hang on a minute, Mr. Wells. We'll catch the next one together."

"Can't, Tom. We already paid upfront for this ride, and can't afford to lose the deposit. Take it or leave it, we're throwing our lot in with this fellow."

Charlie Boles helped Adam up the step and waved his hand at Harlan. "And now for you, sir? Your chariot." Boles looked at Jem and said, "Either ditch them Defeaters in the back or find another ride."

Jem unhooked his gun belt and handed it over to Boles. "You be real, real careful with these now."

Boles took the belt and steadied both dangling guns in his hand before he opened the box and laid them gently inside. "Some serious firepower you got there, Mr. Howard. You ever had a chance to use 'em?"

"Only on what deserved it," Jem said. He hoisted himself into the carriage and Charlie Boles turned the lock that sealed them inside.

Adam stared out the window and panted like a dog, his face near enough to the glass to fog it up with his breath. Harlan rubbed the back of Adam's head, reassuring him that everything was all right. "He gets nervous in confined spaces. We don't travel much." Harlan looked Jem over and said, "But that doesn't explain why you look so nervous, Tom."

Jem's eyes were locked on the narrow port window that looked up at Charlie Boles's boots. Junior tapped his feet ceaselessly on the loose boards. Jem shook his head, "What makes you think I'm nervous?"

"Nothing, I guess. I'm just making conversation. Pay me no mind."

The carriage started moving and shifting from side to side. Adam laughed and bounced up and down in his seat. Harlan put his hand on his son's shoulder, "Like I said, he's worked up about this. If you need to catch some sleep I'll do my best to keep him quiet."

"No. That won't be necessary." Jem looked through the opposite window as the town rolled past.

Several hours later, the destriers were still moving at full gallop. The beasts were in good condition and the signs of civilization disappeared. The wasteland extended into long stretches of red shale with dust that blew in rolling waves. Adam's head was in Harlan's lap, but he was awake, occupying himself by sticking his fingers into his mouth, then taking them out to stare at the strands of drool. The old man's head was cocked back and he snored so loud that he drowned out the noise of the wheels spinning under the carriage.

Charlie Boles Junior's feet tapped away in the forward perch, building to a frantic pace that stopped just as the destriers began to slow. The carriage rolled to a stop. Jem took in a deep breath and held it.

There was talk between the men above that ended when Charlie shouted, "Stop arguing with me and get your candy ass down there like we talked about!"

The lock on the carriage door spun and Junior opened it, pointing a double-barreled Winchester inside the carriage. The boy's hands shook and he stuttered when he said, "Get your hands up, all of you!"

Jem got down from his seat and squatted in front of Junior, putting his chest against the barrel. "Do me a favor, son? Take your finger off that trigger. Professionals keep it on the side of the frame unless they need to shoot."

"Shut up! Wake up the old man and the mushbrain and get out of the carriage."

Jem smiled wide. "Ain't no need for that. These two don't have a dime on them. I, on the other hand, have got something you and your Dad will desperately want. Leave these two out of it and I'll make sure the two of you are more than compensated."

Junior looked from the passenger door to where Charlie Boles was sitting. "Hey, Pa?"

"They out of the carriage yet?" Boles shouted.

"Go on, tell him," Jem whispered. "He won't be mad once he sees how much severian I'm holding."

"Pa? I need you to come here."

"Goddammit, Junior. So help me God, if they ain't out of there yet, there is gonna be hell to pay." Charlie Boles came around the side and cursed when he saw Jem still sitting in the doorway. He cracked Junior across the back of the head so hard that tears showed up in the boy's eyes. Boles snatched the shotgun away and pushed Junior out of the way. "I apologize for the lack of precision to all this, Mr. Howard. He's new and just getting started. I'm sure you understand."

"More than you know," Jem said.

"Now, kindly exit the carriage and stand over there behind it while I remove the other two."

"I was just telling Charlie Junior that there's really no need-"

Boles cocked the gun's hammer and wrapped his finger around the trigger. "I can take your money whether you are alive to know it or not, Mr. Howard. I'd prefer you walk away from this, but I assure you, I will put a hole in your body if you do not extricate."

Jem got down from the door and moved in the direction he was told. Boles poked his head into the carriage and cursed. He handed the shotgun over to Junior. "You keep that scatter gun on him and if he moves, shoot him," Boles said. He pointed a bent finger at Junior, "If he moves and you do not shoot him, I am going to grievously injure you."

Junior turned back to Jem. The boy had a nervous tic that made his eyes squish together and his nose twitch. Jem said, "Don't worry, Junior. I like you, so I'll stand still."

Boles climbed into the carriage, followed by Adam's horrified scream. Harlan Wells shouted in protest and Boles backed down from the doorway, drawing a pistol from his waist. "Get out here right now. Move it, old man. I swear to God, I will either shoot you both or drag that retard out by his ears and when they rip off I'll make 'em into a necklace."

Harlan's head poked out of the carriage, "This is an outrage!"

"Just get out here, Mr. Wells. Adam will be calm if you're calm," Jem said. "Do what they tell you and everything will be fine."

Harlan came down, complaining that his back had stiffened up on the ride and not to rush him. He waved his hand at Adam and said, "Come on out, son. It's okay. I want to show you something."

Adam braced both hands against the doorframe and anchored himself inside the carriage. Charlie Boles kicked the side of the wagon and shouted, "Get out here before I drag you out!"

Adam vanished. Harlan yelled at Boles, "Don't scare him like that! If he gets panicked, he'll have a seizure, you son of a bitch."

"Fine. If the retard wants to sit in there and bake to death, let him." Boles slammed the carriage door shut and Adam started beating the inside of the door with his fists. The thumping stopped abruptly, and they could hear Adam gurgling.

Harlan cried out and tried clawing past Boles to get the carriage door open, but Boles spun and wind-milled the butt-end of his pistol across the old man's forehead. Harlan dropped to the dirt with blood bubbling through his white hair.

Boles hurried to turn Harlan over and keep his blood from staining his clothing. "Can't sell it later if there's blood on it," he said to Junior. "Remember that."

"Ok, Pa."

"You just keep an eye on that one," Boles said. He put his gun down on the ground next to Harlan and patted the old man down. He removed the few dollar bills folded in Harlan's shirt pocket. He continued searching, giving Junior instruction on where else to search for money. "Sometimes they hide stuff in secret pockets, and you got to check, now."

"Ok, Pa."

Jem grabbed the shotgun's barrels and tugged while the boy's eyes were on his father. Junior instinctively yanked the gun back and Jem shoved it forward, slamming the stock into the boy's gut. Junior folded in half and sent a pile of sickness splattering onto the ground. Jem kicked the boy's legs out from under him and sat him down hard.

Boles spun at the sound of the commotion, scrambling for his gun. He nearly had it but froze at the sound of Jem cocking the shotgun's hammer back. Boles put up his hands and said, "You wouldn't shoot a man in the back, now would you?"

Jem pulled the trigger.

The weapon clicked, empty. Jem switched the hammer to the other side and said, "Still got another barrel. Let's try that again." Boles scrambled across the dirt like a crab and sat up to beg for mercy. Jem put the shotgun's barrel against Boles' forehead and pulled the trigger. Also empty. "You are one lucky son of a bitch," Jem said.

Boles grabbed his revolver off the ground and stood up, looking at Jem in disbelief. "You really would have shot me. You crazy bastard!"

Jem dropped the empty shotgun and held up his hands. "I'm guessing Junior forgot to load his gun?"

"I reckon he did," Boles said. "First time in my life I've ever been grateful that boy is an idiot. Junior? Stop crying like a little girl and get up. I'm fixin' to execute this murderous prick."

"That seems kind of excessive, friend," Jem said. He scratched his stomach, feeling the Mantis two-shot tucked away behind the buttons.

"You were going to shoot me from behind!"

Smoke and flame flashed from Jem's vest. The Mantis' bullet hit Charlie Boles in the hip and Jem smacked the revolver out of Boles' hand.

Jem tore off his smoldering vest and threw it down. He pressed the Mantis against the side of Boles' head and hissed, "You really must have an angel sitting on your shoulder today, you piece of trash. I was trying to gut shoot you. I was going to leave you here to die in the desert with your insides spilling out of you. I've got one more bullet though. Where do you want it?"

Harlan Wells groaned and tried lifted his head. "Mr. Wells? Harlan," Jem shouted. He pointed at Junior and said, "Get that carriage door open and check on Adam."

Junior limped over to the wagon to open the door. Adam was splayed across the floor motionless, with white foam spilling from of the corners of his mouth. "Harlan!" Jem shouted. "Get up and check on your son."

Junior helped Harlan to his feet and the old man staggered over to the carriage, clutching his head. He reached inside and checked for a pulse on Adam's neck. "He had a seizure," Harlan said. "But he's passed out for now. He should come out of it soon."

Jem threw Boles against the carriage hard enough to rock it. He stuck the Mantis under Boles' chin and used it to lift his jaw so that their eyes met. "Lucky again, Boles. I was going to shoot you between the legs if that boy was dead, but now I reckon I'll settle for just taking you off the planet."

"Go ahead and shoot, you son of a bitch," Boles said. His foul spittle splattered Jem across the face. "You think I ain't ready to die?"

Jem was about to squeeze the trigger, when Harlan Wells wedged himself between him and Boles. "I won't let you do this," Harlan said.

Jem pushed Harlan away, but the old man grabbed the front of the gun and covered the barrel's opening with his hand. "I said, don't."

"Are you insane? He was going to kill you so he could steal your clothes. Look what he did to your son."

"Look what you're doing to his," Harlan said.

Jem looked at Junior and said, "Walk away, boy. Get going. I'm doing you a favor."

Junior stood in place, covered in his own sickness, begging Jem not to shoot.

Harlan stared Jem in the eyes and said, "Let him go, son."

"Stop calling me that! I am not your goddamn son."

"You let him go. Or you shoot me too."

Jem slammed the Mantis across Boles' face. Boles dropped to the ground and Jem kicked him in the gut several times, then spit on him. Boles fell over on his side and Junior pushed past Harlan to dive on top of him to protect him.

Jem looked down in horror at the boy.

Boles spat out a mouthful of blood and groaned, "I'll find you, you son of a bitch. I'll find you and when I do, I'll kill you."

"I hope you do, Charlie," Jem said. "I'll be at Seneca 6. Just ask for Jem Clayton. They'll know where to find me."

Charlie Boles and his son limped off into the wasteland long before Jem opened the rear of the carriage to remove his weapons. Harlan looked at him and said, "So which is it? Tom Howard or Jem Clayton?"

Jem strapped on his gun belt and said, "I know it must seem a surprise to you, being that you don't associate with people like me and Charlie Boles, but it doesn't pay to get familiar nowadays."

"We were going to Tradesville," Harlan said. "What's in Seneca 6?"

"You and Adam need to see a doctor, and it's the closest main settlement to us. Plus, we need to get to safety. It won't take long for Boles to get fixed up and come looking for us."

"What makes you think he'll come looking for us?"

"Because that's what I would do," Jem said. "Just get in the back with Adam and I'll handle it."

In the distance, Junior was walking beside his father, helping him stay on his feet. The boy looked back at Jem, and Jem paused at the hatred in his eyes. He recognized it intimately. Jem snapped the reins on the wagon and got it moving.

9. Ghosts

Flames licked the soles of his feet, bringing him to consciousness. He started to flail, panicking, ripping off the chunks of red hot metal that left hissing welts on his bare skin. Jimmy McParlan tried yanking his legs away from the fire but was pinned by one of the ship's support pylons. A hundred different pieces of the hull were piled on top of him and all around. McParlan rolled over on his side, struggling to escape from the pylon's weight before his clothing caught fire. He was still strapped to the co-pilot's chair, buried under a pile of smoldering debris.

Ash filled his mouth and he gagged on the taste of burnt plastic. Finally, he managed to unbuckle the restraint and press the column an inch off of his legs. Enough to slide them from the flames. He rolled away and crawled through the wreckage on his belly.

There was the smell of roasted meat. McParlan saw a blackened body on the ground nearby. The hands were not cuffed together. McParlan cursed and poked his head up, looking around. "Elijah? You dead too?"

He tried to get his cybernetic eye to focus, but instead of scanning the landscape, it filled his head with static. McParlan unscrewed the thing and tossed it into the ashes.

A pair of shackled hands raised in the air, ten feet from the frame of the shattered rear wing of the ship. McParlan climbed over sharp paneling and tangled wires and debris. He tore his elbows and knees as he crawled toward Elijah. "Still alive, you son of a bitch?"

Harpe laughed, "The Lord just isn't ready to take me today, Marshal."

McParlan drew his Balrog and put the barrel an inch from Harpe's head, then laid flat and panted, trying to catch his breath. "We'll see about that, Elijah. Here's the deal. I don't think I'm long for this world, but if I feel the claw of the reaper come around my shoulder the last thing I'm going to do is tighten my finger around this trigger." He coughed up something black and oily. "You break anything in the crash?"

Harpe pointed at the thick white bone sticking out of his thigh. "I can't even feel that," he said. "Reckon I'm in shock. God be praised." Harpe laughed again, but his chest was clogged with dirt and smoke. He spat something yellow into the dirt and propped himself up on one elbow, looking at Franklin Carlisle's body. "Got yourself another one? Racking up quite the little body count, aren't you? Honestly, you don't look too good Marshal. You fixing to check out on me now?"

McParlan heard three Elijah Harpes speak and saw twice as many. His eyelids fluttered and he nearly pulled the trigger, but was able to shake his head enough to focus on Harpe's sweaty, snickering face staring at him. "Don't know how long we're gonna be out here, Elijah, but I bet that shock is only going to last a little while. Pretty soon, you'll start screaming for your mama and that thought is what's gonna keep me hanging on."

Jem Clayton looked at the tall tower of black smoke rising over the peaks of Coramide Canyon and strapped the destriers across their hides to move them toward it. Harlan Wells leaned against the window beneath Jem's feet and said, "What's wrong?"

"Some sort of crash down in the Canyon. I'm going to check on it real quick. How's Adam?"

"Seems all right. He woke up, but he's sweating like a dog. I think the heat is getting to him."

Jem smelled burnt fuel and plastic, but there was another smell, the kind that lingers around kitchens. Jem worked the animals up the path to the overlook, and peered down at the canyon below. He eased the animals down the path, drawing one of his Defeaters and cocking the hammer back. There were two men lying together at the edge of the crash site, one wearing shackles, and the other pointing a gun at that man's head. Neither of them were moving. Buzzards circled overhead, waiting to feast.

Jem stopped the carriage at the bottom of the path and knocked on the rear door. Harlan opened it an inch and frowned. "You aren't going over there are you?"

"Just to see if there's any survivors."

"What if it's a trap?" Harlan said.

Jem looked at the crash site and then up at the canyon, checking for snipers. "Doesn't seem likely. Hell of a set-up just to hope somebody comes across this mess. I think this is genuine. You want to hold onto one of my guns just in case?"

Harlan shook his head no and closed the carriage door. Jem removed both weapons and headed for the bodies.

There were dead buzzards scattered across the ground, their carcasses blown to pieces. Jem saw that the old man was holding a Balrog 6K pistol. *Standard issue for PNDA Marshals,* Jem thought. He crouched beside the old man and tapped him on the shoulder with his gun. "You alive, friend?"

McParlan groaned and he tried squeezing the Balrog's trigger. The gun slipped from his grasp and he muttered, "Not yet, damn you. Get your claws off me until it's finished."

Jem picked up the Balrog and slid it into his belt. He rolled McParlan onto his back and inspected him. The old man's lips were white and cracked. Jem waved over to the carriage and called for Harlan to "Bring the water. Hustle up."

McParlan's eyes rolled back in his head. "I can't go with you. Not unless he goes too. It isn't finished…"

Harlan carried two canteens over and handed one to Jem. Jem unscrewed the cap and poured a little onto the old man's grizzled face, letting it trickle between his lips. Harlan went to pour water into the mouth of the prisoner but Jem said, "Keep away from that one until we figure out what's going on."

McParlan's eyes fluttered open. "Keep it coming," he rasped.

"In a minute," Jem said. "Not too much at once or you'll choke."

The Marshal cursed Jem and started to cough. Jem waited for it to pass before he slowly poured another few capfuls of water into his mouth.

Jem let McParlan lay back down and carried the canteen over to Elijah Harpe. He squatted down next to him, keeping his pistol ready. "Give…me some…you son of a bitch," Harpe croaked. Jem splashed him in the face and Harpe swiped his tongue around his mouth, sucking in every drop. Jem held Harpe's head up and poured a little more water into his mouth.

While both men nursed their canteens, Jem had Harlan bring the carriage closer to them. He kicked a few of the feathered corpses out of the carriages way and said, "You shoot all these buzzards?"

"Bastards kept trying to eat us," McParlan grunted. "I'm obliged you came along when you did."

Jem looked back at him. "You with the PNDA?"

McParlan nodded. "I'm Marshal James McParlan. This here piece of human waste is Elijah Harpe."

Jem's eyes narrowed, "Harpe? You're kidding me. I read about those boys." He turned to look at the other body, "Is that his brother?"

"No. Just the unfortunate soul who happened to be transporting us." McParlan's face twisted in pain as Jem pulled him to his feet. He draped an arm around Jem's shoulders and limped toward the wagon. "No matter what, you cannot let that man out of your sight. If he tries to run, kill him. He's done things you couldn't imagine in your worst nightmares."

Jem looked at the empty socket of McParlan's missing eye. "I'll make sure to keep my eye on him."

"What did you say your name was?"

"I didn't." He helped McParlan into the carriage and walked back over to Elijah Harpe. "Is all that stuff they put in the paper about you and Little Willy true?"

Elijah squinted up at him. "Like what?"

"That you some wild boys who go about raping, killing, and pillaging whatever you please. Real barbarians. Take whatever and don't care who stands in your way. That might be my kind of party."

"Well, then I reckon the good Lord has delivered me into the hands of an angel."

"Amen to that," Jem said.

"You believe in the Lord, our God?"

"You better believe it," Jem said, crossing his heart.

"My brother, here is what I want you to do then. Go put a bullet into that heathen of a Marshal's head and send him to judgment. Then me and you can get out of here and figure out a way to signal Little Willy. Parties? Shoot. You ain't seen nothing yet."

Jem glanced over his shoulder at Harlan, who was leaned over the carriage, watching them carefully. "What about the old man? He's got his son along with him. I expect they'll be in the way."

"How old's the boy?" Harpe said.

"Why?"

"Thought you might want to keep him. Who knows how long we'll be stuck out here? Any port in a storm, so they say. A man's physical needs must be fulfilled so that he might do the good work, my brother."

Jem nodded and reached down for the knob of bone sticking out of Harpe's leg and twisted it like a doorknob. Harpe clawed at Jem's hands, trying to wrench them away, but Jem slapped him and twisted again until Harpe screamed and beat his fists against the dirt.

When Jem let go, Harpe laid there panting and said, "You son of a bitch."

"There will be no more speaking from you unless you are spoken to, understand?" Jem said. "You so much as look at that boy and I will cut out your eyes. Speak to him and I'll take your tongue." He waited for Harpe to nod and then heaved him to his feet. Harpe stood there, waiting for assistance, and Jem just pointed at the wagon. "Move it. You're riding up front with me."

Harpe pulled himself into the carriage's forward carry and tried to shift his injured leg inside without bending it. He collapsed into the seat and groaned, muttering a prayer as sweat dripped down the tip of his nose and stained his shirtfront.

Jimmy McParlan knocked on the bottom of the boards and peered up at them. "Hey, Elijah," he said. "Shock wear off yet?"

McParlan slid into his seat and waited for the carriage to start moving before he removed the tablet from his belt and turned it on. He looked at the photographs he'd taken of his rescuer. The interface was broken but he could still access information already stored there. He loaded the photographs and began searching the database for Seneca. The computer verified the man's physical description, and started to provide details about a particular outlaw that made McParlan's eyebrows rise.

Elijah Harpe's open flesh sizzled in the harsh sun and his blood was filling up in the boot of his broken leg. His head rolled forward and stayed there until they would hit a bump, and he'd suddenly cry out. Jem ignored the noise, whistling an old severian miner's tune as he worked the reins. Elijah reached for Jem's sleeve and said, "Put a bullet in me. Give me your gun. I'll do it myself."

Jem yanked his arm away and swatted Elijah across the mouth with the back of his hand. "Keep your filthy hands off me."

McParlan knocked on the window below. "Stop the carriage."

The Marshal limped around the side of the forward carry and frowned at Harpe's leg. "You know how to make a tourniquet?"

Jem looked into the distance and said, "Nope."

"Mind stepping down here for a moment, boy?"

Jem shrugged and came down, walking around the front of the destriers while still keeping an eye on Harpe. "That prisoner is going to bleed out in a few short minutes if you don't tourniquet that leg," McParlan said.

"Sorry, Marshal. Seems I plum forgot how to fix one up," Jem said. "I reckon ol' Elijah is going to perish."

McParlan smacked Jem's hat off of his head and put his face close to the younger man's, giving him a clear view of the dark recesses of his empty eye socket. "I dragged that bastard halfway across the galaxy to see justice served and I ain't about to let you piss it away just because you think it's some kind of sick fun."

Jem looked down at his hat and then back to McParlan. His hands were near enough to the handles of either Defeater to draw them with the slightest effort. McParlan saw the muscles in Jem's arms flex and said, "Oh, is that it? You thinking about stepping up in the world of crime, Jim?"

"Jem. Not Jim."

"I know what I said. What the hell is wrong with you?"

"I just don't like his kind, is all."

"Good, cause I don't either," McParlan said. He reached down to pick up Jem's hat and cleaned it off, making sure the brim was straight. "In our line of work you don't just kill these bastards. You make them suffer. A judge is going to sentence him to a lifetime of hell on a penal colony where every maniac sideshow freak is going to be lined up to play with him. It's our job to deliver him there."

"Who said anything about this being *our* line of work, Marshal?"

McParlan opened the carriage door and said, "Get that tourniquet on him."

Jem cut a long leather strap from the destrier's harness and snapped it in his hand. He tapped his vest, "No badge, Marshal. That means I don't take orders from you."

"You never know. I've got an eye for talent."

"That ain't the one you lost, is it?"

"No, that's the foot I broke off in the last smart ass's rear end. Get that tourniquet on him."

The *visitors station* outside of Seneca 6's fortified security gate was just a computer screen attached to a wooden post. Jem touched the screen and waited. Beyond the gate, dozens of people crowded the sides of Pioneer Way. The closest building to the gate was the Sheriff's Office and Jem only looked long enough to see that not much had changed.

He looked up at the cameras mounted to the gate, waiting for an answer. He rubbed his chin, feeling the stubble in the palm of his hand, and tapped the screen again and the words *security authorization code* appeared. Jem typed in his old residential identification code and watched the gate for signs of movement.

The gate's clear electrical field rippled and a stooped-over man shuffled through it, carrying a clipboard. He looked from his clipboard to the wagon and frowned, pushing his thick glasses up on his nose to squint at Jem. "Where did you get that code, young man?"

"It's the same one I've used since the day I was born. I've been away on business for awhile, but I should still be on your records."

"Clayton?" the gatekeeper said. "Jem Clayton?" Jem nodded and the man looked over the information on his chart. "Well, I see you still listed here, but it shows you haven't paid your occupancy tax in over ten years. You owe quite a bit of money."

"I don't seem to recall any occupancy tax. How long's that been in effect?"

"Over ten years."

Jem reached into his shirt pocket for his small clip of flash money. "And I thought all the robbers were out in the wasteland. Here you go, sir. I reckon that should settle us up and still put me ahead for a few years at least."

The gate keeper frowned at the folded bills. "I don't think I'm authorized to accept such a large sum, partner. You probably need to take that to the Sheriff. He's the one who collects the taxes around here. You can come in, but don't let me find out you didn't go see him and settle up."

"Not a problem. Who is the Sheriff nowadays?"

"Walt Junger, of course."

Jem shifted in his seat and kept his smile plastered tight to his face. "Is that right? What about that old rascal Billy Jack Elliot? He's the deputy, I suppose?"

The gate keeper bristled, "I'd prefer you call him Mayor Elliot, mister. Or even Judge Elliot. He's both."

"Judge *and* Mayor? Don't that just beat all. And here I was worried about what had become of my old home town. We're just on our way to see those boys. I've got a carriage full of prisoners and lawmen and sickly folks who could use some services. Can you send the doctor around to the sheriff's office?"

"I can," the gatekeeper said, cocking his head sideways. "By any chance, was your daddy Sam Clayton?"

"Yes, he was."

"You look just like him."

"That right?" Jem said. "Did you know him?"

"Did I know him? Shoot, boy, we was like best friends! He never told you about Fred Walters? Listen, I have something at my house that might be of interest to you. I live in Tom Master's old house."

"The deputy?" Jem said.

"Exactly. Stop over and see me and I'll show it to you." Walters entered a few codes into his box and the electrical static of the security gate went silent as it opened. "The Sheriff's Office is the first building on your left," Walters said.

"Thanks, but I remember."

A child burst into Anna Willow's office, "Dr. Willow! Come quick!"

"What's the matter?"

"Mr. Walters gave me a penny to come fetch you. Said you're needed at the Sheriff's Office." Anna grabbed her black leather medical bag and locked the door behind her. *Maybe someone finally got sick of that bastard's greed and shot him,* she thought. *Lord, forgive me for even thinking that. On second thought, forgive me for not being upset by the idea.*

Anna stopped at the sight of the man standing on the Sheriff's porch. He spit a cheek full of cut into the dirt and turned to look at her. Anna's knees buckled slightly and she said, "Sam?"

She ran across the street, holding the bag against her chest, when the corner of the man's mouth bent into a sly smile. Jem Clayton tipped his hat at her, "Well, look at you, all grown up and beautiful. Good evening, Miss Anna. Been awhile."

Anna was frozen as he came down the steps, holding his hand out like it would be enough to just take her bag. She threw herself into his arms and yelled, "Jem!"

He embraced her awkwardly at first, but soon held her tight and patted her back. He ran his fingers through her hair and said, "It's all right. I missed you too, Miss Anna."

She pushed him back and wiped a tear from her eye. "Stop calling me that. I'm only four years older than you. Look at you."

"Where's the doctor? Are you his assistant?"

"I am the doctor, thank you very much."

"Well, that's good. I got a whole mess of people in there that need you to take a look at them."

Anna followed Jem up the stairs toward the sound of shouting voices, to see Walt Junger leaning over his desk and pounding it with his fist. "I don't give a goddamn who you are or what you represent, you son of a bitch! This is my office, and my town, and you can't just waltz in here and lay claim to it!"

McParlan leaned across the desk until the tip of his large red nose was only inches from Junger's. "This entire planet operates under a trade agreement with the PNDA, which makes every colony my territory. You can either clear out and let me house my prisoner, or you can share a cell with him until I'm finished."

"I will be filing a complaint with the authorities," Walt Junger said.

Jem whistled as he looked at the numerous plaques and certificates decorating walls. All bore Sheriff Walt Junger's name. A framed medal hung in a shadow box over the desk chair citing Junger's bravery for breaking up a bar fight seven years ago. There was a large plaque near the desk celebrating the bravery of Deputy Tilt Junger with the date of the Beothuk raid etched in fancy script across the center.

The old desk where Sam Clayton had painstakingly typed out his warrants with just his index fingers and a litany of curses for every mistake was gone. In its place, an expensive, hand-crafted one emblazoned with the words *PRESENTED TO SHERIFF WALTER JUNGER, PROTECTOR OF SENECA 6* across the side closest to the door so it was the first thing visitors saw upon entering. Jem said, "Where'd you earn all these, Sheriff? I hadn't heard of any other invasions."

"Some people are able to run such a tight ship that no one would dare invade with them in charge, Jem," Junger said. "I told you to wait outside while I discussed this matter with the Marshal."

"Sounds to me like it's been discussed, and you lost."

Anna let out a gasp at the sight of Elijah Harpe spread out on the floor of the jail cell. The white bone of his thigh protruded into the air like the flagstaff of a ship, its wound covered with bugs that hungrily sucked on the blood and meat. Anna went to open the cell door, but Jem grabbed her arm. "Let go of me. That man needs treatment before he dies!"

"We've got other wounded that need to be seen first, Anna."

She looked at the old man sitting on the bench with his arm around his son, who was contentedly rocking back and forth, flicking his fingers together. "Them?" she said. "I will decide what patients receive priority in this town, thank you very much."

Jem tightened his grip. "That man is a prisoner, and those two are innocent civilians. These two go first, then the Marshal. When they're all cleared, you can come back."

"How long has that tourniquet been on his leg?" Anna demanded.

"Not too long," Jem said. "He'll be fine."

"This is ridiculous." Anna ripped her arm away from Jem and said, "Sheriff, do something!"

Junger held up his hands and leaned back in his seat, "Apparently this ain't my office anymore, Dr. Willow."

Jem put his back against the jail cell and propped one foot against it. Anna ordered Adam and Harlan to get to their feet and remove their shirts. As Harlan stood to his feet he gasped, grabbing his side and had to reach out for Anna to stay upright. In a moment, he had regained his composure and said, "Ma'am, my son has a special condition, and he might not be able to get undressed in front of all these people. I'm afraid if we try to force him, he might have another fit."

Anna sighed and waved her arm toward the door, "Let's go then. My office isn't very far." Harlan thanked her and touched Adam on the shoulder, telling the boy to come along. He winced as Adam grabbed him by the arm to pull himself to his feet. Anna pointed at McParlan and said, "You too. Let's go, so I can get back before this man dies."

Sheriff Junger's head shot up, "You better be taking your prisoner with you if you intend on leaving these premises, Marshal. I surely will not be taking responsibility for him."

McParlan patted Jem as he passed, "Deputy Marshal Clayton will watch him."

"Fine," Junger said, collecting his hat to leave. He looked back at Jem and said, "Don't touch nothing in here. This isn't your daddy's office anymore, boy. We do real law enforcement now."

Jem watched him leave and then turned toward McParlan, "Since when do field agents have the authority to deputize somebody?"

"Since tonight," McParlan said.

Anna put her hand in Jem's and leaned close to him, "Listen, I understand this has all got to be a bit much for you, and I know you have no love for Walt Junger. But please, don't play the tough guy role with me. I've known you since you were just a little boy, and I know in my heart you are not going to let me leave while there is a man laying inside that cell about to die. Now please, for me, let me at least look him over."

Jem looked over his shoulder at Harpe, seeing that his face had turned marble white and his breathing grown so shallow that it took him a second to decide whether it even continued at all. He turned back to meet Anna's expectant gaze and said, "Right after you get finished with the others."

Anna threw the door open and left, and McParlan shook his head. "I see you got quite a way with womenfolk too."

Jem sat on top of Junger's desk and looked over the Marshal. "How is it you're up and walking around so much, while Harpe is ready to give up the ghost?"

"There's more metal and plastic inside of me than this whole complex. You think that was my first crash? Listen, we've got more pressing issues. If I don't make contact with the Agency to let them know where we are and who we have, we're sitting ducks."

"How do you figure?" Jem said.

"Little Willy Harpe makes his brother look like a Sunday school teacher, and I will lay you money he is out there hunting for Elijah right now. If he finds us, he'll burn this whole town to the ground. I need to send a signal to PNDA Control. Is there a long-range antenna nearby?"

Jem shook his head, "No. Seneca 6 never had much need for communication with the outside worlds. The closest one was at Fort Bane, but they abandoned it when I was just a kid."

"If it's still standing, we can use it. Those things were designed to withstand a fusion bomb. How hard is it to get to?"

"It's probably four days ride from here, just past the mountains. But that territory was overtaken by the Beothuk before I was born. The mining colonies let them have it."

"What the *hell* is a Beothuk?" McParlan said.

"It means 'Original Man of Seneca.' At least, to them it does."

"Well, if we can't send that distress signal, everything between Little Willy Harpe and his brother is going to be razed to the ground. If you give a damn about this place, you better figure out a way to get to Fort Bane."

Jem watched McParlan limp down the steps toward Anna's office, and he went around the Sheriff's desk and sank into the deep leather chair. The leather cushion sighed under him and he leaned back, kicking his boots up onto to the desktop. He tapped them together so that dirt fell from their soles onto the desk's immaculate surface.

Jem had been to see Deputy Tom Masters once as a boy. Tom's son Bart was the same age as Jem, but they lived too far apart to spend much time together. Anyway, Bart was a small, pudgy boy with a round face who didn't like to get dirty. Whenever Jem or one of the other boys would pull a snake out of a rock and chase the girls around with it, Bart would run away too. Jem didn't trust that.

The Clayton's house was set toward the rear of the settlement and their closest neighbors were Royce and Katey Halladay. Sam preferred it that way because it meant people were less likely to bother him and his kids, especially if they were sore about something he did on his job. It was Sam's practice to ride the length of Pioneer Way into work each morning, just to make sure nobody had stolen it during the night, he said.

On a summer morning, months before the Beothuk raid, Sam was sitting in his office watching a prisoner everyone called Shoelace Bob. Jem had no idea what his real name was, or why they called him that, they just did. He heard Bob's snores from the street as he bounded up the steps two at a time. Bob's stockinged feet were sticking out from the cell, with his toes curled around the cell bars. Jem opened the door and winced at the odor coming from Bob that was like fermented potatoes.

Sam looked up from his newspaper, "What are you doing here? Who's watching your sister?"

"Miss Katey woke us up for breakfast and told me to bring you some." Jem handed his father the basket of food Katey Halladay had prepared for him. There were biscuits wrapped in napkins, and thick sausages Sam could pick up and eat with his fingers.

"God bless that woman," Sam said. He pushed an envelope across his desk at Jem. "Since you're here, I need you to do me a favor. Take that to Tom Masters on your way home. Tell him not to be so damn careless next time."

Shoelace Bob sat up in his bunk to listen as they talked. There was a huge, swollen lump the size of a fist over Bob's right eye and an imprint of the butt end of one of Sam's Colt Defenders sat in its purple nucleus. Whatever reason Sam had to buffalo the man the night before, it had clearly taken the fight out of him. Shoelace Bob was meeker than a schoolmarm when he waved Jem over and said, "Hey, boy, come here."

Jem hesitated and looked at his father, who considered it for a moment before telling Jem, "Go ahead. Okay, stop. That's close enough."

Bob wrapped his fingers around the bars. "Tell Tom I'm real sorry for what happened, and I didn't mean nothing by it. Ok?"

"Ok."

"You taking his badge back to him?"

Jem felt the hard star-shaped object inside the envelope and said, "If that's what this is."

Bob dug into his pocket and pulled out a coin. He flipped it through the bars toward Jem. "That's for your trouble. Just make sure you tell him."

Jem held up the coin for Sam to see and said, "Is it all right if I keep it?"

Sam said that it was and Jem darted down the steps with the envelope in one hand and the money in the other. He ran to the candy store and bought a cold bottle of soda pop and two honeysuckle sticks. He tucked the second stick in his back pocket for Claire, but as the first one dissolved in his mouth, he began having serious doubts about the second one's life expectancy.

Tom Masters had a small, older home with a well-kept front yard and a wide porch. There was a freshly painted swing at one end that looked out on Pioneer Way. Jem knocked on the screen door and heard someone call out they were coming. Tom Masters opened the door, clutching a hunk of raw steak to his face. His mouth was busted open and he squinted like the sunlight made his bruises hurt even worse. "Jem? What are you doing here?"

Jem handed Tom the package and watched him struggle to open it with one hand. Jem asked for it back and ripped it in half. He handed Tom a badge with the word *DEPUTY* stamped across the front.

"Phew," Tom said. "I thought I lost this in the tussle."

"Shoelace Bob said he's sorry and didn't mean nothing by it."

Tom clucked his tongue and pulled the steak from his face, showing Jem where his eye was completely swollen shut and the bare patch where his hair should be. There were stitches zigzagged across the freshly shaved skin. "My boy cried like a baby when he saw me. I lost a whole day's pay at the mine, and will probably miss a few more. Plus, I still owe Doctor Halladay for these stitches. Ask me how worried I am about what that son of a bitch feels."

"Well, he said he's real sorry," Jem said.

Masters sighed and pressed the steak back to his face. "I guess that goes with the job. Just remember, someday when you're out there rounding up the bad guys, don't ever accept an offer to shake hands with someone you're fixing to arrest."

"Okay."

"I've known Bob since before I was your age. He thumped me like this the second he had me by the hand." Tom rustled Jem's hair and said, "You want me to call Bart down?"

Jem said he had to go, and ran from the porch. He pulled the second honeysuckle stick out and decided that whatever part of it survived the trip home could be Claire's.

Jem heard later that Shoelace Bob had knocked Tom Masters out cold with one punch, but continued to beat the Deputy while he was lying there on the street. Bob ripped off Masters' badge and dropped it in his pocket, laughing right up until the moment Sam Clayton swung the butt-end of a Colt Defender across his face.

Jem thought about Bart Masters' fat face filling up with tears and scowled. I'd never act like that, he thought. Not that anything would happen to Sam Clayton. He's the one that does the swinging, not the one who gets swung on.

Jem rode up to the path to Masters old house, remembering Bart Masters. Wishing he could go back and tell that boy how little he'd really known. Maybe if I see him, Jem thought, I'll buy him a beer and that will make us even.

The house was smaller than he remembered. The same porch swing still faced Pioneer Way, but its chains were rusted and there was a heap of tools scattered across its bench.

Jem knocked on the screen door and Fred Walters called out, "Who's there?" Walters looked up from his seat on the couch and said, "Sam Clayton's boy!"

"Yes, sir."

Walters finished his beer and set it next to a pile of other bottles. "I bought this place from my son-in-law Bart right after Tom Masters died. Bart married my youngest daughter." Someone was washing the dishes in the kitchen and Walters cocked his head in that direction and pressed his hand to the side of his mouth, "That was my pretty one. Anyway, Tom worked for your daddy as a deputy. After I moved in, I found an old picture of him and Sam standing in front of the Sheriff's Office. There's two little kids in it, who I am guessing are you and your sister. What's her name?"

"Claire."

"Right. Let me go look for it." He started up the stairs but stopped halfway and called out, "Hey, Janet!"

The water stopped in the kitchen. "Yes, Daddy?"

"How you gonna fetch a husband if you can't even get a feller a damn beer when he's standing in your living room? We got company. Stop stuffing your face for a minute and come say hello."

Jem waited for Walters to go upstairs and he walked toward the back of the house. There was a woman standing by the sink, stone ugly and bigger than a locomotive, but she smiled kindly at him as she dried her hands on a towel. "I apologize. I didn't hear you come in. Would you like a beer?"

Jem took it from her hand and said, "Didn't we go to school together?"

"We sure did."

"You stopped coming, though. Why'd you do that?"

"My mama got sick, and Daddy needed me to help him," she said, turning the water back on to finish the last of the dishes. "I thought you left this place for good. Whatever possessed you to come back?"

"Made a wrong turn," Jem said with a smile. "Actually, I'm just about to leave out."

"Already?" she said. She eyed him up and down, taking the time to slide her hair out of her face. "Well did you eat yet? It's past suppertime."

Jem held up his finger and asked her to wait a moment. He went to the bottom of the steps and called out, "Mr. Walters? Did you find that picture?"

Janet came out of the kitchen and said, "He's probably passed out in the corner of his closet. I'll find it later and bring it to you. So, do you want me to fix you a plate? A nice, hot, home cooked meal. Bet it's been awhile since you had one."

"I'd love to," Jem said. "But, I told Claire that I'd stop in and see her before I left. I bet she's been cooking all day. How about a rain check?"

Janet nodded and said, "All right. I'll hold you to that rain check."

"I hope you do," he said. He untied his destrier and hopped up on it, heading for Pioneer Way. He was about to turn back toward the security gate when it occurred to him to look back. Janet was standing at the front window. Jem waved to her and muttered under his breath, turning his ride around to head in the opposite direction, toward Claire.

10. Highways

Chief Bill Sutherland tapped his fingers on his desk nervously while staring at the two men walking toward his office on the computer screen. A uniformed officer stood on either side of his desk, both of them holding assault rifles. There was a knock on the door. Sutherland pressed a button and said, "Enter."

Hank Raddiger burst through the door and clutched the edge of the desk, "Kill him. Right away. He can do things. Bad things. Kill him as soon as you can."

"Pardon me?" Sutherland said.

"He's not regular anymore." Raddiger's voice dried up to a squeak at the sound of footsteps coming behind him into the office. He slid to the furthest corner and pressed his back against the wall. Little Willy Harpe paused in the doorway, stroking the black stripe of alien tentacle now sunk into the flesh of his neck like a long, curving tattoo. Harpe whispered something to the creature as he sat down on the chair facing the Chief. "Good afternoon, Bill. Where's my brother?"

Sutherland cleared his throat and said, "There was an incident after your brother arrived. A PNDA Marshal took him into custody and left the premises."

Harpe's eyes narrowed beneath the ledges of his heavy brows. "Is that all you have to say for yourself?"

Sutherland looked at Harpe in confusion. He turned to his officers and said, "Can you believe this guy? He comes into my office, on my station, and talks to me like this?"

"You took our money," Harpe said. "You made the agreement."

"One of my men was killed trying to prevent your dimwitted brother's arrest. If he had just stayed in his ship, everything would have been fine. You are the ones who violated the deal, Harpe. Not me. Get out of my office and go bugger a small animal or whatever the hell it is you hillbillies do for fun. I'll let you know when I have something that's worth it to me to let you know about. Understand?"

"If that's how you feel, then so be it," Harpe said. He stood and stroked the tentacle thoughtfully for a moment. "I have just one last question."

"What is it?"

"Aren't you on fire?"

Sutherland waved his hand in dismissal and said, "That's enough. Arrest this piece of -- Oh my God." His flesh sizzled like raw meat thrown into a red-hot pan. His hands blistered and popped with clear fluids that turned to steam from the heat of his flesh. He thrashed in his chair, knocking everything from his desk. "Put me out! Put me out!"

Both officers stared in confusion at him. "Put you out of what, Chief?"

The Chief dropped to the ground and rolled back and forth, "The flames! I'm burning alive."

"What the hell are you talking about?"

Little Willy stroked the tentacle on his neck and said, "That's enough."

Chief Sutherland stopped moving and crumpled into a ball and sobbed like a child. Harpe used the tip of his toe to turn the Chief over onto his back. "I want all of the data about this Marshal that abducted my brother and the ship they left in."

Someone had scraped off the old, peeling paint from the front porch's pillars and replaced it with a coat of shining pearl. There was a garden along the side of the porch that held fat tomatoes and tangles of greens that coiled around stakes set in the black soil. A ramp had been built over the front steps.

Jem saw a man sitting in a wheelchair at the edge of the garden, reaching down to pluck a vegetable. He inspected it and dropped it into the blanket spread across his lap. Jem called out to him and tipped his hat, "Good evening, sir. I apologize for calling on you unexpectedly like this. Do you know where I can find Claire Clayton?"

The man propped himself up on the chair's hand rails and stood to his feet. His legs looked thin, and unable to support his weight. The man turned his head to point at the ruined clump of flesh that used to be an ear and said, "Ever since the explosion, I don't hear so good out of this side. You said you was looking for Claire Miller?"

"Miller?"

"My wife. I'm Frank Miller. This is our home."

A woman opened the front door. She was tall and lean, with blonde hair cut short like a boy's, but prettier than Jem had expected. Claire's eyes fixed on him briefly, before she turned to Frank and said, "What are you doing out of that chair?"

Frank leaned back down into the chair, and Jem slid from his saddle to offer his hand to Frank. "It's an honor to meet you, Frank. My name's Jem Clayton. I'm Claire's brother."

"You don't say!" Frank said. He grabbed Jem's hand tightly and shook it, smiling at Claire to say, "Your brother's finally here, honey. I told you."

"I can see that," Claire said.

"Hello, Claire," he said. "How have you been?"

"You just passing through, then?"

Her eyes were hard against his with no sign of easing. "I suppose so. Just thought I'd stop by and take a look at you, was all. Make sure you still had all your parts. Nice to meet you, Frank. Take care."

Frank waved him off and said, "Don't be silly! Come inside and have dinner with us, Jem. We haven't had company in ages. Claire talks about you all the time." Frank wheeled his chair toward the ramp, waiting for Jem to tie his destrier and come inside. Claire held the door open for Frank, but let it close behind her as Jem came up the steps.

There were many things Frank was eager to show him inside the house. There were family photos hung on the wall that Jem only glanced at, little knick-knacks set around the house that he instantly recognized, but chose to ignore. Frank looked into the kitchen at where Claire stood with her back turned, slamming her knife on the wood chopping block and said, "Why don't you go on in there. I'll stop hogging up your time and let you two catch up."

Jem took a deep breath before entering the kitchen. He took off his hat and stood awkwardly in the hallway shifting from one foot to the other, watching her cut vegetables. "It wasn't true, what he said," Claire said over her shoulder. "I don't talk about you at all."

"Oh. Well, the house looks nice."

"You paid for it."

He paused. "What?"

"The money that mysteriously showed up in my bank two years ago. You think I didn't know that was you, or how you got it?"

"Maybe it was an insurance policy Pa had for you. Maybe it finally came due, did you ever think of that?" He thought for a second, then said, "See, there was this trust fund--"

She let out a small laugh and went back to her vegetables. "I expect you want to move back in then. I expect you want me and Frank to clear out."

"Don't be stupid, Claire. Why would you even say that?"

She looked over her shoulder at him and wiped the side of her face with the back of her hand. "Frank wasn't born a cripple, or simple, neither. He was strong as an ox when we married. He got hurt in the mines a few years back. It left him a little slow. He doesn't understand things so well sometimes. If you want to run us off because you need a place to hide, that suits me fine. Just keep your mouth shut around him and I'll take care of it."

"I don't even know what to say to that, so I won't. But Frank seems nice. Does he treat you all right?"

"Nice? I know what you're thinking, Jem. You think he's some invalid that isn't capable of taking care of himself, right? Some kind of weak man and not some goddamn lawman or bandit. Well I'll tell you this, I'll take him over someone like you any day of the week. He is good, and he is decent, and he is kind. And if you don't like it, you can go to hell."

Jem waited for her to finish, then he caught her off guard with a smile. "My goodness gracious. You grew up and got meaner than a hellcat. You been waiting to say that to me for years, ain't you? I bet you had the whole thing memorized just in case I came in here, trying to tell you how it was and how it's gonna be. Look at you, holding that kitchen knife like you might stick it straight through my heart." He tapped his left breast and said, "Here it is. I won't even flinch, if you want to try."

She put the knife down on the wooden cutting board. "What do you think happened after I finally got tired of worrying that you were dead or in jail? When that money showed up, it just made me more bitter toward you."

"I told you. There was a trust fund."

She picked up the knife again.

"All right. I sent it to help you."

"You sent it because you expected it might buy you forgiveness for running off all them years ago. I was a little girl and you left me to fend for myself, Jem."

"You had Anna and Old Man Willow. Stop carrying on like you were living in the streets."

Claire gritted her teeth and said, "I think I want you to leave."

Jem cast his eyes down at the dirty white tiles. They were the same ones he and Claire crawled on as babies while his mother washed the dishes. "Listen, when I sent that money, I just wanted to do something nice for you, is all. I didn't mean it any other way. I know I couldn't…how'd you go and get married without me?" He stopped speaking and swallowed, but it was like trying to get a bag of sand down his throat. "Who walked you down the aisle?"

"Nobody did. I made it that far on my own, I figured I could handle the rest as well."

He reached out for her, but she turned away from him and returned to chopping the food.

Before eating, Frank recited a heartfelt prayer where he thanked God for everything under the stars, "Especially the happy return of Claire's brother, Jeb."

"Jem," Claire said. "He just told you that not fifteen minutes ago."

"It's all right," Jem said.

Frank looked at Jem and said, "I am so sorry."

"Just get on with it, Frank. The food's getting cold," Claire said.

"Ease up," Jem said. "It's okay."

Claire scooped piles of peas and mashed potatoes onto both men's plates. "How long are you staying for, *Jem*," Frank said.

"Not long. I have to ride out on business at first light."

Claire stabbed a piece of meat with her fork. "Off to another fast town to do God knows what to God knows who? What would our Daddy say to you right now, Jem? Would he be proud of how his only son turned out? Would Ma?"

"Chances are I'll get to ask them directly before sunrise," Jem said, instantly regretting the anger in his voice. He wiped his mouth with one of the linens and rocked back and forth on the chair while he and Claire stared at one another from across the table. "Dinner sure was tasty," he said. "I never ate so good at this table in all my days. The old man wasn't much of a cook. He did his best, of course, but it was pretty much leaper steaks and beans all year round."

"Venison's my favorite," Frank said.

"Is that right? You any good with a rifle?"

"He can hit a leaper at twenty yards in mid-sprint," Claire said. "He got four last year, right out in the meadow, sitting in his chair."

"That right?" Jem said. "You ever try pheasant? No? Not much eating, but they're good hunting. When I get back I'll show you my dad's old spot." He patted Frank on the back and looked at his sister, "Be good. I'll be back."

All of the businesses were closed along Pioneer Way, except for the bars. They were packed with rowdy customers and working girls who called out to Jem as he passed, trying to lure him inside. Anna Willow was standing on the Sheriff's porch, holding the railing. Her white apron was smeared with dried blood. Jem stopped his destrier in front of her and said, "Rough night, Doc?"

"Your friend, Mr. McParlan, had to sit on Elijah's chest so I could reset his leg. He most likely will never walk right again."

"What a tragic turn of events," Jem said. He waited for Anna to say something, but she ignored his comment. "Hey, did you take up in Roy Halladay's old office?"

"I did," Anna said. "I still have his sign on the door and everything."

"I saw him not too long ago, you know. He was talking about a man's destiny, and what a peculiar thing it is." He looked at the security gate that led out to the wasteland and eventually, Beothuk Country. "Right now, I'd be inclined to agree with that crazy old devil."

"Where you heading off to this late, anyway?"

"Why, you concerned about me out there in the darkness or wishing one of them Beothuk will have a new hat made out of my scalp before dawn?"

"I was just curious where you were going," she said. "You weren't purposefully cryptic as a boy, Jem Clayton. Some might say you've picked up a flair for the dramatic."

"Perhaps they might," he said.

She brushed against his hand and when he did not pull away, she said, "So tell me the fate of Mr. Elijah Harpe."

"A person like you wouldn't understand, Anna. Someone like you helps people. Someone like me does the opposite."

"I wouldn't expect anything less from the baddest man in the world," Anna said.

Jem grinned shyly, "You've been waiting twenty years to fire that one back at me, haven't you?"

"Maybe. Do you remember Zeke that used to work for my father?"

Jem nodded.

"Did you ever hear what happened to me?"

"I heard enough."

Anna's voice was quiet when she said, "When I was a little girl, I trusted everybody. People acted so nice to me after my mother died, I just assumed that's how they really were. Zeke told me I was special. He paid attention to me. Sometimes I wonder if I did something to make him think it was okay to do what he did."

"You were just a kid, Anna. Of course you didn't," Jem said.

"The worst thing about it was that the nice man who treated me so kindly told me he would kill me and my father if I told anyone. I believed him, Jem. I looked in his eyes and I saw evil. I never could tell your daddy what he did to me. Miss Katey had to do all the talking for me, and your daddy hauled Zeke off to the penitentiary."

Jem looked off in the distance. "That's the story I heard too."

"Except Zeke never was at the penitentiary."

Jem did not speak.

"I checked up on him a few years ago, just to see what became of him. The warden said there had never been a prisoner there by that name. So it leaves me with the question as to what became of the man that stole my innocence. Your daddy didn't seem the type to let a man like that go in the desert, now did he?"

Jem shook his head, "No. I don't suppose."

She put her hand in his. "So, you're wrong. Someone like me would understand."

11. Old Time Lawmen

It was one of the three.

In this, she walked at his side, not speaking, eyes cast toward the peaks of Coramide Canyon. Sagebrush decorated the cliffs and crags above, their silvery fullness catching the first light of the rising sun like fire flashing across the mountainside.

It was one of the three, and Sam Clayton knew it would end. He turned to her and moved the hair from her eyes, forcing himself to smile even as she looked away. "Would you like something to put in your hair? Will that cheer you up? I'll get it," he said. "Don't move," he said, holding up his hands to keep her in place. "Don't move."

Sam bolted up the hill toward the sagebrush and grabbed the first handful of flowers and snapped them off at the stem. He turned with them triumphant, waving them in the air, but she was gone. It was one of the three. They all ended the same.

Sam woke up grasping the empty pillow lying next to him on the bed. He sat up in the silent bedroom, bathed in the pale blue light of Seneca's twin moons. Wind pushed the meadow grass from side to side through the bedroom's window, revealing a white wooden cross staked into the ground at the end of the property. There were words written on either side of the cross, reading Beloved Wife, Beloved Mother.

Sam got out of bed, needing to be up and moving, needing to escape from the places the dream dragged him into. He headed for the kitchen and looked into the first bedroom he passed, seeing his little girl sitting up in her bed. Tangled ringlets of hair spilled into her eyes. "Did I wake you up, princess?"

Claire shook her head and said, "No. I'm just up."

"Are you hungry? I can fix you something before I go in."

She slid out of the bed, tiny bare feet catching the edges of the long nightgown as she padded across the wooden floor to her dollhouse. "I'm okay. I'll just wait for him to get up."

Sam got down on one knee and opened his arms. "I'll be back soon, baby girl. Be good for your brother." He took her hand and pressed his chin into her palm. She squirmed but the squirm became a sigh of relief and she said, "It's not stubbly."

"I shaved last night just for you." He kissed the top of her head and moved the hair out of her eyes. He went into his son's room and saw a foot sticking out of the bed, dangling over the floor. "Hey, Jem, I'm going into work early," Sam said. "Mind your sister and fix her some food."

The boy rolled over and yanked the blanket over his head.

Sam patted him on the shoulder, "Don't stay in this bed too long, now. You got plenty to do today."

"Ok," Jem muttered.

Pioneer Way connected the Clayton house to the settlement's main entrance by way of a ten-mile stretch of dirt road. The Sheriff's Office was the first building after the electrified security gate, and it was surrounded by bars, banks, and brothels. Sam enjoyed the morning ride into work. It gave him the chance to look the entire town over and make sure nobody stole it overnight.

If given a choice, he preferred to arrive just after sunrise. Any later than that and the wagons would bunch up against one another at the front gate, eager to get out of the wasteland. Crowds of pedestrians would fill up the square, and it would just be a matter of time before one of the miners getting off the midnight shift tied a load on and did something stupid. It was like clockwork. Predictable as the heat. But before dawn, for a little while, it was quiet.

Sam leaned back in his chair and sipped a mug of coffee, reading the deputies reports that were scattered across his desk. Nothing stood out. A miner got cited for taking a leak in front of a few women. Three patrons of the Proud Lady got in a dust up over one of the working girls when one of them could not grasp the concept of "First come, first served." Sam lifted up one of the reports to read it closer when he saw it mentioned Beothuk savages less than a mile away from the settlement.

The thunder of hooves broke his concentration and he looked up to see Deputy Tom Masters riding hard in his direction. Sam set his coffee down and headed onto the porch. "Trouble, Sheriff. At the Willow Funeral Home," Masters said. "Old Man Willow's got Zeke trapped in the basement."

"His assistant? Why?"

"Something happened with Willow's little girl, Anna." The deputy's destrier snorted and spun around impatiently as Sam climbed up on his own. Sam snapped the reins and both men took off, kicking the sides of their beasts until they were in full gallop, flying down Pioneer Way so fast that their reflections in the storefronts were just clouds of dust and flinging dirt.

When they arrived at the Willow's, Sam jumped off his ride at the porch steps and had his weapon drawn before hitting the ground. He bent low and ducked behind the front door, calling out, "Erazamus? It's Sheriff Clayton. Where you at?"

There was no response. Sam pushed the door open and waited, leaning over to peek inside the living room. "Erazamus? Anna?"

"Back here, Sheriff," a man called out from the rear of the house. "You hear that, Zeke? The Sheriff is here, an' he's gonna strung you up in my front yard until buzzards come for your eyeballs, you pervert."

Crying was coming from the upstairs bedroom. That would be Anna, Sam thought. He kept moving toward the rear of the house, keeping his Defender ready, when he saw Erazamus Willow standing by the closed cellar door with a baseball bat in his hand. "Thank God you're here," Willow whispered. "I gave him a whack across the head with this, but he ran down there."

"What did he do?"

"He violated my daughter, Sheriff."

"How do you know?"

"I was asleep when I heard Anna hollering for him to get off of her. When I went into her room, I saw him standing there and I cracked him with this. He fled down here. Innocent men don't run, Sheriff."

"When you're hitting them with a bat, they do," Sam said. "Did you see him doing anything to Anna?"

"It was dark and she was crying and carrying on. I thought it was more important to get him away from her, thank you very much."

Sam patted the undertaker on the arm and said, "It's all right, Erazamus. You done good. Take a step back for a second." Sam opened the cellar door and said, "Zeke? It's Sheriff Clayton. You all right down there?"

"That crazy bastard tried to bash my brains in!"

"I know. That ain't gonna happen again. You sit tight until I call you up, understand?"

"I didn't do nothin', Sheriff."

"Okay. Just give me a minute and I'll be back. I'm gonna leave Tom up here to make sure nobody comes down and bothers you. You stay put till I say otherwise."

"Yes, sir," Zeke said.

Sam turned to Tom and said, "I'll be back."

Doctor Royce Halladay was standing at the top of the stairs, clutching a bloody handkerchief. He cocked his head at the open door in the hallway where his wife, Katey, was sitting with her arm around Anna Willow. Sam looked at the bloody cloth and said, "Tell me that ain't from her, Doc."

Halladay lifted an eyebrow at the Sheriff and was about to speak when he clutched his gut and coughed violently. He pressed the handkerchief to this mouth and caught the bloody spittle that erupted out of it. Halladay cleared his throat and wiped his face. "Would I be standing here if it were, Sam?"

Sam took off his hat and went into the room, but Anna turned away from him and dropped her face into Katey's lap. Katey stroked her hair gently and said, "She thinks you're going to arrest her."

Sam bent down in front of them both and said, "What the heck made you think a silly thing like that?"

Anna shook her head, and Katey said, "You want me to tell him?"

There was no answer. Katey said, "Zeke told her that if anyone found out what happened, they could both go to jail."

"Come on, now," Sam said. "You known me since you were a baby. You know both my kids. Shoot, Jem's only a few years younger than you and Claire looks up to you like a big sister. Jail's just for bad people, darling. You ain't that."

Anna wiped her eyes and nose on Katey's skirt, leaving smears across the fabric. Sam reached into his pocket and pulled out a handkerchief and said, "Take this before you get snot all over the place."

Anna smiled weakly and took the cloth from him. "Thank you, Mr. Clayton."

Katey patted her on the back. "Anna, tell Sam what Zeke did before your daddy came in."

Anna looked down. "Nothing happened."

Sam bent low to catch her eye, waiting for her to realize he was looking at her. He leaned close, like he was trying to see the fine details of her irises. "What do I see in there?" he said. "Something different than what you just said?"

Anna mumbled something under her breath. "What was that?" Sam said, looking from her to Katey.

"He said he'd come here in the middle of the night and kill us if I told. He said he knows how to get into the house a dozen different ways and slit both our throats."

"That's a damn lie," Sam said.

"How do you know?" Anna said.

"Because that's what bad people do, darling. They try scaring you out of doing what's right. It's called intimidation of a witness. I'll put him in jail just for that."

"Will he stay in jail?" Anna said.

Sam opened his mouth to speak but stopped short. He pursed his lips together in thought and then said, "I can do my best."

"Well that's not good enough," Anna said.

Zeke wrapped his hands around the cell door's bars and leaned back, trying to shake them. "How soon before I can get the hell out of here?"

Sam kicked his boots off the desk and sat up, fishing in his vest for his pocket watch. "Doc Halladay should be finished his examination soon. After that, it depends."

"On what?"

"On what the Doc finds out."

"Well he ain't gonna find nothing."

"I hope, for your sake, you're right," Sam said.

"I'm gonna tell people how badly you been mistreating me. Holding me here with no proof of nothing is a goddamn disgrace!"

Sam snapped his fingers at the cell and said, "Sit your ass down and shut your hole. What I have and don't have is none of your concern."

"The hell it ain't!" Zeke shouted. He slumped onto the cell cot and stuck his fists under his chin, muttering, "The hell it ain't."

Sam saw his deputy come out of the doctor's office across the street and reached into his desk drawer. He stuck a pinch of sweetweed cut into his lower lip and sucked on its bitter essence until he'd worked up a mouthful of juice. He walked out onto the porch and spit a black arc over the railing. "Give me the good news, Tom."

"I wish I could," Tom said. "Doc Halladay said it's clear something happened, but he can't say for certain. Anna still ain't talking."

Sam chewed and spat and wiped off his mouth. He chewed again and spat again. He started to chew once more, then stopped and said, "Prepare the prisoner for transport to Seneca 5 to see the judge."

Tom Masters looked up at him, not moving until the Sheriff looked back at him. "Yes, sir," Tom said. The deputy walked into the office and pointed at Zeke, "Get your hands up against that wall."

"I'm going to tell that judge what you been treating me like," Zeke said, turning around and sticking his hands against the bricks above the cot.

Tom stuck the iron key into the door's lock and turned it. "You stay like that until I say otherwise, else I'll shoot you in the spine and leave you pissing in a bag for the rest of your life."

Zeke giggled, "I bet you'd like that. We'll see how tough you are after I see that judge."

Tom snatched Zeke's wrists and pulled them behind his back and slapped cuffs on them. He leaned close to Zeke's ear and said, "There ain't no judge at Seneca 5, stupid."

Sam plucked a sagebrush flower and twirled it under his nose, inhaling the fragrance. He crumpled the stem in his fingers and blew the leaves into the wind, watching them sail off the edge of the cliff. He checked the rope and it was taut. "Can you hear me down there?"

The rope was looped around a tree stump and stretched across the ground all the way to the side of the cliff where it vanished. Sam walked to the edge of the cliff and looked down, seeing the bottom of Zeke's feet. Zeke's ankles were raw and bloody under the rope's tight knot as he swayed side to side in the wind. Sam nudged the rope with his boot, "You didn't pass out on me, did you, boy?"

Zeke lifted his head to look up at Sam. His face was purple and swollen and he spat out grunting noises when he tried speaking.

"Zeke?" Sam said.

"What?"

"Is that a yes or a no that you can hear me down there?"

"Go to hell!"

Sam reached down and gave the rope a shake, making Zeke bounce up and down on it like a fish on a line, making him scream until he went hoarse. Zeke begged and pleaded with Sam to stop and the Sheriff stood up and wiped off his hands. "You're gonna wiggle yourself straight into a freefall if you don't quit messing around."

Zeke curled his head up to his chest then straightened himself out and breathed in as much air as he could fit in his lungs. "HELP ME SOMEBODY HELP ME!"

Sam tilted his head back and looked up at the streaks of purple and orange across the sky as the sun descended. "You're gonna need to save your voice for the drop, Zeke. It's a doozie."

Both of Seneca's moons crested the mountaintops of Coramide Canyon, full and shining with white light that showed off the frozen rivers and craters etched across their surfaces. The canyon turned the color of gold. Sam pulled out a wad of chewed sweetweed from his lower lip and chucked it over the side of the cliff. He reached down for a jug of water and held it out for Zeke to see. "You thirsty?"

Zeke's face turned up and Sam splashed him with water. "Hold steady now," Sam said. He let the water trickle out and watched Zeke squirm to try and catch each drop with his mouth.

"Give me more, Sam," Zeke gasped. "I'm gonna die of thirst. I'm withering inside."

Sam was about to tip the jug again but stopped halfway. "Why'd you violate that little girl?"

"I didn't violate anybody. Old Man Willow is a lunatic!"

"She says you did."

"That's a damn lie. I woke up in the middle of the night to piss and I heard her calling for me from the bedroom. 'Zeke, Zeke, come here,' she says. 'What's wrong, Miss Anna?' I says. She tells me she had a bad dream and needs me to stay with her a minute."

"Then what happened?"

"I went in to check on her, and next thing I know I'm getting bashed across the head with a bat."

Sam stuck his finger in the dirt and made shapes. He drew a fish and then wiped it out of existence. Just like that, he thought. Just like it never was.

He was covered in dust and dirt from the canyon. He looked down at his Sheriff's badge and licked his thumb to smear away the grime. The lettering was worn out and it was badly in need of a polish, but Sam's old Sheriff had told him, "Never clean your badge, son. It gets older just like you do and picks things up along the way. Stuff you'll need in times to come."

He reached into his vest and pulled out his watch, checking the time and wondering what Jem and Claire were doing. Had Jem done his chores? Had Claire eaten a decent supper? He took off his hat and ran his hand through his sweaty hair. "Hey Zeke?" he said. "You know the sad part about all this is that Anna was more upset about you getting into trouble. She thinks you two are fixed to get married. She said she'd rather be with you than her daddy because you treat her better."

"That's because he treats her like a kid," Zeke said. "Ever since his wife died, he wants to keep her as his little baby, but she ain't."

Sam nodded and let out a soft chuckle. He smacked himself in the forehead and said, "I can't believe I'm so stupid. Why didn't you say so from the beginning?"

"About what?"

Sam wagged his finger at Zeke and said, "You jest a regular ol' tom-cat, ain't you?"

"A what?"

"You and Anna is sweethearts, Zeke. I can see it plain as day. All this fuss for nothing. Boy, you almost got dropped off a ledge and for what? For nothing. Thank God I figured it out in time."

Zeke looked up at Sam and said, "You did?"

"I really do apologize, Zeke," Sam said. "Let me get you back up here. Anyway, you got bigger problems than me to worry about now."

"Like what?"

"Anna's pregnant, boy. Doc Halladay confirmed it when he examined her."

Zeke stopped squirming and closed his eyes, letting himself sway back and forth. He turned back to Sam and looked him square in the eye, "I swear to God, Sheriff, I will do the right thing and marry her. I'm gonna stand by her an' that baby."

Sam reached up and scratched his head under the rim of his hat. He looked down at Zeke and sighed, "How'd I know you were gonna say that?"

Sam leaned back from the ravine and took a deep breath, looking back over his shoulder at the miles and miles of never-ending desert that surrounded the canyon. The sun was down now.

The wind turned for the cold. Sam slid one of his Colt Defenders out of the holster real quiet and cocked the hammer back. He crept toward the edge of the cliff, called Zeke's name, and fired.

12. Wilderness

Jem rode until the lights of Seneca 6 were tiny white dots in the darkness. He let his destrier run loose over the hard, red clay of the wasteland. Her hooves echoed like a cavalry charge as they flew through the twists and turns of Coramide Canyon. Riding at night was better because daylight riding drew swarms of stinging bugs to the flop sweat soaking the destrier's hide.

A fierce howl stopped the animal dead, nearly throwing Jem from the saddle. He righted himself and patted the destrier's neck, telling her to calm down. The canyon was covered in shadows, but nothing seemed to move. Jem drew one of his guns and waited.

Anyone who'd grown up in Seneca knew about the werja. Jem had never seen one. Most that did never lived to talk about it.

Morning began like a spark of flint in a corner of the sky that soon set fire to the distant mountain peaks. Jem rode into the open plains pulling his hat down over his eyes, trying to see ahead. In that moment he pictured Sam, twenty years prior, emerging from the same canyon, looking up at the same sky.

He thought about what Sam's reaction would be to Jem taking the time to ponder such things and laughed. It was like Sam was sitting next to him, looking at him sideways, chewing a cut of sweetweed. "You expecting that signal to send itself, son?"

Jem spat a mouthful of sweetweed juice into the dirt, and worked the rest of it into the crook of his lower lip with the tip of his tongue. "No, sir," he said, and started up the path.

The pass was overgrown with thick brush and spiny branches, every inch of them covered in curved thorns. Jem dismounted and grabbed a handful of vine that speared his glove and left broken thorns in his palm. He pulled off his glove and tried to dig them out with the tip of his knife.

One of the thorns was deep and he had to cut away the skin to pry out its hooked tip. He stuck his head up to yell in frustration and saw a half-naked young man looking down at him from high above, on a ledge. His long black hair whipped in the wind and two younger boys, kids really, were crouched at his side, trying to stay hidden. This one stood his ground, staring down at Jem in defiance.

Jem stuck the knife back in his hand and cursed as he dug out the rest of the thorn. He cleaned the knife on his pant leg and sheathed it, then whistled for his destrier. He pulled himself into the saddle and started up the pass when the boy raised a stick high over his head and shook it, letting out a high-pitched screech.

Jem waited for him to finish and looked up. "I know who you are. Heard that scream once before when I was just about your age. Didn't scare me then neither."

By nightfall, his stomach was growling. There were birds perched on the bushes, but they hardly seemed worth the effort to shoot. His Defeaters would leave little except a pile of wet feathers and the meat would taste like gunpowder. He had a bottle of whiskey in his saddle. He reckoned he could eat raw bassaricus as long as he had the right thing to wash it down with.

He rode until he came upon a herd of leapers crashing through the brush. They ran in a pack, their long legs kicking high in the air at each step. The herd's alpha was obvious. A large, muscular brute with antlers that spread out as wide as Jem's arms. A smaller buck ran behind him, racing to keep up. Jem drew one of his pistols and fired, dropping the leader in the dirt so that the rest of the herd had to jump over him to get away.

Jem grabbed a hold of its antlers and dragged it off the path. He slit the animal lengthwise, cutting through the tendons and separating the carcass to remove its internal organs. It had been years since he field dressed a leaper. Sam had been a good instructor.

He laid out the tenderloins and ribs on a blanket of hide and went to gather an armful of dry branches that would go up like an inferno with one match strike. By nightfall, he was turning the meat over a roaring fire and the dripping grease sizzled in the flames.

Jem ate until he was full and drank a portion of the whiskey. The temperature started to drop. He stoked the fire, trying to build up the flames enough to burn long into the night, thinking of the howl he'd heard earlier. Whatever made that noise was still out there and would be walking around while he slept in the open. Jem swallowed whiskey until the howling, the cold, and night under the open sky ceased to matter.

Jem removed the rest of the meat from the fire and set it aside, saving it for morning. He laid out a blanket and leaned back to watch the flames dance and interweave, thinking of the Alvarez sisters, thinking of Anna Willow…

He opened his eyes at the sound of a step so light on the ground it could have been just a leaf blowing across the dirt. The oldest Beothuk boy was creeping past the fire, reaching for the meat. Jem cocked the hammer of his gun, freezing the boy in place.

The gun was aimed at the center of his chest and he stuck out his chin and pulled back his arms, daring Jem to shoot even though his lips quivered slightly and his shoulders rose and fell with excited breaths. His chest was finely muscled and hairless. There was a light growth of baby hair across the boy's lip that looked like it might crawl off the side of his face. Jem made him out to be fourteen.

"You're the one that squawked at me. Where are the others? You come alone? Must be the brave one." He waved his gun at the meat and said, "Go ahead. Take it. I don't know what the hell you all are doing out here, but you must be hungry. Have it."

The boy remained motionless.

"You understand anything I'm saying?"

The boy looked at the gun, then back to Jem. Jem decocked the hammer on his Defeater and put it into his holster. As soon as the gun was out of his hand, the boy took off into the shadows.

"I'm not going to hurt you," Jem called out. He thought he could make out where the boy was, or at least had a rough idea which patch of darkness he'd vanished into. Jem picked up the spit and held it out. "Here. Take it. It's all right. I've got enough for all three of you."

Hours later he shivered himself awake and opened his eyes to see the pale sky. His fire was a pile of smoldering ashes and the food was missing from the spit. He checked for tracks around the campsite, but saw neither animal nor Beothuk boy footprints. The destrier was standing only a few yards away, gnawing on branches. Jem tucked a pinch of sweetweed behind his lip and climbed up into the saddle.

It was noon. Sweat dripped from the brim of his hat when Jem took it off to wipe his forehead. Coarse thorn-ridden vegetation spilled over the edges of the cliffs above him in long vines that swept the trail on either side of him. There were piles of leaper bones tangled in the vines, their blood spattered across the rocks beneath.

Jem stopped his destrier and dismounted. The bones were picked clean but the blood was fresh. Strange paw prints were stamped into the ground around the kill site from an enormous animal with razor sharp claws. No, he thought. Several animals.

His destrier snorted and stomped impatiently for Jem to climb back on. He unholstered a Defeater and cocked the hammer back, scanning the trail and cliff walls. "Easy," he said, patting its neck. "Nothing to worry about."

He steered through the vines, forcing her to walk slowly as he kept his head on a swivel and his gun at the ready. The trail bottomed out into a dried riverbed with massive stones sunk in the clay. The damp muck sucked the destrier's hooves as they travelled the embankment, searching for a path that would let them up onto the other side.

Jem saw them enough times that he gave them names.

He called the oldest boy Squawk. All three of them would ride along the edge of the cliffs above Jem, but it was only Squawk who stayed whenever Jem looked up. Squawk who stared back. Squawk who let Jem know he was not afraid of the White Man.

The second boy was thin and long-limbed with a hooked nose and inverted chin. His appearance reminded Jem of a character from a book that his mother once to read to him. He called that boy Ichabod.

The smallest had long, dark hair and a face that resembled Squawk's. He scurried out of sight whenever Jem looked, but laughed and made it a game. Squawk reproached the boy every time, looking thoroughly annoyed. It didn't matter. The game continued. Bug, then, Jem decided. Your name is Bug.

The mountain pass ended at a wide meadow made of tall, swaying grass and cool air that blew across Jem's face. The destrier licked the air with its long red tongue, lapping at it playfully. He eased her down the embankment and she trotted across the flat land, kicking her knees in the air and flinging mud from her hooves. "Feels good to be back on soft ground, don't it?" he said, patting her side. The destrier snorted and spun around in the air, whipping her tail.

A cheer broke out from the mountain behind him and Jem saw the three boys sitting on their destriers, watching him. Bug had his hands raised in the air and Ichabod was clapping. Squawk barked at the both of them, and Ichabod said something back, then pointed at Jem and made circular motions with his finger. Squawk sneered and bunched up his destrier's mane in his hand and kicked it in the sides.

Squawk's destrier bolted down the path toward Jem and trotted around him in a circle, both rider and animal prancing with their heads held high in defiant arrogance. Jem folded both of his hands on the saddle horn and said, "You gonna do something beside try and make me dizzy?"

Squawk slapped the rear end of his mount and gave a command that sent it rearing up on its hind legs with both front legs sticking straight in the air. Squawk let go of the mane with one hand and leaned back, keeping that pose until the animal finally came back down. Jem stuck his fingers in his mouth and whistled loudly. When Squawk turned around to join the others, Jem noted a small smile on the boy's face.

Jem waved to the other two and said, "Come on, now. Let me see what you've got."

Ichabod rode into the meadow. His brow was furrowed in concentration as he brought the destrier's speed up, reaching a full gallop before gently pressing himself out of the saddle. He stood to his feet, grasping the mane with both hands and shifting hesitantly from one foot to the other. He suddenly let go of the mane and clapped both hands over his head, then dropped back down onto the animal and hugged it for dear life. Jem whooped and hollered as Ichabod rode past.

He looked over at Bug and pointed. "What about you, squirt? Got any tricks?"

Bug kicked his small mount into motion and took off running with an excited shout. He passed Jem at full speed and jumped to his feet, surfing on her back with one hand high in the air. The boy stood straight legged as the animal whipped around Jem, and he let go of the mane and spun in the air, landing backwards on the beast with his arms folded in a relaxed pose. The animal seemed to steer itself while the boy smiled and patted his mouth, pretending to yawn.

Jem's mouth fell open and he said, "Holy shit." As Bug spun back around to ride back to the others, Jem grabbed his hat and stood up in saddle, waving it and cheering.

The sun retreated from the mountains and Jem gathered the collar of his coat under his chin to keep out the cold wind. He gathered sticks in a pile and built a ring of stones around them then lit a match and flicked it into the kindling. He rubbed his hands over the blaze and sat down.

The boys were watching him from a safe distance. Only Squawk refused to cross his arms over his bare chest and shiver. The other two looked pitiful. Jem waved for them to join him and said, "Come on. Don't be stupid."

Squawk gave a command and the other two boys nodded and ran into the darkness. Squawk bent low in the grass and moved into the shadows. "Have it your way," Jem said. He uncapped his whiskey flask and took a sip and tended to his fire.

That Beothuk boy I shot wasn't much older than Squawk, he thought. He took down a full grown deputy in the darkness and scalped him. Jem took a second, longer sip of whiskey. He was gonna come kill me and Claire, too. Screw that. I'm glad I shot him.

Jem thought about the story Walt Junger, Billy Jack Elliot and Old Man Willow told about finding Sam's body. A Beothuk *massacre*. So bad they couldn't bring the body home. Jem took his knife out of its sheath and twirled it in his fingers, watching the firelight reflect off its blade. He drank again. "*Sheriff* Walt Junger," he said.

A fat conejo landed dead on the dirt in front of him.

Jem looked up to see a triumphant Bug raise his hands in the air and cheer.

"Let me guess. It was a contest and you just won," Jem said. He grabbed the conjeo by its ears and slit it open with his knife. Bug bent next to him, watching in fascination at how he prepared it.

Branches cracked and something heavy was sliding across the dirt toward them. Squawk came into the light, dragging a doe by her legs. He deposited the animal at Jem's side with a grunt and looked down at the conejo in Jem's hands. In the flicker of the firelight, for the briefest moment, the brave warrior was just a disappointed little boy.

Jem looked over the doe and said, "That has got to be the biggest female leaper I ever seen. I'm impressed." He patted the animal on the side and nodded approvingly at Squawk. Squawk plopped down cross-legged in front of the fire and sulked as he waited for Jem to finish gutting Bug's catch.

Jem got the meat roasting in minutes and showed Bug how to work the spit. He watched the boy try it himself and then said to Squawk, "All right. Stop pouting, we'll do yours now."

Squawk's head shot up and he held his hand up to tell the other to stop talking. All of the muscles in his body coiled like springs.

Bug whispered something, but Squawk hissed at him to be silent. Jem searched the darkness but saw nothing, heard nothing, until a high-pitched cry rang out like an animal being torn apart at the joints. Squawk leapt to his feet and ran in that direction.

"Lakhpia-sha," Bug gasped. The child's eyes went so wide that Jem could see white on nearly all sides of them. "Lakhpia-sha!"

"What the *hell* is a Lakhpia-sha?"

There was a second scream and Jem realized Lakhpia-sha was Ichabod. He scrambled to his feet and ran until he could make out Ichabod's flailing hands and feet pinned under the form of a massive, silver-furred beast.

The creature was shaking Ichabod by his left arm, its drooling fangs sunk deep in his flesh. Squawk leapt onto the beast's back and wrapped his arm around its throat, trying to wrench it off of Ichabod enough to free his arm.

Jem raised a pistol and shouted, "Get out of the way!" but Squawk could not let go. Jem yelled as loudly as he could, trying to scare the thing off but Ichabod's arm was clenched in its mouth, shredded to a tangle of bone sinews.

Jem grabbed Squawk by the shoulder and ripped him off of the animal's back. He grabbed a tuft of the creature's thick hide and jammed his knife into its throat. He pumped the knife back and forth like he was trying to get water out of the beast's neck, and finally, a jet of hot black blood spurted onto his hand.

The beast let of Ichabod and ran off, taking Jem's knife with it.

Jem raised his pistol and fired twice into the darkness but heard nothing. Ichabod moaned, lifting his ruined arm and staring at it in disbelief.

"What the hell was that? Son of a bitch." Jem looked up and saw Bug riding for them on his destrier, coming across the meadow at full gallop. Two small flames appeared in the darkness near Bug and Jem realized it was the shining yellow eyes of a second creature. Bug's destrier screeched as the beast leapt and bit its neck, splashing Bug with her blood.

Jem grabbed the boy by the ankle to pull him free of the thrashing mount. He fired at both animals rapidly, shooting Bug's destrier and its killer until both of them were writhing on the ground in a mewling mix of bloody fur.

"Werja," Bug shouted, spinning around and around, pointing into the shadows. "Werja!"

A third beast had been creeping up behind them and had its jaws open for the back of Squawk's head when Jem turned and fired a bullet past Squawk's ear that cleaved the animal's skull in two.

Squawk did not flinch. He tore pieces of his loincloth into small strips with his teeth, hurrying to get them around Ichabod's arm. He chattered to Ichabod, smacking him on the cheek and shaking him, but the boy had stopped moving.

Jem thought he saw movement in the darkness and pulled the trigger. His gun clicked, empty. Two werja ran forward so quickly that Jem barely had time to get his other gun free. He fired blindly, counting his shots, conserving his bullets until he had a clear target even if it meant waiting until the things were right on top of him. He needed to save three bullets, he thought. I'm not letting these kids get eaten alive.

Jem cocked the hammer back and waited, trying to breathe. One of the beasts roared, coming close enough that Jem could see its bright eyes as it leapt from the ground at him but did not strike. The animal's open jaws sagged and it dropped at Jem's feet with an arrow sticking out of the side of its skull.

Whistles filled the air as arrows showered down around them, followed by the thunk-thunk-thunk of struck targets and the roars of dying werja.

Jem held his arms in front of the boys as shadowy figures approached them, coming through the steam escaping into the cold air from the bodies of the werja. He heard their beads rattle and saw their tall bows first. Their arrows were trained on him now and Jem did not move away from the boys as the dozen Beothuk warriors closed in.

"This boy's hurt," Jem said. He pointed down at Ichabod and said, "He needs help."

One of the men broke through the ranks and shoved Jem out of the way, looking down in horror at Ichabod's injuries. He scooped up the boy in his arms and held him to his chest, then lifting his head to shout, "Mahpiya! Mahpiya!"

The warriors parted as a withered-looking savage limped through the crowd. He was dressed in long white robes and used a staff to support his lame right foot. He bent to inspect Ichabod's arm and reached into his robe for a small bottle. He uncorked the top and poured something foul-smelling onto the wounds, making them sizzle.

Ichabod groaned, and the adult savage rocked him back and forth, wiping the boy's hair out of his face. The old man poured the last of the liquid onto Ichabod's arm and removed a clean cloth from his bag that he gently wrapped around the wound. He spoke rapidly at the men nearest to him and waved for them to come over. They picked up Ichabod and carried him to a destrier, then laid him across the back of the animal and secured him there. One of them leapt up onto it and galloped away.

The warriors lowered their bows but kept their arrows notched as a tall, handsome savage came toward, moving anyone in his path aside with one look. His long grey hair was twisted in braids that were intertwined with feathers. Beads rattled from the fringe of his boots as he walked.

Bug ran to the man and wrapped his arms around his waist, saying "Noshi."

Squawk stood up and took his place at Jem's side, thrusting out his chest and swallowing so hard that Jem actually heard it. Jem looked from Squawk to the man, then to Bug and said, "Let me guess, Daddy's here."

The man stopped in front of Jem and began to speak, but as he looked at Jem's face his words stopped and his eyes widened.

Squawk seized the chance to step in front of Jem and start in, chattering non-stop while the man continued staring.

Squawk started to act out the attack of the werja and smacked Jem across the chest, pumping his fist for emphasis. The man folded his arms and waited for Squawk to finish speaking. Squawk finally ran out of breath and the man waved him out of the way with the back of his hand. He lifted Jem's chin and inspected both sides of Jem's face. He looked down the length of his nose at Jem and smiled gently before letting go and turning to seek out one of the fallen werja.

He rolled the animal's carcass over and grabbed the handle of Jem's knife that was sticking out of its neck. He grabbed the handle with both hands and put his foot against the beast's head to draw the blade from its hide. He peeled back its thick black lip and stuck the knife into its gums, prying the longest razor-sharp fang until it popped out in his hand.

He held the fang up to the several dangling from his own neck and nodded with approval. He wiped it on his loincloth before dropping the tooth into a pouch on his belt. "I am Chief of this tribe. My name is Thasuka Witko. We camp nearby and you will come with us."

Jem looked at the Chief and said, "Uh…I…am Jem Clayton."

Thasuka Witko turned to walk toward the others and said, "I already know who you are."

13. The Medicine

They called the elder "Mahpiya," and he remained seated at Ichabod's side within a tent, fanning the boy with a smoldering plant that smoked white and fragrant. He draped talismans on the boy's chest and painted symbols on his body while singing and chanting. Jem looked through the tent flaps and watched, but Mahpiya did not acknowledge him.

Squawk tugged on Jem's sleeve and pulled him away from the tent toward a clearing where the rest of the group was gathered. The men were seated in a circle surrounding a roaring fire. They stopped talking and sat up straight and became tight-lipped at Jem's approach. Only Thasuka Witko leaned back and relaxed, playing with a long, unlit wooden pipe as Jem joined the circle and sat down.

Two Beothuk warriors moved aside from Jem and both he and Squawk sat down. Those two watched Jem from the corners of their eyes while others only nodded curtly. Thasuka Witko raised his voice to say, "Welcome to the circle of warriors, Jem Clayton. You take your place amongst the true people of Seneca and have earned the right to sit among us. Only one white man has ever earned the right to do so in my lifetime, and it was also through an act of bravery and humanity toward the people. He lives in our stories as El-Aquila."

The name brought murmurs from the men and many of them looked at Jem with renewed curiosity. Thasuka Witko waited for everyone to be silent before continuing, "When El-Aquila sat in our circle, he asked Chief Hoka-Psice how the Beothuk came to this place and why we make war on the outsiders. Our stories had never been shared with a white man before."

The Chief looked at the faces of the men seated around him and said, "It was my father's belief that by telling the white man about our people, he would take our stories back and enlighten the rest as to the ways of the Great Spirit. I argued that no white man's ears could hear our truths and it was a waste of time to try. Hoka-Psice was a wise Chief, and ignored me, as I will ignore those who sit here and would try to stop you from hearing the same story."

Jem looked around at the brown faces in the circle, seeing that none of them looked very pleased. "If your young ones are an example of your people's character, there is much more I'd like to know."

The flames flickered in the Chief's dark eyes and he looked up at the sky and pointed his finger at the stars, "In the first days, the Beothuk were slaves in a far away land, made to work for cruel masters. It was The Enlightened One who led our people to freedom and told them to take a fire wagon by force and escape. They found this place where no one would bother to look for them. Many of our ancestors complained that this place was not fit for them. They saw no forests or oceans. They said the land was too hard and the sun was too hot, but the Enlightened One scolded them, for this was a place he felt they could live in peace. If this planet had no riches for the White Man to plunder, the White Man would never come.

"The Beothuk populated the planet and learned its ways. They harvested the harsh ground and plucked fruit from the agave plant. They fed on the fast, long-legged awiyusti and the slow, fat agana. They fought the mighty werja and fashioned their skins into blankets to protect themselves during the cold desert nights.

"Our people made trinkets out of the strange glittering stones that sometimes appeared at the mouths of caves, or rattled around the bottom of our water jugs when we filled them in the streams. The Enlightened One could not have dreamed that someday Outsiders would come with enormous machines that bored holes in the ground to drill for these stones.

"My grandfather was a young boy when the first mining company signed the original treaty. They promised that if the Beothuk allowed them to drill at the far end of the planet undisturbed they would trade food and blankets with us, and never venture any further from that location.

"The first treaty was broken within a month, when more machines landed and deeper veins of these so-called precious stones were found. Our leaders approached the Outsiders again, demanding the mining company return to their area. They were promised it would be the last time, and offered crates of alcohol and chewing weed in return for their agreement.

"Even as the Outsiders broke their word to us again and again, we did not rise up. Until one fateful night when a small group of young men were sent out to scout a new settlement made by the white man deep in the heart of our territory. They were so eager to go, they left with no weapons or food. We call these the Ayawisgi, and to this day, we celebrate their bravery by sending our own young men into the wilderness," Thasuka said, eyes shifting to Squawk.

"The Ayawisgi were captured by the white men, who tortured them for sport. Our people went to find their sons, and there was a great battle when we first showed our valor to your people. We have been at war ever since." Thasuka fell silent and he stared into the fire for a long time, before saying, "I grew up hating the white man and killed as many of them as I could. My thirst for revenge drove me to raise my first son, Goyathlay, to ride with me into battle as soon as he was old enough to hold a weapon.

"The boy was careless, but I was too proud to see it. On the night I led my warriors into Seneca 6, I lost track of him. Our mission was to raid the supply houses, but he ran off into the homesteads and attacked a young deputy. He must have been mad with bloodlust." Thasuka's eyes rose to Jem's and locked on him.

Jem froze in place, feeling the older man searching him for a reaction. Jem did his best to remain impassive and said, "So what happened to your son?"

"The deputy shot him through the chest as Goyathlay was trying to take his scalp. It does not matter. He died because of me. I failed to raise him to be anything other than a murderer." Tears filled Thasuka Witko's eyes as he spoke, but then he looked at Squawk and smiled. "Now, one of my other sons sits with the son of El-Aquila within the sacred circle. The Great Spirit is at work."

The rest of the tribe nodded and murmured, their voices like a low rumble. Jem leaned forward and said, "Wait a second. The *son* of El-Aquila?"

The Chief made shapes with his hands to show a man riding on a wagon, coming across the wasteland. He continued to make shapes and act out the story when he said, "El-Aquila came to us with a carriage full of our dead and the tribe thought it was a trap. Hoka-Psice ordered everyone to hide, thinking that the white man had filled his wagon with patient fire. El-Aquila left the wagon and came into our camp on foot, unarmed, to show his bravery.

"Hoka-Psice asked him why a white man would come such a long way to return our people. He said that he had a son named 'Jem' and could not bear the idea of keeping any other man's son from coming home."

Jem opened his mouth to speak but nothing came out. The smoke from the fire must have stung his eyes too keenly, because when he touched his cheek, his fingers came away wet.

"What El-Aquila could not have known is that the Beothuk believe a spirit is doomed to wander the world until it is laid to rest. We call them the wanagi, and they travel the desert searching for their home." Thasuka Witko stopped speaking and looked away from Jem, giving him the chance to clean off his face and collect himself. All of the men seated around him did the same, keeping their eyes fixed on the ground until Jem was finished.

Thasuka Witko held out his hand and said, "Osceola, father of Lakhpia-sha, has asked to speak. I will translate for you."

The same warrior who had shoved Jem out of the way to get to Ichabod stood up at the far end of the circle. His body was lined with taut muscles and scarred with lines that created strange diagrams in his chest. He spoke, and Thasuka Witko said, "Thasuka-Witko has told the white man of the sacred Ayawisgi rite where we send our young warriors into the wilderness.

"One week ago my son was sent off on his own Ayawisgi." Osceola pointed at Squawk and said, "It was a great honor that he would join our Chief's eldest, Haienwa'tha. But many of us were surprised when Mahpiya had a vision that told them to also take Haienwa'tha's younger brother, Thathanka-Ska. I told the old man that Thathanka-Ska was too young, and would burden the older boys. He told me that it was the Great Spirit's will.

"The Ayawisgi go with no food, no weapons, no means to make shelter. They must endure until the tribe comes to find them. Who among us does not remember their own trial? The suffering is forgotten and all you remember is the embrace of your fellow warriors upon your return.

"I have other suffering that cannot be forgotten. My father and brothers were murdered by the white man, and all of my life I have vowed to kill them wherever I find them. It has been this way since my great-grandfather was a little boy, and the great birds called the El-Aquila were so thick in the skies people thought they were storm clouds. Smoke from the white man's machines destroyed their nests, and no one has seen an El-Aquila for many years.

"I thought it was Hoka-Psice's joke to name the legendary white man El-Aquila. A white man who is peaceful and honorable to the Beothuk is like that great bird. Something many wish to exist, but will never see. When I heard the thunder of this white man's guns and told you our sons were being attacked by the Outsiders and raced toward them, expecting a great battle where many would die. I could not believe my own eyes at what I saw instead."

Osceola stopped speaking and unraveled a cord with his hands to display the fang of the werja that Jem had killed that dangled from it. He passed the necklace through the crowd to Thasuka-Witko, who inspected it and nodded, then passed it to the man next to him. The necklace was handed around that way until it reached Jem.

Osceola pointed at Jem and said, "On this day I, Osceola, tell you that this white man is my brother and under my protection. They say in the south there is a new bird faster and stronger than El-Aquila, and our medicine men tell us it is a great sign for the Beothuk. Tonight, I believe. They call this bird El-Halcon, and that is the name I give my new brother."

All of the men sitting next to Jem clapped him on the back and spoke words that he did not understand, but sounded encouraging regardless. Thasuka-Witko lit his pipe and passed it to the man next to him, each of them putting their lips on the stem and sucking in the fragrant smoke that they then lifted their head and blew toward the heavens.

The pipe came to Jem and he put the stem in his mouth, tasting bitter sweetweed juice and he inhaled, filling his lungs with what felt like fiery embers of coal. He held it in as long as he could, then lifted his head and breathed it all out at once, watching the smoke change shapes in the air and conform to the pattern of the stars.

Thasuka Witko lifted his head to see Mahpiya emerge from the medicine tent. The old man wrapped both withered hands around his walking stick and waited. The Chief nodded and waved for Jem to come sit by his side.

"So where did you learn our language?" Jem said.

"Many of the Beothuk can speak like Whites, but it is not something we reveal often. We never want them to know that we can understand what they are saying if we are captured. Very few choose to actually make the words. They consider it to be a great disgrace."

Mahpiya eyed Jem with lizard-like eyes that bulged under half-lids and did not appear to ever blink. His skin appeared made from saddle leather, so smooth and brown and hairless that Jem had no idea if he were sixty, eighty, or two hundred years old. Thasuka Witko patted Jem on the back and said, "You must go with him. He says there is much at stake, for both our people."

"Right now?" Jem said. "Where are we going?"

Thasuka Witko shrugged. "He would not tell me."

It was so dark at the bottom of the hill that Jem could not see his hands unless he held them in front of his face. The sky was empty, devoid of star or moon. There was a brief flicker of flame as Mahpiya lit a handful of desert sage and held it out like a torch. The sage's smoke was sweet like incense, as Mahpiya fanned smoke onto Jem, he sang in low, rhythmic tones.

Jem's guns rattled in their holsters as he walked. Heavy winds rolled across the plains, louder than mining drills, lifting like waves that gathered dirt and debris in their procession and crashed into Jem's face.

He lifted his hands to hold down the brim of his hat and protect his eyes, and followed the old man's song. It carried on the wind, but he lost its direction, and he stopped. There was dirt in his nose and mouth. He pulled his black bandit's scarf from his pocket and tied it around the back of his neck. He called out for Mahpiya, but there was nothing but wind.

Two destriers charged past him, their hooves shaking the ground like locomotives, and Jem leapt aside to avoid the wheels of the wagon they were hauling. The wagon bounced as the animals raced, and a gun went off in the distance. Two masked riders flew after the wagon, their pistols raised and firing until it slid to a halt.

One of the riders leapt from his destrier and walked up to the rear of the wagon and knocked on the door. Screams came from the passengers inside, high-pitched and feminine, high-pitched and adolescent. The bandit said, "Gentleman Jesse Alcott has come for your money, boys and girls."

Jesse opened the door, put his gun inside of it, and fired until the screaming stopped.

Jem's own screams were drowned out by the rising winds. He drew his gun and ran forward blindly, never finding the bandits and never finding the wagon. He lowered his head into the storm and kept walking until the wind died down enough that he could look ahead. There was a campfire with a man sitting in front of it, tending the fire, his face hidden beneath the brim of a battered hat. He poked the fire with a stick but no smoke rose out of the pit, and he did not look up when Jem walked up to him and said, "Hey, partner. Did you see any of that? A couple bandits shot up a wagon."

The man turned a log over with his stick but did not respond. Jem held his hands over the flames, but felt no warmth coming from them. "How about an old man? You seen him?" Jem said.

The man continued stirring the flames, and finally muttered, "I ain't talking to you, because you ain't real. So just get along."

"I'm real enough, friend," Jem said. "I'm lost in this storm just like you are."

"This storm? This storm is a joke compared to what's coming."

Jem looked around but saw no tent or even a bedroll. There was a wagon on the other side of the fire and Jem said, "You got any other shelter?"

"You ever been out in the wilderness so long that it felt like everything you ever were was an illusion. Like your whole life was just some story you dreamed up. You couldn't go home if you tried, because nobody there would remember you anyway." The man bent forward and spat a mouthful of sweetweed juice into the dirt between his knees.

"I think you've definitely been out here too long, friend." Jem wiped the dirt off his pants and said, "That man I'm looking for is a Beothuk. He would have stood out if you saw him come past. Did you see any Beothuk?"

The man lifted a finger toward his wagon and said, "Only the ones in the back of that carriage, and I brought them with me."

Jem got up to inspect the wagon and saw the words WILLOW FUNERAL HOME written across the side. There were dead bodies of Beothuk warriors laid out in the back, their injuries painted over and their bodies carefully arranged in positions of respect. Jem spun around to face the man, and saw Sam Clayton look up at him from under the brim of his hat.

Sam leaned back from the fire into the shadows and an enormous bird with wings wider than Jem's arms and curved talons that flashed in the firelight sprang into the air, flapping only once and it was enough to send the bird high into the sky and out of Jem's sight. Jem stumbled backwards, losing his footing, and falling toward the ground but never hit it. He fell and fell, end over end, through space and time and everything else until finally, he reached nothingness.

Jem awoke in the dirt, smelling smoke from the remains of a smoldering fire set outside the entrance of a tent standing over him. Harsh light streamed through the tent's flaps and Jem had to cover his eyes and squeezed his skull between his palms to ease the pounding inside his head. He saw a jug of water and a bundle of salted beef inside the tent and grabbed the jug and swallowed water until it threatened to come back up.

He stepped out of the tent and tore off a piece of beef with his teeth. He shook out the cramps in his leg and stretched, looking around the flatland outside of the tent. He was standing in a long, tall shadow. He turned around and saw the radio tower. Jem scratched the top of his head and said, "I'll be damned."

14. Darkness

Hank Raddiger begged and whined until Little Willy Harpe finally lifted one of his fingers and said, "Fine, as long as you shut up already. Euphoria." Hank's head snapped back like he'd been shot in the forehead and he convulsed all the way to the ground where he squealed and kicked over a whole row of books on one of the shelves in Bill Sutherland's office. Papers and pamphlets scattered into the air and Sutherland took cover behind his chair.

"That's enough," Little Willy said after a few moments. "We have things to do."

The connection broke and Hank pounded his fist against the floor. "You said I could have a full ride, Willy! Goddamn it, you promised."

"It makes me disgusted the way you beg, Hank."

Hank's expression softened and he pressed his hands together and got down on his knees. "Master? Please. I'm begging you. Just a little more."

Little Willy stroked the long black oily streak around his neck and said, "Tell you what. I'll make you a deal. Go find me a rat, there should be one scurrying around in the lot, and when you come back take that rat and stick its head in your mouth. If you can bite the rat's head off before it bites your tongue off, I'll give you a ride like you ain't never had."

Sweat beaded like grease bubbling inside a skillet on Hank's forehead as he weighed the challenge. Finally, he nodded and raced out of the office, ducking between ships to search for his prey. Bill Sutherland stood up from behind the chair, clutched his stomach for fear that the sickness boiling in his gut was about to spill out.

Little Willy sighed sadly and said, "I know my associate can be a little bit pathetic. It's a shame, really, but that boy would do damn near anything for some of that Euphoria. And I mean, *anything*. I could *make* him do anything I wanted, of course. Same as I could make you, Bill. But it's the desperation that makes it exciting, if you see what I mean?"

"No. Not really." Sutherland pressed his back against his office wall and steeled himself.

Little Willy frowned and said, "You know what? Me either. I think when he gets back I'm gonna tell him the trash furnace is a swimming pool and we can watch him dive into it. Better yet, I'll tell him there are bugs crawling under his skin and that he has to peel it off to get rid of them! Should make for a fun evening's entertainment, what do you say, Bill?"

Sutherland struggled to find words to respond with when the center console on his desk beeped twice. Sutherland dove for desk and pressed the button eagerly, "Yes? What is it?"

A uniformed Customs officer appeared on the screen. *"We intercepted a PNDA distress signal coming from a planet that matches the trajectory of the Marshal's ship."*

Harpe spun the console around to face him, "Where did it originate from?"

"A small mining planet called Seneca."

Sutherland turned the console away from Little Willy, in his own direction. "Did the signal make it any further?"

"We killed it immediately, sir."

"Good work." Sutherland shut the screen off and sat down at his desk. He resisted the urge to sigh with relief and instead used his most professional tone to say, "I can have a ship outfitted and ready to take you and your friend within the hour, Mr. Harpe. I am sure you want to be on your way as soon as possible."

Little Willy presented his hand to the Chief and Sutherland grabbed it enthusiastically. "Pleasure doing business with you, Mr. Harpe," he said. *As soon as your ship is clear of my station, I am going to blow you into cosmic dust.*

Harpe stopped smiling and looked down at Sutherland's hand. He cocked his head sideways, admiring it. "You have nice hands, Chief." He stroked the skin on Sutherland's hand with the tips of his fingers. "But you're a nail biter, I see. You do that when you're nervous?"

"Not really. Just out of habit, mainly," Sutherland said. He tugged, trying to free his hand from Harpe's grip, but Harpe held him fast.

"Not because you're hungry? Speaking of that, it's gonna be a long day for me. You think I should eat before I go?"

"That sounds like it's a good idea. Can I have my hand back?"

"It does sound like a good idea, doesn't it?" Harpe said. "In fact, you're hungry now too."

"Yes, I am," Sutherland said suddenly. He smiled with embarrassment that he'd needed Little Willy to remind him. "I could damn near eat anything."

"You don't say," Little Willy said. He looked down at Sutherland's hand and stroked it gently.

Ten minutes later, Hank Raddiger hurried back to the Chief's office, holding a long-tailed rodent by its throat. He was careful not to kill it, but wanted it to be stunned a little before he had to put it in his mouth. He thought about slamming its head against the wall a few times, but was in too much of a rush to get back. "Willy!" he called out. "Willy, I've got it-"

Little Willy stepped in front of him at the doorway to block his entrance. "Stop yelling, you damn fool."

Hank lifted up the rat. "I've got it," he said. His hand was dripping with blood from where its claws tore him when he snatched it. It squirmed in his hand and squealed. "I'm ready," he said, opening his mouth wide around the creature's head.

"Get rid of it," Little Willy said. "We're leaving."

"What about our deal?"

"Get rid of it."

"Aw, goddamn, Little Willy. You swore." Hank threw the rat as hard as he could against the wall and continued to whine, but Little Willy ignored him.

Little Willy kept his head turned to inside the Chief's office and he nodded with approval and said, "There you go. That's how you do it." Something was making a sickening crunching and slurping noise inside the office. "Keep going, Bill. Finish your meal."

Bill Sutherland's mouth was full of something wet and he garbled his words, saying, "So good. So unbelievably good."

Hank tapped Little Willy on the shoulder. "Is the Chief coming with us?"

"Bill's slightly occupied. Go find me a ship," Little Willy said. He looked back into the office and said, "Okay, Bill. Time's about up. Wake up and tell me what you see."

Hank tried to look past Little Willy's enormous form, but a shriek burst out from inside the office so full of horror that Hank immediately ran off into the docking bays to find a ship.

Four days after Jem Clayton had come to her house, Janet Walters summed up the nerve to go and see him. She knocked on the Sheriff's Office screen door, and when no one answered, she put her face against the screen and frowned when she saw a grizzled old man sitting at the desk . "Go away," he said.

Janet folded her arms and did not budge. "Who are you? Where's Sheriff Junger?"

"I'm Mr. Never You Mind, and this other feller is Nobody Cares, now beat it."

"Where's Jem Clayton?"

"Not here."

"Are you gonna let me in?"

"No."

Janet banged her hand against the door and said, "You open up right away, whoever you are. I've lived here my whole life and I'm not leaving until I get to speak to someone in authority."

McParlan grunted and came to the door. "We're closed. Your so-called Sheriff ain't here. I'm a PNDA Marshal and I'm housing a prisoner in this facility, which means I don't have time to investigate who stole your ears of corn or why Miss Mary Lou played fiddle at the ho-down instead of Old Billy Bob."

Janet folded her arms across her bountiful chest and said, "Lister here, Mister Fancy Off-World Newcomer, I didn't come to make no complaints. I came to bring something to Jem Clayton." She held up a framed photograph and said, "It's a picture of Jem's daddy, Sam, back when he was the Sheriff."

McParlan opened the door to take the picture from her, and Janet wedged past him to look at the man inside the cell. Elijah Harpe was lying on his back with his bandaged leg propped in the air, snoring. Her eyes widened, "Is that your prisoner? I heard he's famous."

"Don't go anywhere near him," McParlan said. "He's only famous for all the disgusting things he does to innocent women right before he slits their throats. Ain't that right Elijah?"

The man in the cell did not respond, but his snores paused long enough for McParlan to see a slight smile at the corners of his mouth. McParlan looked back at the picture. "Is that Jem back when he was a boy?"

Janet peered over his shoulder and nodded, "Sure was. And that's his little sister, Claire. She's married to a man that got gimped

172

in the mines, poor thing. She's been taking care of him for most of their marriage. Everybody says it's a shame how she got stuck taking care of a cripple, being so pretty and all, but I think it's sweet." Janet pointed at the man standing in the middle of the photo wearing a gold star on his vest, "That's their daddy, Sheriff Sam Clayton. Wasn't he handsome? Everybody says how much Jem looks like him."

"Is that your daddy?" McParlan said.

"That was Deputy Tom Masters. I live in his old house down Pioneer Way. That's how I came upon this. My sister married his son Bart. I was going to take it to Claire myself, but she lives all the way at the opposite end of the settlement at the last house on Pioneer Way. I hoped to see Jem before he left. Everybody says he won't stick around for long."

"He'll be back," McParlan said. "I'll make sure he gets this."

"I'm much obliged," Janet said. "I work just down the street, across from the Proud Lady." Janet looked around the office and said, "Are you stuck in here all this time?"

McParlan shrugged and said, "Somebody's got to stay here and guard the prisoner."

"When's the last time you had a home cooked meal?"

The old Marshal scratched his chin and took a second look at the young woman standing in the doorway. She was heavy, sure, big as a truck, but she had real pretty eyes and her bosoms were bunched together to create a deep crevice that looked like the kind of place he might be able to rest his head and stay awhile. McParlan said, "It's been a long, long time, Miss Janet."

"You come see me tonight and I'll fix you up something special," she said. "You gonna hold onto that picture for Jem?"

McParlan stood the photograph on the edge of the table so it would be the first thing anyone saw when they walked in the door. "Maybe if they see this, they'll remember what a real lawman looked like."

Janet said good day and let herself out the door. McParlan watched her go down the street and smiled despite himself when she turned around and looked back, checking to see if he was still standing there. Elijah Harpe's voice ruined the moment. "Hey, Marshal?"

"What?"

"Can I see that picture?"

"Why?"

"I just want to."

"No."

"How old's the little girl?" Harpe said. "Is she young? Is she pretty?"

McParlan ignored Harpe's thick snorts of laughter as he kicked his feet up on the Sheriff's desk and laid his head back. "I get a contented feeling when I think about you spending the rest of your miserable life on a penal colony, boy. I really do."

The heater in the basement made an unstoppable clanking noise that sounded like a freight train running through Anna's office basement. Anna had taken the contraption apart a dozen times. She changed the filters and tightened every bolt, but it still rattled enough to shake the operating room floorboards overhead.

She picked up a heavy wrench and smacked the units thick metal side. She proceeded to curse it out when she was interrupted by a polite cough coming from the stairwell. Harlan Wells said, "Miss Anna, you all right down here?"

She wiped a grease-smeared hand across her forehead and nodded. Harlan's boy, Adam, was hunched over behind him, watching her. Anna dropped the wrench on the workbench and said, "I'm fine, it's just that this dang heater hasn't worked right since Doctor Halladay was here. I'm ready to rip it out and just buy a new one."

"Listen, you've been real kind to us since we got here. Let my boy Adam take a look. He's got some kind of special gift for fixing things. Do you mind?"

Anna looked at the young man, who seemed too obsessed with the movements of his fingers to comprehend keeping his mouth closed to stop drooling all over the place, let alone fix her heater. "I'm just going to get rid of it anyway, Mr. Wells. Let him have as much fun as he wants with it."

Harlan patted Adam on the arm and said, "Go ahead, son. Fix that thing for Miss Anna."

Adam looked back at his father with no obvious signs of recognition.

"Adam," Harlan repeated, pointing at the heater and coaxing Adam to look at it. "Go over there and fix Miss Anna's heater. It's making an awful racket." Harlan mimicked the heater's BONG-BONG-BONG sound, and Adam said, "BONG-BONG-BONG."

Harlan stuck his fingers in his ears and made an ugly face. "Make that sound stop. There you go. Good boy."

Adam approached the heater and looked it over. He ran his fingers over the coiled wires and touched the pressure gauges attached to them; he laid his ear against its wide metal belly and listened.

The boy sifted through the tools on the work bench and started to disassemble the bolts connecting the water lines. The clanging stopped. Adam continued working and Harlan said, "He might look simple, but he ain't."

Marshal McParlan's muffled voice hollered Anna's name from outside and down the street. "Damn," Anna said. "I was supposed to go watch the prisoner for a spell. I'll be back, Mr. Wells."

"I can go," Harlan said. "Adam will be fine here. I promise he won't blow up your office. You go get freshened up. Jem should be back by nightfall, and you'll want to wash that grease off your face and make yourself all pretty."

Anna put her hands on her hips. "Just what does that mean?"

"It means I'm an old fart who's been around long enough to know what it means when a woman can't take two steps without bumping into something and spends a long time looking through the security gate. She's waiting for her man to come home." Harlan tipped his hat and smiled at her before turning to go up the steps.

There was dust on the road outside of the office, kicked up by passing carriages, and Harlan covered his face with his neckerchief before he crossed. Jimmy McParlan was leaning on the handrail, watching the older man limp out of the way of an oncoming carriage. "How's that forehead, Mr. Wells?"

Harlan lifted his cap to show the Marshal the line of stitches that ran under his hairline like railroad tracks and said, "At first, I was afraid it was gonna ruin my modeling career, but Miss Anna told me scars are *sexy*."

McParlan laughed and opened the door for Harlan. "This sum-bitch hasn't moved in two days except to eat and use the toilet. I need to go scout this town's layout and see if we can't set up some sniper nests, or choke points, or something we can use to our advantage. We got us a fight coming, and if Jem don't come back, we're dead men."

"Well, you go do what you need to and I'll make sure Mr. Harpe stays put," Harlan said.

"If he talks to you, ignore him. If he begs and pleads with you, ignore him. If he wants you to come close to listen to him, ignore him. I've seen prisoners throw a handful of their own filth at guards just for laughs. You follow me?"

"I do. I won't go anywhere near him."

"And most especially, if he does anything that remotely looks like he is trying to escape, pick up that pistol on the desk and shoot him. Can you do that?"

Harlan looked at the old pistol laying on the desk. "I will do my best."

"Okay. Good." McParlan took a deep breath and made sure he had Harlan's full attention, "I hesitate to say this because it probably won't happen, but maybe it's one of those things that can still happen unless you say it might happen. At which point it won't. Kind of like a reverse-jinx."

"If you say so, Marshal."

"If any hostiles show up to try and take this fool before I get back, you need to understand one thing. They might try to convince you that if you give them Elijah they will go away peacefully. That is a damn lie. They will do unspeakable things to every man, woman and child in this town just to send a message. If they show up, you take that pistol and kill as many as you can, but kill *that* son of a bitch first."

Harlan watched the Marshal ease down the steps toward the road and looked back at the gun. He'd never fired one before. Harlan picked it up and stuck it in his belt, and when he turned around, he saw Elijah Harpe sitting up in his bunk, staring at him. Elijah smirked and laid back down on the bench, folding his hands under his head before closing his eyes to go back to sleep.

McParlan stuck his fingers in his ears and waited for the high-pitched whining to cease. He walked past the mining site's entrance toward the column of massive machines all gathered around a massive crater. They were larger than buildings and shot white hot laser beams into the quarry in bursts that shook the ground and blew gusts of rock dust into the air. The Marshal tapped one of the workers on the shoulder and asked to speak to someone in charge and was directed toward a young man holding a clipboard.

McParlan walked over to him and touched the badge on his dusty coat, "Marshal James McParlan of the PNDA. Who're you?"

"Bartholomew Masters, but you can call me Bart." When he stuck out his hand to shake McParlan's, his fingers were tattooed black and tipped with cracked fingernails that would never heal. His skin was colored grey from so many years spent down in the mines.

"I need explosives," McParlan said.

"Sorry, but we don't use any. The entire settlement drills strictly by laser so we don't risk damaging any of the product."

McParlan looked at the laser drilling machine and said, "Actually, these might work even better. Can I see one in action?"

"You sure can. Come back tomorrow at seven AM. We're all done for the day."

McParlan put his hands on his side and said, "Actually, I'd like to see it a little sooner than that, son. Like, now."

"No can do, Marshal. The machines take forty minutes to work up enough charge to fire. We can only use a single machine twice in the same day. I don't have any left to give you a demonstration with, Marshal."

"Damn," McParlan said. "Don't you have anything else?"

"Just a few handheld's."

"Show me."

Masters took the Marshal to the equipment lot and showed him a bulky backpack contraption with a hose connected to a barrel.

"These things are heavy as hell, but nothing works better for delicate detail work."

"What's their range?"

"About a foot and a half."

"Can it be expanded?"

"To what?"

"Fifty feet."

Masters laughed and said, "No. They'd blow up."

"Let's just say I'm looking to increase security around here," McParlan said. "The Sheriff around these parts couldn't handle an invasion of old ladies with knitting needles, and I'm afraid something much worse than that is coming. You got any interest in helping me?"

Masters looked over his shoulder at the men leaving the worksite to head home. The men waved to Masters and he waved back and said, "Goodnight." He turned to look at the Marshal and said, "This sounds like an over-a-beer conversation to me. You thirsty?"

An hour later, the sound of rattling keys woke Elijah Harpe. He rolled over on his side to face the cell door, and saw Harlan Wells selecting the right key to fit into the lock. The old man put a heavy iron one into the door and started to turn it. Elijah rubbed his eyes and waited for the dream to end.

Harlan yanked the door open and said, *"Come on out, you idiot."*

Elijah laid back down on the bunk and folded his hands behind his head. "You are stupider than that potato-headed son of yours if you think I'm dumb enough to fall for that. You think I'd let you shoot me in the back as I walk down the steps just so's you can claim a reward?"

Harlan's voice was deeper when he said, *"Little Willy says you might even be stupider than you are ugly. And that's quite an achievement."*

Elijah's eyes flew open and he bolted upright. "Well, I'll be damned. How in the hell did he manage to get to one of you all the way out here?"

Harlan's eyes fluttered and his face twisted. He gasped and reached out to clutch the door to try and pull it shut and keep it open at the same time, with one arm struggling against the other. "No! Get out, you son of a bitch. Get out!"

Elijah watched the old man with amusement and said, "I'm getting." He pushed Harlan away from the door as he limped out on his bad leg. "Back up, you damn fool."

Fat droplets of sweat spilled off of Harlan's face. He had to hold onto the cell doors just to stay on his feet. Through clenched teeth he said, *"Meet by the crash site. We've got a weapon now that will change everything, forever."*

Elijah walked over to the Sheriff's desk to look at the framed photograph. He popped the frame open and took out the picture. He tore off the end that showed the little girl with pigtails, smiling up at her daddy. Elijah ran his finger over her face and whispered, "I bet you're real pretty now, Claire." He looked at Harlan, "Tell Willy I'll meet him right here in the morning. I have some reckoning to attend to."

"Stop…stop…" Harlan muttered as he struggled to pull the pistol from his waistband. Elijah Harpe limped down the steps of the Sheriff's office and just as he reached the street, Harlan got the gun free and raised it to his back. *DO NOT TRY TO DEFY ME.*"

"Get out of my head," Harlan gasped. He tried squeezing the trigger, but watched in horror as his arm began moving toward a woman walking down Pioneer Way. The woman was completely unaware as she strolled along the shop windows, admiring the items within, when Harlan's gun erupted, blowing a hole through the back of her hat and splattering its light blue fabric with dark blood.

People looked up from all around the town square to see the woman crumple to the ground. They waited, like it was a street performance and did not want to be thought a fool for acting surprised. Men in front of the Proud Lady lowered their mugs of beer and stopped talking. Children in front of the candy shop stood still as the old man holding the pistol groaned in misery, and blood spread out on the dirt under the woman's hat.

Women screamed and snatched their children up, dragging them back into the stores or into the alleyways. Three miners waiting to cash their checks at the Savings and Loan ran at Harlan, yelling for him to stop, but he turned on them and fired. Harlan moved like a machine across the street, turning his gun on anyone who looked at him.

Anna Willow threw her office door open and stood open mouthed at the sight of Harlan Wells coming toward her, gun at the ready. "Mr. Wells!" Anna shouted. She saw the bodies lying on the street behind him, but the cold, expressionless mask of his face terrified her more than anything. Harlan raised his gun to her face.

"No!" she cried and everything slowed down and magnified. The mouth of the barrel widened to reveal the spiraled rifling within. The flat steel surface of the bullet inside the chamber seemed larger than her fist. The only sound in the world was the mechanical click of the revolver's cylinder turning as Harlan squeezed the trigger. The gun fired and chunks of the doorframe exploded above Anna's head, showering her with wooden splinters as she dropped to her knees and covered her head. "Why are you doing this?" she screamed.

"I can't stop!" Harlan's gun hand shook and his pale cheeks exploded with burst blood vessels. "He's making me do this! Somebody help me!"

The office door opened behind her and Adam Wells came out of the office, looking in wonder at the way Anna cowered in front of his father. He turned to look at Harlan and smiled.

Harlan turned the gun on his son and said, "Please, please, no. I beg you. I will shoot myself if you want, right now. Adam, run away! Run away!"

Anna stood up in front of Adam, backing him toward her office while shielding him with her body. "Harlan! Listen to me. You don't have to do this. Your son didn't do anything wrong."

Harlan's jaw sawed back and forth and when he spoke, his voice was not the same. *"You never wanted him anyway. When you saw how he was you thought about drowning him in the bath, old man. You hated what he took from you."*

"What is wrong with you?" Anna shrieked. She yanked Adam down onto the ground next to her and covered him with her arms. "Leave us alone."

Tears streamed down Harlan's face and blood collected in his nostrils and spilled down his chin, dribbling between his lips. "I will not do this! You cannot make me, you son of a bitch!"

Marshal James McParlan ran down the street yelling, "Put that goddamn weapon down, Harlan! What the hell has gotten into you?" He raised his Balrog and fired at the ground by the old man's feet, but Harlan did not even notice.

"McParlan?" Harlan said. He let out a laugh and said, *"Marshal James McParlan?"*

"Stop talking and put the gun down, Harlan. You don't want to hurt anybody else."

Harlan turned on him and said, *"Oh, but I do, old man. You took my brother, and now I'm going to kill every person in that little shit town. You know what happens to people who mess with my family, Marshal?"* Harlan Wells lurched forward, dragging the soles of his boots in the dirt. *"I mess with theirs."* Harlan aimed the gun back at Adam and started to squeeze the trigger, but managed to get the gun into the air and fire it at the sky. *"Stop resisting me, old man."*

"What the hell's gotten into you?"

"All of Hell." Harlan's mouth twisted and his eyes bulged and it was his own voice that cried out, "Don't let me do this. I can't stop him! He's inside my mind. He's going to make me shoot them! Please, for the love of God, don't let me do this."

"Who's inside of you, Harlan?" McParlan shouted.

"The brother of that man you arrested. It's too late," Harlan gasped. He lowered the gun again at Adam and said, "I can't— Adam—Please, Marshal, save him."

McParlan's gunshot cracked the air and Harlan Wells collapsed. The Marshal holstered his Balrog and kicked the gun away from Wells' hand, standing silently over the body as people closed in on him.

Claire Miller carried a large basket of vegetables up to her front porch door and kicked it with her boot. "Frank? Frank! Come open this door up. This stuff is heavy."

She put the basket up against the wall and braced it there as she pulled the screen door open and turned the interior door's handle. She heaved the basket through the entrance, calling for Frank again. Claire set the basket down and wiped her wet forehead with the sleeve of her shirt. The light was on in the back bedroom. "Stop pretending like you can't hear me," she said. "I know you got one good ear. Don't try to get out of helping me."

Frank's chair was turned over in the entrance of her childhood bedroom. She hurried into the back room but stopped at the sight of a dirty-looking man sitting on her bed. He was resting a bandaged leg and picking his fingernails with a knife.

In the corner of the room farthest from her, Frank was standing on a wobbling stack of books. He was naked and shivering and had a noose tied around his neck. There was a sock stuffed in his mouth and the noose was taut from his neck up to the ceiling beams above. Frank's hands were bound behind his back with what appeared to be a pair of her pants and he was moaning when she walked in, tears spilling from his eyes.

The man on the bed held up a torn piece of a photograph and looked at Claire. He nodded with satisfaction and said, "I knew it. You did grow up to be a pretty one, Claire."

"Who the hell are you and what do you want?" Claire hissed.

"I'm a friend of your brother's," he said. Then he grinned and said, "Well. That might not be the entire truth. The Lord hates it when I lie. Jem and I ain't friends at all. Now me and you? We're gonna be real, real close friends before the night is over."

"Get out of my house, and leave us alone."

Elijah Harpe smiled to reveal a dripping cesspool of yellow and brown. "I'm trying to be nice to you. Trust me. This is the easy part. It's what comes next that you got to worry about."

15. Judges 19:25

Claire Clayton was six years old when her daddy died. Most of her memories of that time were covered by the kind of fog that renders faces blurry and voices faint. She remembered how Sam Clayton smelled, though. Something like good pipe tobacco and worn but well-oiled leather. She remembered sitting in Sam's lap and him always pressing his chin into the cup of her palm, he'd rub his scruff against her skin until she giggled and tried to get away. Sam let up just enough to let her catch her breath, and did it all over again.

She remembered the night Deputy Frank Banner was murdered in front of their house, and telling Sam, "I'm proud of Jem for protecting us and killing that bad man."

Sam looked at his little girl and bent down to her level, like he always did when he wanted to talk to her. He wasn't the kind to stand over her and issue edicts. He was the sort that got face to face with a little girl to tell her why it was necessary for her to go to bed on time. Sam said, "I know that's the truth, but I want us to agree to pretend that it was Frank who killed that Beothuk."

"But why?"

"Because it would be bad for Jem if people thought he'd already shot a man before he's even old enough to shave. They'll be proud of him for a little while, but if anything bad ever happens, they're gonna say he got a taste for killing and it never went away."

"Did he get a taste for it?"

"Of course not. I'm just as proud as can be for him, and of you too, darling. But for now, let's just keep it between us as a family, okay?"

She did not remember anything about Jem and Anna coming home to tell her that Sam was dead. Anna told her that she sat on her bed and stared at the wall saying nothing until Jem went into his room and slammed the door. Claire remembered the inhuman howling coming from his room. She remembered things crashing and breaking in his room and the gut-wrenching sobs.

Anna put her arm around Claire and rocked her back and forth. "Jem is gonna be all right, Claire. He just needs to let it out. Do you?"

Claire looked up at her and said, "No, ma'am."

After a time, Claire decided that she and Jem just saw things in different ways. Jem had real memories of their Mama and had lived through her death. For as long as Claire could remember, they'd been alone. The people she loved were already in grief. She never had a chance to think any other way than that you don't own anything in this world, you can't control it, and what you love can go away in the blink of an eye.

That's why Jem was a fool, she thought. He still believed you could hold onto what you love.

The only other thing that stood out in her child hood was an incident that she'd never spoken to anyone else about. It was two years before the night of the Beothuk raid, which made her about four years old. One evening, Katey Halladay knocked on the door and said their daddy was going to be working late. Jem was outside running loose with some local boys, and Claire helped Mrs. Halladay cook dinner and clean up. Sam had never imposed much in the way of chores on the children, and Claire was baffled as to why Katey wanted her to wash her hands and put on a clean shirt. "It's not like we're going to church, Miss Katey," she said.

Katey Halladay put three plates on the table and told Claire to arrange the silverware. "How come you aren't staying to eat with us?" Claire said.

"I am, sweetie. Your daddy won't be home for dinner."

"Where is he?"

"He just had to work is all, Miss Nosey Thing," Katey said. "Now go call Jem in."

Over dinner, Jem was shifting in his seat with excitement. "Did you hear what happened?"

"Did I hear what, dear?" Katey said.

"There was some sort of trouble at the Willow Funeral Home with Old Man Willow's assistant, Zeke. Daddy and Tom Masters had to arrest him and cart him off to the penitentiary all the way out at Seneca 5."

"Is that right?" Katey said. She tapped Claire's plate with the tip of her fingernail. "You need some more greens, young lady."

"Yes, ma'am. So what did the man do?" Claire asked.

Jem shrugged, "Nobody would say. Just that it was pure awful and Old Man Willow was chasing him around with a bat when Daddy got there." Jem looked over at Claire and said, "I wonder if he hurt Anna?"

"All right now, let's eat," Katey said.

"I reckon that's the only thing that would make Old Man Willow mad enough to chase Zeke around like that. I'm just guessing."

"That's enough guessing," Katey said abruptly. "I said to eat."

That night, Katey brushed Claire's hair and complained the entire time that it was like trying to run a brush through a net made of sailboat rigging. Claire grimaced every time the brush tore through another knot, but after it was done, she looked at herself in the mirror and smiled at the sight. Katey tucked her into bed and read her a story, then gave Claire a little kiss on the forehead and said, "Goodnight."

Claire closed her eyes and turned over, but could hear the discussion in the living room between Katey and Jem as to exactly how late Jem would be allowed to stay up and wait for his father. The conversation ended with Katey saying, "Until I say so."

Hours later, Claire felt a hand touching her face. She smelled that familiar tobacco and leather scent and felt Sam moving the hair out of her eyes. "I'm sorry, Princess," Sam said. "I didn't mean to wake you. Go back to sleep."

Claire rubbed her eyes and told him it was okay. She laid back down and pulled his big hand back to her face. "I'm glad you're home."

"Me too. I just wanted to make sure my little angel was okay."

"I'm ok," she yawned. "Why wouldn't I be?"

"Sometimes, a daddy just needs to check. You know that if anybody ever tries to do anything bad to you, you need to tell me right away. Don't hide it, don't be ashamed of it, and don't keep it inside. You just come let me know and I'll take care of it."

"How would you take care of it?" she said. Her eyes started to close on their own. Sam kissed her on the face a few times and stood up without answering.

The next morning, Jem ran into Claire's room and told her "Hurry up and get dressed! I've got to show you something."

He waited anxiously for her in the hallway, and when she came out he held his finger to his lips and whispered, "Keep quiet."

They could hear Sam snoring in his bedroom, and both kids crept through the front door and onto the porch. Jem said, "I stayed up till Pa got home and overheard him talking to Miss Katey. She asked him if he was okay, and he told her he was fine, but *then* she said that Doc Halladay told her the penitentiary was filled up at Seneca 5 and they weren't taking any new prisoners. She asked him where he'd been all that time and what happened to Zeke."

Jem looked back through the door and made sure they were still alone. "Pa wasn't even mad that she caught him in a lie. He just said that he'd been out in the desert. She asked him again where Zeke was, and he told her never to mind."

"Why was he being mean to her?" Claire said.

"He wasn't," Jem said. "He sounded all sad and emotional when he said it, and Miss Katey gave him a hug and told him he was a good man." Jem took Claire's hand and led her down the steps, taking her around the side of the house. "This morning, I was tending to his destrier and looking around when I found something."

They went around the house to the rear and Jem bent down to sweep aside the long grass under the porch. He waved for Claire to come look, and she stared at Sam's blood-splattered shirt and pants bundled and hidden in the grass. Claire backed away and put her hands around Jem's arm, trying to pull him away. "Come on," she said. "We weren't supposed to see this. We're gonna get in trouble."

Jem let her pull him up, but as they walked back toward the house, he said, "I'm glad he done it."

Elijah Harpe hobbled around the corner of the bed, using the frame to keep himself upright. He came within arm's reach of Claire and said, "You don't talk too much, do you."

Claire stood her ground, but could not keep her eyes from flickering at her husband as he squirmed on his gimpy legs to keep his balance. His toes gripped the edges of the topmost hard-bound book, but the stack was uneven. It teetered under his feet as he danced back and forth on the books, whimpering a series of unintelligible pleas through the stuffed sock in his mouth.

"That ol' boy can't stand up there much longer, gorgeous," Elijah said. Claire recoiled as Elijah sided up next to her and touched her cheek. He smirked at the way she stared back at him. "Behold, said the old man to the sons of Belial as they beset his house and beat upon his door. There is a good man within, and to him you shall do no vile thing. But instead, take my daughter, his concubine, and humble her."

Elijah looked back at Frank and winked. "You know what those sons of Belial did next, partner?" He ran his finger down the length of Claire's neck toward the center of her chest. "They abused her all the night, until the morning. Later, the good man divided her into twelve pieces and sent her all across the land. That's in the Good Book."

When Claire did not answer, Elijah grabbed her by the hair and pulled her close. He pressed his mouth against hers, and to his surprise, Claire's mouth opened. He pushed his tongue against hers and swirled it around just as Claire chomped down with her teeth.

Elijah squealed and tried to push her away, but it felt like her teeth were about to tear his tongue in half. He went to stab her with the knife, but Claire caught his wrist with both hands and held his arm tight. Elijah landed a hard punch to her stomach with his other hand that doubled her over. He dropped an elbow onto the back of her head that dropped her to the floor in a heap.

He hopped back around the bed and shoved Frank off of the stack of books, making Frank's face turn purple as he swung by the neck. His cheeks puffed out like they were going to burst and his legs dangled in the air.

Claire was trapped on her back like a turtle and Elijah showed her the knife and started to tell her about blowtorches and hot irons. About cutting pieces off of her husband's body and feeding them to her. About how long it would take before she finally was allowed to die.

Claire slammed the heel of her foot into the thick bandages wrapped around Elijah's knee and he looked down with his mouth open wide, but he was too stunned to scream. His eyes rolled into the back of his head like a slot machine coming up empty spaces and the knife slid out of his hand as he dropped to the floor.

Claire laid there, waiting for the room to stop spinning. Fireworks had exploded behind her eyes when Elijah hit her and she was still seeing flashes of green and white while she lay there looking up at the ceiling. It was Frank's gurgling that lured her back. She grabbed a handful of blankets on the side of the bed and started pulling herself up.

Frank was swinging free on the rope and his face was turning black. Claire stumbled around the bed, and as she walked near Elijah, he snatched her by the ankle and wrapped himself around her leg.

Claire stomped him like an angry chicken, but he held her fast and managed to drag her down on top of him. She balled up her fist and slammed it into Elijah's face with all her might and strained back to grab the bed and shove it as hard as she could.

The metal frame slid across the floor, just close enough that Frank was able to get the balls of his feet onto the mattress and stand up to take a quick breath.

Claire lifted her head and shouted, "Don't you give up on me!"

Elijah grabbed a handful of her hair and twisted, winding it around his fist and cranking her head down until her ear was next to his mouth. "I was going to be nice to you before, you bitch, but now I'm going to show you what evil really is."

Elijah Harpe slithered on his belly like a worm, coming out of the bedroom to get to the kitchen. He could only see out of one eye and it stung worse than a thousand needles stuffed inside his eyelids. He tried pushing up from the floor and collapsed. He tried again, but had to lay flat and catch his breath.

Claire was crawling out of the bedroom behind him. "Where…where… you going?" she said between two broken lips. Her whole face was swollen until both her eyes were just slits and the skin around them was green and bulging like the face of a fly. "Had enough… sissy?"

Elijah shook his head, "You are one twisted woman." He braced himself against the wall and was able to get up on his good leg to limp into the kitchen. At the edge of the counter, he lost his grip and toppled onto the tile floor. He groaned and wheezed with laughter at his own misfortune. Elijah reached up for the ledge of the countertop and fished around the pile of utensils and pricked his finger on the blade of a sharp knife.

Claire was still coming, calling to him from the hallway, "We're gonna finish this."

Elijah rested on his elbow on the floor for a moment before taking the knife down. He wrapped his fingers around the handle and said, "I could not agree more."

Claire did not respond as Elijah crawled back out of the kitchen. "You fought like a tiger, gorgeous. I hope you still have some fight left in you." He came into the hallway and came face to face with Claire, who did not look at him. Her eyes were turned toward the other end of the hall, by the front door and she mouthed the name, "Jem."

Elijah laughed at her and said, "It's just us, honeypot. And I'm gonna enjoy this more than you can—"

A hand grabbed Elijah Harpe by the ankle of his bad leg and yanked him down to the floor. Elijah looked back in disbelief and saw Jem Clayton standing over him, his eyes blazing with hellfire.

Jem dug into his pocket for the balled-up mask of black fabric. He shook it into the dusty winds that swept through the canyon.

The wrecked ship's parts were no longer smoking, and were now covered over with dirt and sand. The charred body of the pilot was gone. Jem reasoned that it had been picked over by birds and other scavengers, and the bones were carried off by creatures that were gnawing on them in caves at that very moment.

He unfolded the mask and tied it around the back of his neck, then pulled it up over his mouth and nose. He tapped Elijah Harpe on the cheek and peeled one of his eyes open. "Anybody home, Elijah?"

Elijah tried to speak but couldn't. He toppled over on his side and shot up on one shoulder to keep the torn flesh of his back off of the scalding sand. There was a rope tied around his waist, and its harsh fibers were thorns digging into his raw wounds. Jem had dragged him from the back of his destrier from Claire's homestead. His bandages had long-since ripped off and the stitches on his leg had torn open. His old wounds were leaking, and so were all the new ones.

"You recognize where we are, Elijah? Back where we first met. I should have killed you right there. Time to correct that."

Elijah squinted and looked around at the canyon where the ship had crashed. His shoulder gave out and he rolled over on his back, no longer able to feel the burning sand and rock on his open skin. He smiled at Jem. "None of us can hide from God."

Jem fished in his shirt pocket for the torn photograph he found on the Sheriff's desk. "Good thing you left this behind," he said. "Otherwise, I'd probably still be looking for you." He dug into Elijah's pockets for the torn piece, and found it. Jem reached behind his back for the long kitchen knife and drew it out to show Elijah.

The blade reflected light into Elijah's eyes, but he ignored it and stared straight at the sun's fiery surface. He forced his eyes to stay open until tears ran down his cheeks and everything around him became opaque. "I can see it," Elijah gasped. "I see the glory."

"Well, just keep looking at it. Let me know if you get there."

Jem stuck the tip of the blade into the soft flesh at the center of Elijah's throat and pushed until blood bubbled through. He sawed at the skin and tissue until his knife caught on bone. Elijah did not scream or even struggle. He laid there, grunting as Jem worked the blade back and forth, cutting until he was able to grab a handful of Elijah's hair and tear the head the rest of the way off.

He lifted Elijah's head and stared into the wide, vacant eyes, watching as the muscles in the face continued to twitch and the mouth worked up and down with no sound coming out of it.

Jem carried the head through the crash site, looking for a place to mount it. There was a length of metal sticking out of the hull, and Jem jammed Elijah's head onto its tip, twisting until it was firmly seated.

He wiped his hands in the dirt and scrubbed them with sand, wiping away the clumps of blood from his fingers and flicking them into the dirt. He pulled off his mask and wiped off his hands, then balled up the black mask and threw it to the ground. A destrier snorted from the cliff above. Someone was watching him.

The destrier's rider coughed into his fist and lifted up his hand to wave to Jem. Royce Halladay walked his mount down the cliff and into the canyon, eyeing the burnt equipment littered across the valley, then coming to the place where Jem had spiked Elijah's head. Halladay smoothed his mustache with the tip of his finger as he admired the sight and said, "Well, now I suppose that I should be angry with you, Jem Clayton. Had I known that you were interested in barbering, I would never have paid those thieves in Seneca 5 so much money. I fear the finer points of the art may have escaped you, however." Jem turned away from Halladay and headed back toward his destrier.

"Forgive me if the situation did not call for levity, Jem. Let us not lose our heads over it, what do you say?"

Jem pulled himself into the saddle and looked back, "Twenty years is a long time to be away, Doc. Why the sudden interest in returning to Seneca 6?"

"I heard there might be trouble."

Jem spurred his ride to close the distance between them. He leaned close to Halladay and said, "Let's just cut the shit, old man. I know what you are and you know what I am. If you followed me here to try and lure me into a trap, you're going to suffer for it. I swear on my father's soul that no reward money in the world is worth the misery I will impart on you for trying."

Royce Halladay's eyes narrowed and he said, "Do you recall an incident when you were ten years old? Sam brought you to see me because you had spots all over your face and he was worried you were coming down with the clumps. Do you remember?"

"I remember I bit you."

"Correct!" Halladay said. "I tried placing a thermometer into your mouth and you bit me because you were an ungrateful, mean little bastard that didn't know when someone was trying to offer you assistance."

"That was then. You ain't a doctor anymore and I ain't ten. You expect me to believe a vicious killer like you gives a damn about me or anyone else on this rock?"

"I expect you to show me the proper respect due a man who is faster than you, a better shot than you, and only tolerating your continued existence out of respect to a dear, departed friend."

Jem opened his mouth to speak but found nothing came out. Halladay smirked at him and pulled on his reins, turning away from Jem to head back up the trail.

"You ain't *that* fast, old man," Jem said.

"Fast enough for you, boy. Fast enough for you."

16. Smells Like Snakes

Harlan Wells was still twitching when the crowd piled on top of him. His frail limbs retracted and quivered even as the townsfolk stomped him, turning his face to jelly and his body into a bag of crunching bones. "String him up!" a miner announced.

Jimmy McParlan cracked him across the back of the skull with his pistol and fired into the air. "Back up you sons-of-bitches! Anybody so much as takes another step and I'll start putting holes in all of you."

Several men rushed him and tackled him around the waist, driving him to the ground. They peeled the gun out of his hand and one of the miners leveled it at McParlan's head and squeezed the trigger. The gun clicked uselessly and a computerized voice emitted from the barrel: *Fingerprint identification failure. Initiating security precautions.*

The gun vibrated in the miner's hand and glowed red, turning hot enough to sizzle the flesh inside his palm. The miner dropped the gun and ran screaming through the crowd. Boot heels cracked McParlan across the ribs and a finger gouged his good eye. McParlan batted them away from his face and tried fighting back even as more of them jumped onto him and started swinging freely. He gave up fighting and instead used his remaining strength to cover his head and hope to hold on long enough for them to get tired. They didn't get tired. It only got worse.

The Marshal woke up in the dark, groaning for the bastards to get off of him. Someone was grabbing him, holding him down and McParlan shouted, "You don't understand! Elijah Harpe has escaped!"

"It's all right now, Marshal," Bart Masters said.

"Where the hell am I?"

"Dr. Willow's office. I dragged you in here to get you away from those maniacs out there."

"I'm much obliged, now where the hell are my guns? I've got a fugitive to look for."

"I honestly hope you weren't too attached to that prisoner, Marshal. Jem Clayton caught him at Claire and Frank's house and dragged him all the way out to Coramide Canyon."

McParlan closed his eye and was struck by the image of Harlan Wells aiming a pistol at Adam, begging him to shoot. He thought about the strange voice coming out of Wells.

"I am ashamed of what happened to you out there, sir," Masters said. "People disrespecting the law like that, it makes me sick."

"I ain't been much impressed by the law I've seen in this town so far," McParlan said. "I'm not sure I can blame `em."

"It wasn't always like that, Marshal. "My daddy was a deputy under Sheriff Clayton. Helped him fight off the Beothuk on the night of the invasion and escorted the wounded across the wasteland out to the hospital in Seneca 5. He never told anybody about his own injuries and they say he collapsed in his saddle the second the last person was picked up on a stretcher. With him and Sam both gone, it was easy pickings for Walt Junger and Billy Jack to swoop in and take over."

"So what are we gonna do about it?" McParlan said.

"Right now, you aren't in shape to do much of anything," Masters said. "And I'm just a miner."

Anna Willow knocked on the door, and let herself into the room. "Thanks for minding the Marshal for me," she said.

Bart Masters tilted his hat at her and left as Anna moved into his chair. She handed a cold compress to McParlan and told him to press it against his face. "You looked better after they dragged you out of the wreckage of that spaceship," she said.

McParlan waved his hand at her, "That wasn't my first angry mob. They all hit like women."

Anna sat on the edge of the bed and folded her hands in her lap. "Thank you for saving my life today, Marshal."

He ignored her and said, "How's Adam?"

"He's fine," Anna said. "I sent him to stay with an older couple I know. He was just sitting by the window, rocking back and forth, like he was waiting for Harlan to come home. I thought a change of scenery would be good."

McParlan nodded and said, "Good thinking. Plus, you got your hands full."

"That woman that Harlan shot was a widow. She had two little girls. I guess someone will have to look after them now. That other man was shot in the hip. He'll live, but probably won't walk right ever again. But at least he'll live. Why in God's name did he do that? Why? It was like he was possessed by the devil."

"In a way, I believe he was."

"What does that mean?"

"I'm still not completely sure. But trust me, that wasn't Harlan who shot them folks."

Anna went to the next room and knocked gently before poking her head in. Frank Miller was sitting in his wheelchair next to the bed where his wife was laying. Frank's face was swollen and crusted with blood, and there was a massive burn mark collared around his throat that he refused to let Anna even look at until she finished tending to Claire.

Frank pressed his fingers to his lips and said, "She finally fell asleep."

Claire's head was bandaged like a turban. Her eyes were swollen shut and her lips looked like she was wearing a pair of wax ones from the candy store down the street.

"She isn't dead," Frank said. "She isn't going to be dead."

"I know, honey," Anna said.

"You fixed her, right? You fixed her and she isn't going to die."

"I fixed her," Anna said. "How about you let me look at your neck now that she's situated? If you get an infection, you won't be able to take care of her."

Frank nodded silently. Anna had to peel the shirt collar away from the injured skin, making Frank wince as it came unstuck. She rubbed ointment gently into the wound and Frank settled. "Does that feel better?"

"It stings pretty bad, to be honest."

"That means it's working. Whatever you do, don't itch it. I want you to get some sleep now too, Frank."

He ignored her and leaned forward, re-tucking the blanket around Claire's shoulders. Anna shut the door rather than argue with him and took a moment to appreciate the quiet. Bart Masters coughed lightly to let her know he was watching her from down the hall. "Why don't you go home and get some rest, Dr. Willow. I'll stay with the patients and send someone for you if there's a need."

Anna thanked him and grabbed her coat. She stepped outside and saw a dim light from the Sheriff's Office. Walt Junger was sitting at his desk, hunched over, scribbling on a stack of documents. Anna had heard rumors that Junger was applying for warrants for McParlan's arrest, sending off letters to every government agency in the sector. She shook her head and was about to turn away when someone sitting on a porch swing outside of her office caught her eye. Anna squinted to make him out and said, "Jem? What in the world are you doing lurking around out here?"

"I didn't have anywhere else to go. I figured I'd stay nearby if you needed me, but not disturb you."

Anna held out her hand and said, "Come on. You're coming with me."

There were no lights on in any of the businesses along Pioneer Way as they walked. Even the bars were closed. "So tell me the fate of Mr. Elijah Harpe," Anna said.

Jem looked down and said, "A person like you wouldn't understand, Anna. Someone like you helps people. Someone like me does the opposite."

"I wouldn't expect anything less from the *baddest man in the world*," Anna said.

Jem grinned at her. "You've been waiting twenty years to fire that one back at me, haven't you?"

"Maybe. Do you remember Zeke that used to work for my father?"

Jem nodded.

"Did you ever hear what happened to me?"

"I heard enough."

Anna's voice was quiet when she said, "When I was a little girl, I trusted everybody. People acted so nice to me after my mother died, I just assumed that's how they really were. Zeke told me I was special. He paid attention to me. Sometimes I wonder if I did something to make him think it was okay to do what he did."

"You were just a kid, Anna. Of course you didn't," Jem said.

"The worst thing about it was that the nice man who treated me so kindly told me he would kill me and my father if I told anyone. I believed him, Jem. I looked in his eyes and I saw evil. I never could tell your daddy what he did to me. Miss Katey had to do all the talking for me, and your daddy hauled Zeke off to the penitentiary."

Jem looked off in the distance. "That's the story I heard too."

"Except Zeke never was at the penitentiary."

Jem did not speak.

"I checked up on him a few years ago, just to see what became of him. The warden said there had never been a prisoner there by that name. So it leaves me with the question as to what became of the man that stole my innocence. Your daddy didn't seem the type to let a man like that go in the desert, now did he?"

Jem shook his head, "No. I don't suppose."

She put her hand in his. "So, you're wrong. Someone like me would understand."

She led him to the front steps of her house and he stood there while she unlocked the front door. "Well, don't just stand there. Come on."

Jem followed her through the dark house toward the washroom where she turned on the taps above a large washtub. The pipes whistled and hot water sputtered into the tub. Anna started to unbutton his shirt, and Jem stopped her. "I'm a little old to be given a bath by anyone, let alone you."

She continued to unbutton his shirt. "I am a doctor, Jem Clayton. I want to make sure you weren't injured today. Anyway, it's not like it's anything I haven't seen when you were a kid."

He pulled her closer to him so that they were pressed against one another. "You might be surprised."

Anna's cheeks turned crimson and Jem smiled before stepping back from her and yanked off his boots. They were caked in mud and he set them down next to the door. "I'm just playing with you, Anna. Besides, you're a little too old for me."

"I'm only four years older than you!"

"Yeah, but that's in woman-years. A woman thirty-six years old is like a man at fifty. At least, by my math." She rolled her eyes but did not look away as Jem started to unbutton his pants.

They laid down together after his bath and started on opposite sides of the bed. "It's cold in here," Anna said.

"You want me to go put on the furnace?"

"No."

Jem wrapped his arm around her and pressed himself against her back. "Is that better?" When she did not respond he lifted his head to look at her and saw she was already asleep.

The next morning he woke up alone. There was a pitcher of coffee on the table next to the bed with an empty cup in a saucer. Beside the pitcher was a locked wooden box with an old key laying on top of a note that read: *Whatever is in this box belongs to you. I have kept it all these years waiting for you to come home.*

Jem folded up the letter and regarded the box. He studied the rusted metal lock as he twirled the heavy iron key in his fingers before fitting it into the opening and turning.

The box lid creaked open and the first thing Jem saw were several pieces of paper folded together. He removed each page and placed them on the bed to smooth them out. There was the same shaky handwriting on each page. He read the first one.

Dear Jem:

I do not know how this letter will find you. Perhaps you will be an old man like me when you finally read it. All the men written of within it may have long since passed on and you will be left with nothing except maybe a few answers.

However, it is my hope that you are not so old, and that those men have not quite so easily escaped from their past deeds.

I entrusted this box to my beloved daughter Anna, who has always taken a fancy to your family. It is my sincerest hope that she is healthy and happy as you read this, and while I entreat you not to tell her anything else that you read here, please tell her that.

It has been ten years since I last laid eyes on you. You rode out one day searching for something that I suspect was taken from you when you were just a boy. Whatever it is you went looking for, I don't believe you will have found it. Not out there, anyway. It's here.

I am going to tell you the truth about your father and his passing.

I pray to God Almighty that you are man enough to stand it, and I hope more than anything else that you are strong enough to forgive me. I am already dead, as you read my words. I've heard death's footfalls creep toward me for weeks now and he will be here soon. I am looking forward to it, actually. By the time you have lived to my age, and seen what I have seen, you will not fear death. You'll fear life. You'll look forward to taking a nice long rest, and to the end of having to lose the things that you love.

Only four people know the truth about what happened that day in the wasteland. One of them died finding out. I suspect I'll be gone soon, so count me out as well. Of the two that remain, it is my dying wish that they have a chance to witness your reaction to all I am about to say.

It had been a week since Sam Clayton had left us for Beothuk Country with that wagon full of dead bodies. He went on a damned fool's errand to try and make peace with those savages by showing them a more noble way of existence. Nobody, including myself, thought this was a good idea.

Sam was a popular man, and there were rumblings of forming a search party that didn't amount to much beyond tavern talk. It took me by surprise when I came to find out that Walt Junger and Billy Jack Elliot had taken it upon themselves to ride out into the desert to look for him. I saw Walt loading up a destrier in front of the Sheriff's Office and asked him when he was headed out. "First light," he said.

"I'm going with you," I said.

By that time, Billy had come out to stand on the porch, and Walt looked up at him. Billy nodded and shrugged, telling me that was fine.

We went past the security gate and headed into the mountains. To my surprise, both the other men hunted for your father with ferocity, determined to find him. I'd never put much stock in Walt Junger, but he cut sign for Sam Clayton like he was born to do it.

Truthfully, I wasn't eager to find him.

I thought we would get to the border of Beothuk country and find your father's body displayed like some kind of goddamn waypoint marker, a warning to all us civilized folk that this is what happens to them when you venture too far from home.

Imagine my surprise when I spied a rider in the far off distance, making his way down the mountain toward us.

I called out his name before we were even close enough to recognize one another, out of sheer hope. I spurred my ride forward, taking off toward him, but the other two stayed behind. I looked over my shoulder to see Billy side up to Walt and start talking.

Sam smiled at me as I came near. "What the hell are you doing all the way out here?"

"We came to rescue you, Sheriff," I said. "But you certainly don't look any worse for the wear."

He asked who I'd brought with me, and when I told him, he frowned and stared straight ahead. "How are my kids?"

"Fine," I said. "They're with Anna. You'd see her skin a werja with her bare hands before anybody messed with those children."

"I know," he said. He was about to say something else, but Walt and Billy started riding toward us. Sam waited, taking their measure as they approached.

"Hello, Walt," he called out. "Billy, your damn nose still looks crooked. Did you go see a doctor to get it set? You having trouble breathing out of it?"

Walt rode in front of Billy Jack's destrier, blocking both our views of him for a moment. Walt made a big show of greeting Sam and telling him how proud everyone was of him, but just as Walt got close enough, he cut to the side. Billy Jack Elliot was aiming a rifle at your daddy. I remember thinking that it was some sort of joke, but then I heard the gunshot.

The noise sent my destrier up on her hind legs, and by the time I got her back down, Sam was slumped over in the saddle. He was already gone by the time I ran to his side.

The bullet had gone clear through his heart. I was reaching for my pistol when Walt Junger put the barrel of his gun against my forehead. "Time for you to make a decision, Old Man Willow."

"Go to hell, you murderous son of a bitch." Tears were streaming down my face and filling up my eyes to the point that I could hardly make out either of them.

Billy got down from his saddle and came up beside Walt. He pushed Walt's gun down and said, "Calm down. Mr. Willow's mind is spinning right about now. He needs a few moments to process."

I got my pistol free and shouted, "Process this!" like I was some sort of dimestore hero. I feel funny writing it, but it's the truth. The look on both of their faces was priceless. It would have been perfect if I'd shot them both right there, but I squeezed the trigger and nothing happened. Either the damn thing jammed or it was never loaded in the first place. I've never been much of a gunman. If anything, I kept it with me for show.

They laughed when I sank to my knees in the dirt and cried like a fool. Jem, I cried for you kids and I cried for my dear friend Sam. I'm not proud to say that I cried for myself and Anna too, because I was convinced that they were going to kill me next.

But I did not beg.

I cursed those sons of bitches and told them to get on with it.

Billy squatted down in front of me and said, "I think there's been enough killing for one day. Especially since you got that pretty little girl back home."

"Imagine what could happen to her if you don't come home tonight. We might have to go visit her, just to check on her," Walt said.

"I heard how that old boy who used to work for you got real friendly with her," Billy said. "I heard he had her do all sorts of things. Sounds to me like she's got some experience. What do you say, Walter?"

"I could use a sweet young thing that knows what she's doing," he said.

"Unless of course we can all agree that we found Sam Clayton dead out here. I think if we all made that agreement, we could all live together in peaceful harmony."

I looked at both of them and cursed them harder than any man has ever cursed another human being. I cursed them, Jem, and I told them to shoot me, but they didn't.

They laughed at me.

Both of them dragged Sam's body off to the side of the road just to leave him there. I wouldn't allow it. I dug out a shallow grave for him with my bare hands at the crest of the mountain. When they weren't looking, I took his Sheriff's badge and stuffed it in my pocket.

Before we left, I memorized where we were and when I got home, I drew a map to his grave.

Justice died in Seneca 6 the day Sam Clayton was murdered, Jem. It's been sitting inside this wooden box ever since. My hope is that by writing this, I might bring the day that it returns closer.

I pray with all my might that you forgive me, Jem.

May God have mercy on my soul, and none on the bastards that murdered the finest man I have ever known.

    Yours Eternally,

    Erasmus Willow

Jem folded the pages of the letter and removed a map from inside the box. The map was a crude drawing with a stick figure for Sam's body and various symbols designating the terrain. Old Man Willow had drawn dots across the map to show footpaths and scribbled notes along the margins about the terrain.

At the bottom of the box was a small object wrapped in black velvet cloth. Jem felt the heavy object inside the cloth, weighing it in the palm of his hand, before he unwrapped it. He peeled away the corners of the covering slowly to reveal the tarnished bronze star hidden within. The word *SHERIFF* was etched across the front.

Jem laid back on the bed and inspected the star, turning it over in his hands. It looked smaller than it had when he was a boy, even though this was the first time he'd ever actually held it. Sam had never taken it off of his coat.

Jem twirled the badge between his fingers, feeling that the grooves of the letters were worn smooth. He studied his reflection in the dull brass surface and could not deny that the image he saw looked a lot like the badge's previous owner.

But he'd been a good man, Jem thought. A law-abiding man of respectable character. Decent as the day is long. Sam Clayton was a *good* man, and you sons of bitches took him away, he thought. He picked up the letter and looked at it again, thinking, *you all are about to die.*

17. Mercy

The newest Ayawisgi entered the sacred circle, surrounded by the warriors of the tribe. A trio of drummers pounded a skin of stretched hide in unison with a slow beat that made the boys bend over and sweep the ground with their hands. The pace of the drum increased and the drummers sang in high-pitched tones of an ancient battle between the Beothuk of the Plains and the White Man.

Lakhpia-Sha winced as he tried to lift his thickly bandaged arm at the elbow to point it toward the sky. Haienwa'tha hovered close by, keeping the excited Thathanka-Ska from bouncing into them both.

Osceola stood outside the circle, stone-faced as he watched the boys dance save for the movement of his lips as he recited the choreographed movements he'd carefully imparted to them. His eyes clenched shut each time one of them missed.

Chief Thasuka-Witko entered the circle and held up his hands, "All Ayawisgi join us inside the circle, and celebrate your fellow warriors' ascension into the tribe of men." Everyone began to dance, and even ancient Mahpiya limped with his staff into the circle to join them.

Mahpiya had been a grand-champion in his youth, competing against other tribes and returning with ribbons and blankets in prizes for his people. He mastered the dances of the Northern tribes and Eastern tribes and even now as his steps were limited and stilted, everyone stood aside at his approach lest they give off the appearance of challenging him.

Mahpiya watched his people dance and held out his hand to the four winds in thanks for another season. He closed his eyes and swayed to the drum's beat, feeling the wind rise and blow across his face.

Mahpiya stopped dancing.

Everyone quickly noticed him standing still, face into the wind, chanting. Thasuka-Witko made his way toward the old man cautiously, not wanting to disturb his trance. Mahpiya's eyes opened and he said, "Clear the circle."

The drumming stopped and the dancers filed out of the circle behind the Chief, leaving the medicine man standing alone in the center. He raised his stick and lifted it high in the air, then drove it into the ground. He held out his hands and uttered a prayer, drawing circles in the dust with the edge of his staff until it started to swirl on its own.

Mahpiya guided the small cyclone from side to side, as it grew in force and started toward the edges of the circle, whipping past the faces of the men who stood watching. The cyclone spun around and around, circling Mahpiya as he reached into his pouch and threw a handful of green leaves into the winds.

His eyes darted back and forth to read the shape the leaves took as they flew past, and suddenly the old man clapped his hands and the wind stopped, sending dust and stone raining toward the ground. Mahpiya looked at Thasuka Witko and said, "You must gather the women."

Chief Thasuka Witko greeted the Women's Council by nodding at the ones who surrounded the fire and assessed him with their stares. The eldest woman on the Council was called Agaidika. She was older than the small mountains; older than even Mahpiya.

Agaidika had outlived everyone she loved, including her own children, and the many years alone had brought her the kind of wisdom that is born of having no sympathy for anyone or thing. At the opposite end of the circle were young women, only a few years older than Thasuka Witko's oldest, Haienwa'tha. They held babies to their young, full breasts then bounced them on their knees, trying to keep them silent when the Chief made ready to speak.

Thasuka Witko spoke directly to Agaidika, loud enough for her deaf ears to hear, but also for his sons, who hid nearby so that they might listen and learn. He had done the same when Hoka-Psice went before the old woman, and he would not have bet that she would not still be alive long after he too joined the Great Spirit. "Mahpiya has told me that there are bad signs coming from the West. He claims a great evil comes to those lands, with wicked medicine to destroy the Wasichu who live there."

Agaidika smacked her toothless gums together like she was chewing her words before she leaned forward and squinted at the Chief in the dim firelight. "Why should the People concern themselves with the Wasichu? If anything, we should celebrate their demise."

The rest of the women murmured in agreement, and Thasuka Witko said, "Hoka-Psice always admired you, Grandmother

Agaidika. He said if you had been born a man, you would have made a formidable General. You have guided our people for many years, and I value your counsel. I intend to lead a scouting party west to determine if this evil poses a threat to us."

The women closed in around Agaidika. Each of them took turns whispering in her hairy ear. Thasuka Witko wrapped a blanket around his shoulders while he waited for an answer and walked away from the circle, toward the shadows where he saw two pairs of dark feet standing under a bush. Haienwa'tha whispered, "Why do you even have to consult with them? You are the Chief. They are only women."

Thasuka Witko chuckled and said, "I once asked the same exact question of Hoka-Psice. I expect that your sons will someday ask you the same. This is what I was told: A Chief of the tribe gives the orders, but it is the women who enforce them, or see to it that they are not enforced at all."

When he walked back, the women were separated from Agaidika and waiting for him to sit down. The old woman said, "It does us no good to endanger the lives of our brave warriors on something that is not of our concern. If Thasuka Witko insists on interfering in the concerns of the Wasichu, let the new Ayawisgi go."

"I said I was going to lead the party."

Agaidika smiled with a mouthful of rotten teeth and said, "You have said what you said, and so have I."

The women withdrew from the fire, and Thasuka Witko stood up and called out to Haienwa'tha to bring the warriors of the tribe to him. Soon, the men were advancing up the hill toward the fire, talking amongst themselves excitedly about the upcoming battle. They boasted to one another about how many they would kill and the amount of scalps they would return with.

Thasuka Witko waited for them to gather around him before he said, "It is decided. All of us will remain here, except for the new Ayawisgi. They will ride west to act as our eyes and ears."

There were responses of disbelief and anger at the women's decision. The Chief held up his hand and said, "The point of the Ayawisgi is that they have proven themselves as warriors. What right do we have to question their abilities?"

Haienwa'tha stuck out his chest and said, "We will honor our ancestors and give all of you many things to sing about in our memory! When do we leave?"

Thasuka Witko looked at his son with concern and said, "Gather your things."

The three boys hurried down the slope to return to camp. Osceola watched his son run and grunted with approval. "He is not afraid, even with only one arm."

"Lakhpia-Sha is not going, old friend," Thasuka Witko said. "He is too weak to ride."

Osceola's face twisted at the insult and he turned to his Chief and said, "My son is not weak. Be cautious with your words."

"Listen to me very carefully," Thasuka Witko said. "The scouting party is too small to send someone who is not healed. The old woman insists only the new Ayawisgi go, but according to the old laws, if one of them is not suited for the journey, I can select a replacement."

Osceola nodded in understanding and said, "Do you have a replacement in mind?"

Thasuka Witko patted him on the arm and said, "There is only one man I would trust with the lives of my two remaining sons."

Osceola bowed his head and said, "I will get my things ready."

Mahpiya limped toward them and said, "I too will go with them."

"The women's council did not mention you, old man," Thasuka-Witko said.

"This is true."

"So I must forbid it."

"Ah. Well then, so be it. In that case, I am going out to look for new herbs for the tribe and will most likely be gone awhile."

"And just where will you be going to look for them?" Thasuka-Witko said.

The medicine man looked toward the west and said, "I think, in that direction."

Charlie Boles Junior watched his father sit up in the hospital bed and said, "How does it feel?"

Boles braced his hand against the bandage around his thigh and said, "It hurts like hell, stupid. How much money do we have left?"

Junior reached into his pocket and took out the small fold of bills. "Not much. It cost a ton to get you fixed up. We have maybe enough to rent a room here long enough to find work."

Boles snatched the money from his son's hand and said, "Work? Go and find a sturdy mule that can carry us all the way to Seneca 6. Don't buy nothing bow-legged now or I'll make you sorry."

"Why Seneca 6? We ain't going looking for that man, are we?"

Boles' eyes narrowed. "Just do what I tell you."

Four days later, Charlie Boles Junior tapped his father on the arm and pointed up at the sky. A small transport vessel was descending from the clouds into a canyon, its thrusters popping jets of flame and smoke. Charlie Boles snapped the reins on their stolen, scraggly-legged mule, and headed toward the edge of the cliff to watch the ship's landing gear extend as it lowered into the valley.

The boarding ramp extended and two uniformed Customs Agents carrying large rifles exited the ship. Little Willy Harpe and Hank Raddiger followed behind them. Little Willy surveyed the wreckage of a spaceship scattered around the canyon and said, "Go find that homing beacon and turn it off."

He passed the burned out hull and pieces of engine to see a flock of black birds piled onto the carcass of a body, picking it clean. Harpe stomped his feet and chased the birds off, and as they fled from his approach, he saw that the body was missing a head.

Hank shouted, "Over here!" There was panic in Hank's voice as Harpe walked around the wreckage toward him. Hank put up both hands to stop him and said, "Now calm down for a second, Willy. I don't want you to get upset."

Harpe shoved him aside, seeing nothing more than scattered ship parts and the burned out hull of a small spacecraft with a pole sticking out of it. Something was placed on top of the pole. Something that looked like it had hair that blew in the wind.

Little Willy stared at Elijah's head, spiked on the pole. Elijah's eyes were staring back at him as Little Willy reached up and grabbed the head by both sides and started to twist it free. It popped off with a sucking noise and Little Willy held the head between his hands and collapsed to his knees, screaming with such ferocity that Hank Raddiger's insides felt wet. Hank kneeled in the dirt beside him and did not speak.

Little Willy swept his sleeves across his eyes and swallowed. "He's going to tell me who did this to him."

"I don't think he's going to do much talking, Little Willy."

"SUFFER, you imbecile."

Hank convulsed and contorted and his teeth smashed together so violently they cracked. Little Willy turned Elijah's severed head upside down and peered into the open gullet of his throat before rolling up his sleeve and sticking his bare hand into the mushy pulp beneath Elijah's chin. He slid his fingers around the neck bone and pushed past the muscle and connective tissue until he could touch the base of Elijah's skull. He grabbed the brain stem and yanked it out of the way, guiding himself along the gelatinous surface of

Elijah's brain. "Show me what happened, Elijah," Little Willy said. "Show me."

Little Willy closed his eyes and felt the creature ripple with energy. He reached out with his mind and tried to reignite the spark of existence inside Elijah's brain. It was cold and dark, unlike anything he'd ever encountered.

Elijah's presence was out of reach, and Little Willy commanded him to return over and over until the eyelids on Elijah's face began to flutter. Little Willy stroked the decomposing flesh on his brother's cheek and said, "I'm here, Elijah. Don't be afraid. I'm right here."

Elijah's mouth opened and closed and Little Willy focused until the brain matter surrounding his hand grew hot, as if he were holding a scalding cauldron of boiling water. He tried smashing the skull against the hull of the ship, frantic to free his hand. The creature started to peel away from Little Willy's body, its dark purple color turning pink and spotty as it unseated itself from his flesh.

Hank Raddiger gasped as soon as Little Willy's spell over him ended. He sat on the ground in silence, feeling a cool breeze blow over his aching body. When he sat up, Little Willy was sitting cross-legged next to him, looking down at the creature sunk into his armpit, sucking on the fluids in his body. "What the hell is this thing?" Willy said.

"Something evil!" Hank said. "Something I wish we'd never found. Let's get rid of it right now while it's weak."

"How long has he had it?"

"How long has *who* had it?" Hank said.

"My brother," Harpe said. "It's amazing."

"What the hell are you talking about?" Hank said. "We fought those military bastards for it last week and you've been letting it crawl all over you ever since."

Little Willy looked at the severed head on the ground and whipped his head away. "Get rid of that thing, Hank. Get rid of it right now. I don't want to see it ever again."

Hank got to his feet and brushed himself off. "Ok, Little Willy."

"Elijah," he said. "Don't call me by my brother's name."

A hundred yards above the canyon, Charlie Boles grabbed his son by the shoulder and said, "We're getting the hell out of here and going home."

A rifle's battery pack hummed in Boles' ear and he looked over his shoulder to see one of the uniformed Custom's officers aiming the weapon at him. "Don't move."

18. Pale Horse

Dr. Royce Halladay set his cards down on the table and shook his head mournfully. "I apologize for my lack of knowledge, but I am not certain if having four of the same card is a good hand. And these do not even have the decency to be a proper number. Tell me, is the letter 'A' a good card to have?"

The other men at the table threw their cards down in disgust. "Go to hell, Halladay," one of them said.

Halladay stared at the men in affected confusion as they stood up to leave. "But what about all this money you've left on the table, gentlemen? Well, I suppose I must take it then, if only to keep it safe until you return." He raked the pile of coins and bills toward himself and chuckled. The chuckle became a cough, then a bark that left him gagging on phlegm and blood.

He looked up as the Proud Lady's doors swung open and Sheriff Walt Junger came through them, looking all around the bar until their eyes met. "There are four warrants for your arrest on this side of the planet alone, Royce," Junger said.

"I would prefer if you called me, 'Doctor,' if it's all the same to you, Walter." Halladay slid the money inside his shirt pocket and stood up to walk over to the bar with his empty glass. He set the glass down and tapped it for the bartender to fill it up again.

People standing around the bar had stopped what they were doing to watch the scene unfold, and Junger's face started to twitch. He hitched up his gun belt and loudly announced, "I'll call you anything I damn well please, blood-spitter. And it's *Sheriff* Junger to scum like you."

Halladay turned toward him with a raised eyebrow, "Now why would I call you that, Walter? Doctor is a distinction I earned, while the title Sheriff has only ever truly belonged to one man, and we both know what happened to him."

"He was killed by the savages out in the wasteland. I saw his body, which is a damn sight more than you did after you ran off and hid when we were under attack."

"Has that story passed through your lips so many times that you actually are starting to believe it, Walter? I wonder." Halladay swallowed his drink and set it on the bar. His eyes were bloodshot and ached from lack of sleep. His legs jittered with restlessness and there was fire in his chest that boiled his guts, yet when he looked at Walt Junger standing there, all red-faced and affronted, Halladay suddenly felt right. He stood up straight and said, "Do you want to talk about what Tilt told me right before he passed on? It is a hell of a story."

Junger backed away and struggled to unsnap his guns, shouting, "You are under arrest!"

Halladay produced two pistols, both aimed an inch from the Sheriff's face. He cocked back both hammers and waited for Junger to lift his hands away from his weapons. Halladay smiled gently and said, "I *apologize*, Walter. You were not prepared."

Halladay decocked the pistols and twirled them in his palms twice before dropping them back into their holsters. Both men stood facing one another, unarmed. Halladay said, "Are you ready?"

"Seneca 6 is a *civilized* town, Doctor Halladay! We have laws. This is not how we do things."

Halladay started to answer when his face suddenly contorted and he bent forward, as if to begin a great fit of coughing. Junger grabbed for his pistols, when Halladay snatched both of his guns out of their holsters and jammed their barrels against Junger's forehead. "That was called theatrics, Walter. And the cuckoo on your clock just crowed."

Junger turned for the Proud Lady's doors and ran through them, screaming for help. Halladay walked slowly down the steps after him, aiming his pistols near Junger's feet. Halladay fired and the ground exploded next to Junger's boots, sending him sprawling across the road. Halladay cocked the other pistol and shot it into the ground near where Junger lay and said, "Get up."

Junger got up to his feet and let his hands hang loose at his sides.

"Arm yourself, cur," Halladay said.

Junger stood there shivering, clutching his arms around his chest and he said, "Go to hell, Royce. You're gonna have to gun me down in cold blood."

Halladay smiled when he said, "Oh, but I assure you, mine is colder than a crocodile's." He went to pull the trigger, but the metal barrel of a rifle tapped him on the shoulder and stayed his hand. Halladay looked back at the young man holding the weapon and said, "Bartholomew Masters? Tom's boy? I was always fond of Tom. Now, kindly remove from this conflict before you become perforated."

"I can't allow you to gun down our Sheriff, Doc. Especially when he doesn't even have the decency to arm himself."

"I will *kill* you and a dozen more who remotely look like you just to eliminate this son of a bitch, Bartholomew. Stand aside!"

"I have no doubt you will," Bart said. "But it don't change the fact that I can't just stand here and watch you do it."

Junger backed away from Halladay and said, "That's a good lad. You'll be well compensated for this."

Bart scowled at him and said, "Just run off and don't show your face again until things've calmed down." He waited for Junger to disappear between the two nearest buildings to lower his rifle and said, "I'm awful sorry, Doc, but we still need to have some law in this town, even if the people we trust to enforce it aren't worth the slime on a ring worm."

Halladay groaned and secured both his pistols back in their holsters. He turned on Bart to say, "Twenty years ago I put five stitches in your father's head after he was attacked on the same spot you are now standing. I do not believe he ever paid me for them. I will take my payment from you, immediately, in the form of liquid nourishment. I'll also agree not to put a canoe through your forehead for interfering with my plans."

"It would be my honor, sir."

William James Elliot, the Honorable Mayor and Judge of Seneca 6, stood on the porch of the Sheriff's Office with his thumbs hooked through his pearl white suspenders. He was a thin man in a tailored suit made of fabric that shimmered in the morning light. He propped one foot up against the railing and swept dirt from the heel. The shoe was made of an exotic animal's skin that had been imported off-world.

Elliot took a puff of his cigar and blew the acrid smoke into the air as he watched Marshal James McParlan come out of Anna Willow's office down the street. He smiled at McParlan but kept the cigar clenched in his teeth.

The Marshal waited impatiently for the wagons to let him cross. The bruises on his face were dark now, and he appeared to be favoring his left side. McParlan looked up at Elliot and said, "Can I help you?"

"No, you cannot. But I assure you that I can be of great help to *you*." Elliot tapped ashes on the railing and said, "Why don't we go inside and discuss it?"

McParlan opened the door and saw Walt Junger sitting at his desk behind a stack of carefully arranged documents. McParlan removed his hat and sat on the visitor's bench while Elliot leaned against the jail cell and re-lit his cigar. "My associate and I were wondering when you might be leaving?" Elliot said.

McParlan looked him up and down, "Just who in the hell are you supposed to be?"

"This here is the town Mayor *and* Judge. You will address him with the proper respect while in my presence."

"Why, you got Bart Masters hiding in the back to protect you in case I pull a gun?" McParlan said. He turned to Elliot, "The answer to your question is simple. I'm not leaving until the threat is eliminated."

Junger opened his mouth to speak, but Elliot silenced him with a sideways glance. "Your prisoner is dead, Marshal," Elliot said. "Your authority here ended the moment Jem Clayton dragged that poor bastard out into the desert. Now, as the highest elected legal authority in this territory, I'm advising you that your services are no longer needed. Your continued presence here is also no longer needed, nor welcome."

McParlan saw the satisfied look on both men's faces and said, "Both you hotshot hillbilly cousin-kissers might be able to push people around in this town, but I'm not from this town, so excuse me if I don't piss my pants in awe of your 'legal authority.' Right now there's a mass murderer on his way here with a highly-classified military weapon that he will use on every last man, woman and child in this settlement."

"What proof do you have of that, Marshal?" Elliot said. "A deranged old man, who I might add, you brought here. The same man you shot to death right outside this very door?"

Junger waved his hand around the office at his multiple plaques and awards and said, "I've kept this town safe for twenty years without your assistance. Why should I need it now?"

"You'll have the corpse with the most medals after Little Willy gets through with you, Sheriff. That's the parts of you he doesn't eat, of course. Now, speaking of eating, if you're done wasting my time here, I'm going to go get some breakfast."

Junger watched McParlan limp out of the office and slammed the door shut behind him. "Son of a bitch, Billy. It's only a matter of time before that Marshal starts sticking his nose into things that don't concern him. I'm telling you, it's a bad omen that Halladay and Jem Clayton are back and that they brought this one-eyed bastard with them."

Elliot stuck his fingers between the blinds and watched people passing the office along Pioneer Way. "Here's what we're gonna do, Walter. We're gonna lower the prices at the Proud Lady and the interest rates at the Savings and Loan. That should keep the locals stupid and happy for the time being."

"And what about the trouble makers?"

Elliot re-lit his cigar and took it out of his mouth to blow on the tip, making it glow bright red. "Deactivate every security gate on Seneca 6. Let's leave the doors open for a little while and see what wanders in."

Little Willy Harpe squatted in front of Charlie Boles Junior and waved his hand in front of the boy's face. The boy's stare was vacant. Harpe snapped his fingers in front of Junior's nose and there was no response. "Did I break him?"

"I don't think so," Hank Raddiger said. He was careful not to get too close to the man. The voice coming from Harpe's mouth was markedly different than before, but Hank was suspicious that Little Willy was playing games with him.

Harpe shook Junior by the shoulders. "Come back to us, boy."

Junior's eyes opened. His pupils were dilated and would not focus. Finally, Junior smiled stupidly and said, "Hey, Elijah."

He looked around for his father and saw that the two Customs Officers were taping plastic explosive packets around his midsection. They squeezed each packet flat and sculpted them to Boles' body. Charlie Boles grinned at Junior when the officers handed him his gunbelt. He buckled the belt and said, "Now I'm ready!"

Junior lifted his shirt to show his father the plastic explosives wrapped around his own waist and said, "I am too."

Harpe looked at him and said, "Do you know what you are prepared for?"

"For glory," the boy said.

Harpe's voice was patient and instructional, like a teacher reviewing a lesson with his pupil. "And what are you to do?"

"Find Jem Clayton and tell him my Pa has a score to settle with him."

"How will you recognize this servant of evil?"

"He's the man that stole our wagon and beat my Pa."

"What will you do after you find him?"

"Let everybody know there's gonna be a big fight, and get them all to come out into the street."

"Blessed truly are the children," Harpe said. "What then?"

"I press this button." Junior showed Harpe the toggle switch in his hand, connected by wires that disappeared beneath the cuff at the wrist of his shirt. The wires snaked along inside the sleeve, winding down his chest to where they connected to the set of plastic explosives wrapped around his thin, hairless stomach. "Then, I walk to wherever the biggest group of women and children are standing, and all I need to do it let go of it. That's when I go to glory and all of them get to come with me."

Harpe pulled Junior by the shoulders and kissed him on top of his head. "You long for the spiritual milk, my son, and it shall it be yours. Before nightfall you will look upon the face of the Lord All Mighty and drink all that you desire."

Junior smiled and nodded as Harpe walked over to Charlie Boles. He told Boles to hand him his gun and proceeded to remove all of the bullets from the weapon. "Why you doing that, Little...Elijah?" Hank said. "I thought you wanted him to duel Clayton?"

Harpe handed the gun back to Boles, who holstered it. "Do you think I want to chance Clayton getting gunned down in the street and for it to all be over?" Harpe checked the dead man's switch in Boles' left hand, making sure the wires were hidden inside the sleeve. "I want my good friend to bear witness to this, Hank. And I want him to know it is just getting started."

Harpe watched Charlie Boles and his son get onto the same destrier and trot up through the canyon. "You did say my brother considered you his Lieutenant, right?"

"That's right. I was the one figured out where you were taken, and how to get here. He was so grateful he gave me what he called 'The Rapture.' He would just look at me and speak that one little word. I was thinking we could have that same agreement."

Harpe frowned and said, "That don't sound much like my brother."

Hank felt feverish with need. He pulled on Harpe's shirt and said, "Your brother and me had special arrangements, Elijah. Please, just a little?"

"Suffering introduces a man unto himself, Hank," Harpe said. "You want me to arrange a more intimate introduction?"

"No."

"Good. I'm looking for two long pieces of metal. Thick enough to hold the weight of a man, and twelve feet long, at least. Have you seen anything like that?"

Hank removed his hat and looked around the scene of the wreckage. "I'm sure we can find something in this mess."

The Boles were near the top of the canyon, about to descend on the trail that would take them to Seneca 6's security gate. "I spent my whole life believing that I was doing the Lord's work, and that when the time came, he would take me to his side and thank me for being his loyal servant. You cannot imagine my surprise when the time of my death came and there was no glory waiting. Nothing…just oblivion. It was a never-ending darkness more horrible than any hell you could possibly imagine. I admit it, for a moment, my faith was shaken. I thought I'd backed the wrong horse, Hank. You follow me?"

Hank nodded and said, "I think so. I'm not sure."

"My job wasn't to serve God," Harpe said. He cast his eyes skyward and touched the creature embedded in his chest. "It was to become Him."

Bart Masters guided his destrier down Pioneer Way, ignoring the stares from people he passed who looked at the mining device strapped to his saddle. "Taking your work home with you, Bart?" someone said.

"That's right. Our stove's broken and I need it to heat up the water," Bart replied.

He pulled up his reins in front of Anna Willow's office and removed the backpack from the saddle. "I'm here, Marshal."

Jimmy McParlan came out and looked the device over. "Did they give you a hard time taking it off the site?"

"When they find out about it, I'll probably get fired."

McParlan sucked on his teeth and said, "Show me how this thing works again."

Masters lowered the pack to the ground. "This here is the battery and charging cells." He held up the hose and wand connected to the pack. "This is the barrel where the laser comes out. You can adjust the intensity of the beam here." He handed the unit to McParlan and said, "I don't see what use it's going to be, Marshal. The beam only comes out about a foot no matter how high you adjust it."

"That's just cause you don't know how to adjust it right."

"And you do?"

"No. But Adam Wells does." McParlan looked over as a destrier approached the security gate with a man and boy riding together. They did not stop to enter a code and went through the gate unhindered. "What the hell?" McParlan said. He handed Masters the mining device and said, "Take this into Adam and tell him to make it better. I'll be right in."

The Marshal held up his hand to stop the riders and said, "How you folks doing. Did you enter a special code to get in here?"

The boy shrugged and said, "No, sir. We entered by the Lord's grace."

"You wait right here." He limped up the front steps to the Sheriff's Office door and banged on it. "What the hell's the idea of leaving the gate open, Junger?"

Walt Junger put his pen down and looked at McParlan with feigned astonishment. "Why, Marshal, you made it quite clear that my assistance was not needed."

"This is no time for foolishness. Secure that gate."

Junger shook his head and said, "I'm afraid it doesn't work that way, Marshal. This was a directive that came straight from Mayor Elliot himself. Feel free to take it up with him."

McParlan slammed the door and searched for the newcomers but they were already gone. He ran the image of them through his mind over and over. They were dirty looking, simply attired folk, probably just trying to resupply before heading off. They had calm, easy expressions and nothing about them looked ominous. The man had been armed, but that was common enough in this area. McParlan decided he could not think of what it was, exactly, and that was enough to make him want to go find out.

At noon, the sun was bearing down with such fury that Jem Clayton wondered if it was possible for his hat to melt. He walked through the swinging doors of the Proud Lady and was relieved to be out of the heat. When his eyes finally adjusted to the dim light, he saw Dr. Royce Halladay sitting at a poker table, eyes half-lidded, but still upright, still drinking, and still holding his cards.

"Jem Clayton," Halladay slurred.

Jem put his hand on Halladay's shoulder. "You've been hitting it pretty hard, Doc. Why don't we go get some food?"

Halladay flicked his empty whiskey glass with his finger and said, "I prefer to drink my breakfast, sir."

"I need to talk to you. Let's get some food."

Halladay looked up from his cards and cast a suspicious eye at Jem. "I do not appreciate your tone, Jem. The last time I checked, I was a grown man. In fact, I was an adult when you were just a whiny little brat buzzing around my office trying to bite me." Halladay leaned over with laughter and Jem had to put out his hand to keep him upright.

Jem went to the bar to order a coffee. The men seated beside him were covered in the grime of the mines and had finished the first of many bottles they would drink that day.

Jem looked over to see that Halladay was still playing and giving the dealer a hard time about dealing him the wrong cards. The swinging doors opened behind Jem and he heard a boy call out, "Found you, Jem Clayton! My Pa is right outside waiting on you."

Jem returned to his coffee and sipped it. "Go away, Junior. Tell Charlie I'm not interested."

"Coward!" Junior shouted.

Jem turned to look at the boy, then returned to his coffee and ignored him.

Outside, peopled stopped in the street to watch Charlie Boles kick up a cloud of dust as he stomped around, hollering, "I'm going to stand here until you come out, you yellow-bellied rat bastard!" Boles turned to face the onlookers and said, "Jem Clayton jumped me and my boy out there in the wasteland and left us to die! And now I come for him, and he's scared to show his face."

The Proud Lady's doors swung open and Royce Halladay staggered onto the porch, grimacing at the bright noon sun. "Jem Clayton would not waste the bullets on a mongrel such as you. I, however, have several extra that I would be glad to contribute."

"He told me to come meet him in Seneca 6 after he robbed me and stole my wagon. He left me and my boy in the desert with no food and water. You either produce him or I will be forced to seek other reparations!"

"I seem to have room on *my* dance card." Halladay grinned stupidly as he drummed his holster with the tips of his fingers.

"I don't have no quarrels with you, old man," Boles said. He moved his hand to his weapon. "I just want Clayton."

Halladay went down the steps, "Alas, now I have one with you."

A woman stopped her three children from walking into the sea of people, afraid of losing them in the crowd. She kept them behind her as Halladay and Boles squared off and pulled the littlest one into her wide skirt. She put her hands over the two older children's eyes and said, "Don't look."

Charlie Boles Junior walked over to her and pulled on her sleeve. "Don't be afraid, ma'am."

"You shouldn't watch this either, sweetheart," she said. "Stand behind me and keep your eyes closed. I will say a prayer for your daddy."

Junior pressed the device's button with his thumb and said, "I'm not afraid. When I let go of this, we're all going to glory."

"What did you say, dear?"

The crowd roared as Jem Clayton came out of the saloon doors and drowned out whatever response the boy gave her. Jem Clayton called out to Dr. Halladay, "I'll handle this."

Halladay kept his hand near his gun as Jem came down the steps and stood in front of Boles. Boles nodded eagerly and said, "Yeah, time we settled up."

Jem lifted both of his hands to show Boles they were empty. "I will not fight you, Charlie. We had our disagreement, and it's over with. I've got too much else on my mind to worry about you right now. Accept my apology and take your boy home. You can have your wagon back, it's parked near the Sheriff's Office. I'll even take you to it."

"Won't be no apologies," Boles said. "Draw." Boles snatched his gun from its holster and aimed it at Jem's face.

Charlie Boles Junior tugged on the shoulder of the woman. He leaned up to her ear and whispered, "Your children are going to love it in Heaven."

Charlie Boles started to squeeze his trigger when he looked across the street at his son approvingly, seeing that the boy was about to detonate his device. *Detonate his device?* Charlie thought. What the hell am I saying? He threw up his hands and screamed, "Junior! No! Don't do it!"

Jem turned to look where Boles was yelling, but Royce Halladay shoved him out of the way and fired one bullet into Charlie Boles' stomach and a second into the center of his forehead. Boles dropped his gun and weaved from side to side, taking steps in his son's direction. He held up his hand and said, "Junior, don't do it, son. Fight it."

The electrical charges wrapped around Boles' waist popped like blown fuses and smoke billowed out of his shirt. He let go of the toggle switch and it dangled by the wires hanging from out of his sleeve.

"Pa?" Junior said. "Pa!"

Charlie Boles shirt caught fire and the flames raced across his clothing and through his hair. He fell to the ground in a smoldering heap. Jem turned to look at Junior and the people around him who were too busy watching the burning body to notice Junior let go of his dead man's switch. The boy's bomb detonated and there was a flash of light that sent Jem hurtling backwards.

19. Golgotha

Harpe stood at a peak on Coramide Canyon and watched the scene unfold miles away in Seneca 6. It was smoky, and hard to get a clear view of any particular person, but the chaos was evident. Harpe measured the blast radius to be at least ten feet in every direction of the boy. Luckily, he'd been standing close enough to a building to take out one of its load bearing walls.

"How's it look down there, Elijah?" Hank Raddiger said.

"The boy's device worked fine, but something went wrong with his father's explosives. I'm hoping he goes up any second now. My word, Hank, this is the best damn entertainment I've ever had. When I give the go ahead, send them Customs boys in to acquire our package."

A fire-brigade wagon rolled toward the site with men clinging to its side. Another truck came up behind that one, a large, industrial vehicle with heavy front end scoop to clear away the rubble of the building.

"There you are," Harpe said.

He saw Marshal McParlan standing knee deep in the rubble, scooping out handfuls of ash and dirt with his bare hands. The old man tossed away whole sections of wall and he dug like a beaver until a hand reached out from the rubble and McParlan grasped it, pulling with all of his strength.

"I hope you enjoy playing Savior, Marshal," Harpe said. He put down the binoculars and looked around the crash site. A pair of large metal beams bolted into an X leaned against the hull of the ship. "Is it sturdy enough to do what I need it to do, Hank?"

Hank patted the crossed beams and said, "Yes, sir."

"You'd better hope so," Harpe said.

Anna Willow waded through the rubble of the destroyed Savings and Loan building. People were still buried beneath it. Burn victims' clothing had melted into their blackened skin. The lucky ones were dead. Anna shouted for someone to bring her more medical supplies as she dug through smoldering building materials. She stuck syringes of morphine into the necks of any patient that was still moving and was running out fast.

There were at least a dozen dead bodies. People ran frantically in every direction, choking on smoke as they screamed for their loved ones. She tried to help them all. She did what she could.

Marshal Jimmy McParlan dragged someone out of the rubble and stuck his fingers in their mouth to clear out the mud. McParlan couldn't tell if it was a man or a woman. He pushed the person aside and dove back into the wreckage for more.

Bart Masters ran through the smoke and started grabbing pieces of the wall at McParlan's side. "Pull, pull!" McParlan shouted.

Water jetted at the flames from the fire brigade wagon, filling the air with moist black smoke. McParlan looked over to see Royce Halladay staggering to his feet near the steps of the Proud Lady.

Halladay clutched his head and coughed, spraying mouthfuls of blood across the ground in front of him. McParlan grabbed him around the waist and pulled him from the fumes and dust. He dragged Halladay over someone laid out at the bottom of the Proud Lady's steps and realized it was Jem Clayton.

McParlan set the doctor down in an alleyway away from the blast site and said, "Catch your breath." He hurried back to Jem and lifted his head to check for injuries. He looked into Jem's eyelids and saw that his eyes were rolled back in his head but he was breathing steadily. "You got your bell rung real good, I reckon, but you'll be all right," he said.

Jem moaned and reached for McParlan. His words were garbled when he tried to say, "Another bomb."

"What?"

Jem pushed up from the ground and got to his knees before collapsing again. He stretched his hand out to point at Charlie Boles smoking remains and the Marshal saw packets of grey plastic strapped around Boles' waist.

"Everybody get back!" McParlan shouted. He ran over to Boles' body and cleared away the charred fragments of shirt covering his waist. The fire had consumed most of the clothing but left the explosives untouched. McParlan grabbed the sizzling wires and started ripping them out of the packets. The metal threads and melted plastic from the wires stung the Marshal's fingers and made them blister but he kept at it until each one was cleared. "Masters! Bring me a bottle of clear liquor."

McParlan backed everyone away from Boles' body and waited until Bart Masters returned with a bottle from the Proud Lady. McParlan grabbed the cork with his teeth and splashed liquor onto the plastic explosives around Boles' waist. "Does alcohol neutralize them?" Masters asked.

"No," McParlan said. "But fire does." The Marshal struck a match and dropped it onto Charlie Boles' stomach. The match lit the pool of clear liquid and the packets started to crinkle and turn black.

Someone called out McParlan's name through the thick fog. Sheriff Walt Junger emerged from the smoke, wearing a smile wider than a canal. "There's some men here who say they received your distress call."

McParlan's look of relief turned to disgust when he watched a uniformed Customs Officer come up through the smoke to stand beside Junger. "These boys want you to go with them to discuss the situation," Junger said.

A second Officer drove Charlie Boles' wagon up to them. There was a high-capacity rifle in his hand. Junger said, "Get in, Marshal. There's a man who wants to speak with you. He says that after you come, his business here is through."

"I won't give up my guns," McParlan said. "We can shoot it out right here if you want."

"They don't want your guns," Junger said. "I already ensured you would be allowed to keep them."

"Wait a second, Marshal," Bart Masters said. "I'm coming too."

"Like hell. Stay here and make sure this mess gets cleaned up." McParlan looked at the Sheriff and said, "God knows there's nobody else here worth a squirt of piss to get the job done. Hey, Bart?"

"Yes, sir?"

"Make sure that sister-in-law of yours is all right."

Anna Willow watched him going and shouted, "Marshal! Where are you going?"

McParlan got into the carriage's rear and stood in the doorway with his hand on the handle. He turned to look back at her and said, "Time to put a stop to this before anyone else gets hurt, Anna." He said goodbye and swung the carriage door shut.

Lightning struck the side of the house so close that it woke Jem from a sound sleep. He opened his eyes to see the flash of white and blue in his room, followed by a deafening clap of thunder.

Jem got out of bed and went into Claire's room. She was snoring gently and holding an old teddy bear that he had never seen before. The bear was missing an eye. Jem walked to his father's room to tell him that there was a storm, but the bedroom door was locked. Jem raised his fist to knock, but lighting struck again, and Jem ducked and covered his ears.

A gust of wind knocked the front door open, and rain pelted through the screen. A dark-skinned young man stood on the porch staring at Jem. His long dark hair clung to his face in the rain and war paint dripped down toward the bleeding bullet hole in the center of his chest. "Goyathlay?" Jem whispered. "It's you."

The Beothuk turned his back to Jem and walked down the steps into the meadow. Jem followed him through the door, calling his name, telling him to wait while lightning arced across the mountains and illuminated the valley. A campfire flickered in the meadow, surrounded by people who gathered close to the flames and tried to warm themselves.

Goyathlay turned around in the darkness and held his hand out to Jem. Jem started to follow him but had to lift his arms to shield his face from the rain.

Charlie Boles Junior stood by the fire, huddled next to his father. The boy's teeth chattered from the cold and he pressed himself tightly to Charlie. The people surrounding the fire looked at Jem and moved aside, making room for him. Junior held out his hand for Jem to come sit.

"Jem!" a man's voice boomed from the porch that stopped Jem in his tracks. The voice made him turn around ever so slowly to see Sam Clayton waving at him, holding a torch. "Come back here, boy. Don't you go with them."

Goyathlay waved for Jem to hurry, and Jem looked back at his father, "They want me to go with them. I belong with them."

"No you don't," Sam said. "You belong with me."

"If that were true, you would have never left. Not this place and not me."

Sam came down from the steps, holding his torch high in the air like a beacon. "I left here, Jem. But I *never* left you."

Jem awoke with a start, sitting up in his old bed at Claire and Frank's house. Claire and Anna Willow were seated on stacks of boxes and bundles of clothing that had replaced all of the things he'd left behind in that room. "Easy, Jem," Anna said. "Try not to move around too much."

He gasped and grabbed his side, feeling like someone had smacked him with a hammer. There was a sharp pain when he tried to breathe and he felt the bandages wrapped tightly around his ribs. "How many are broken?"

"Just a few," Anna said. "But you're going to be mighty sore for awhile."

"I remember smoke was coming out of that boy's shirt, and I smelled something burning. Nothing after that. What happened? Was it a bomb?"

Anna looked at Claire, and neither of them responded. "Why don't you lie back down and get some rest, Jem?" Claire said.

"There was a woman and her children standing next to him too. What happened to them?"

Anna shook her head and said, "We'll talk about it later."

Jem cursed and swung his legs from the bed onto the floor. He gritted his teeth and tried to breathe. "Where are my guns? I'm putting an end to this right now."

"It already ended, Jem."

"What are you talking about?"

Claire put her hand on his shoulder and pushed him back down on the bed. "Help finally showed up from that crazy Marshal's useless agency. He went with them to sort it out. There hasn't been any trouble since. Now lay your ass back down before you tear something."

"Really?" Jem let it sink in and sighed with relief. He held his side as he laid back down and said, "The signal must've worked. God damn, I can't believe it. Did they get Little Willy?"

"I have no idea, but you are just gonna lay here and get some rest," Anna said. "Claire will cook you something to eat. You've been asleep for over twenty-four hours."

"I wish I'd seen it when they showed up to get Little Willy. I bet he wasn't so tough then. Those Agency boys have some serious firepower. They probably just launched a few rockets at him from space and came in to clean up whatever was left."

"It wasn't anything to be impressed by, Jem," Anna said, patting his hand. "Just two men in uniforms driving that rickety old wagon you came here in."

"Uniforms? What kind of uniforms?"

"Their patches said Customs, I think. They wanted McParlan to go with them, and he went."

Jem struggled to get out of the bed, saying, "Where the hell did you put my guns, Claire?"

The wagon ride had been uneventful. The Customs Officers ignored McParlan's questions as they rode through the wasteland. The incline grew steep, and the wagon stopped at the edge of a cliff overlooking the canyon below. "We have to go the rest of the way on foot," they said.

McParlan saw that the other paths leading down to the canyon had been blockaded, leaving only a narrow trail that wound down the edge of the cliff. He followed the officers down to where

Little Willy Harpe was sitting on a square piece of scrap metal, watching them. "Hello, Marshal."

"Little Willy Harpe. Put your hands up, you are under arrest."

Harpe smiled at that and stood to his feet. He was shirtless and appeared to be rubbing some kind of long black tattoo that spread out from his armpit to cover his neck and chest. McParlan eyes narrowed when he saw the bulbous creature seated under Little Willy's armpit and that the tattoo was actually the thing's tentacles buried in his skin. "My God…is that what I think it is, you maniac?"

"Do you like it?"

McParlan grabbed for his Balrog and had the weapon aimed at Little Willy's head faster than the Customs Officers had time to react. Little Willy spoke a single word before McParlan could pull the trigger and it was as if he were turned to stone. He struggled to fire, wrapping both hands around the gun and squeezing with all his might.

Little Willy Harpe lowered his forehead against the barrel of the Marshal's gun. "I once watched a man get fed into a threshing machine. He went in feet first, and it took awhile for the gears to grind up something vital enough that he died." Little Willy looked up at McParlan and said, "Go ahead and imagine what that's like."

McParlan shrieked and flopped around in the dirt. Harpe looked down at him and said, "Welcome to Golgotha."

McParlan's chin was low against his chest but he managed to summon the strength to lift it and spit at Little Willy's face, but his mouth was too dry, and all that came out was a rasp of air.

Little Willy signaled to Hank Raddiger to bring the beams. Hank struggled to drag the enormous metal X across the dirt toward them. Hank dropped the beams and bent over to try and catch his breath. He set a drill on the ground next to the X and placed four bolts beside it. "Here you go, Elijah," he panted. "Just like you said."

"You need to get better underlings, Little Willy. This one's too stupid to remember your name."

Harpe lifted McParlan's head by a handful of hair and said, "You lack faith, my son. Use this time to reflect and repent your sins." He walked over to the X and waved to the others, "Bring him."

Hank and the two Customs Officers hoisted McParlan into the air and carried him over to the X. They laid him down on top of it and spread his arms and legs along the tops of the crossed beams. McParlan started to struggle and Harpe said, "You will lie STILL." The Marshal went limp, and Harpe said, "But you may talk. And you may scream."

"Don't hold your breath, you piece of shit," McParlan said. He watched Harpe bend over to pick up one of the thick bolts with a pointed steel tip.

Harpe notched the bolt to his drill and gave it a spin, listening to the motor whir with satisfaction. Harpe bent over the first beam and pressed the tip of the bolt against McParlan's right wrist. "You ready?"

"Go to hell."

Harpe gave the trigger a light squeeze that sent chunks of McParlan's skin flying in every direction.

"Remember you can scream," Harpe said.

20. Always Outnumbered, Never Outgunned

Claire sat on her front porch, watching the sun hover over the mountains. She rocked back and forth and did not look at Jem as he came through the front door and stood by her. He dipped into his pocket for a pinch of sweet weed and tucked it into his lower lip, working it there until there was something to spit, but as he bent over the side of the porch Claire said, "Don't you get *any* of that filth on my steps. And I don't want it splashed all over my yard either."

Jem walked over to the other side of the porch and spat over the railing into the dirt. He wiped off his mouth and presented her with a sealed envelope that contained Old Man Willow's letter. He'd put a second letter with it that told her a bag of pure severian was under the floorboards in his old bedroom. He told her to look in the same place he'd hidden all of his secret stuff as a boy.

In his letter was a set of careful instructions on how Claire could find and hire a bounty hunter that could be trusted to dispatch two well-known politicians like Walt Junger and Billy Jack Elliot. He warned her not to reveal their identities until the bounty hunter agreed to the price and told her to keep half of the money until the deal was finished. Or, she could just let Royce Halladay read Old Man Willow's letter and he would probably take care of it for free.

"What is this?" Claire said.

"Some interesting reading in the event I don't come back. If I do come back here and it's already opened, I'm gonna be madder than hell at you."

"That stopped being a concern of mine years ago, Jem." Claire's blonde hair blew gently in the breeze and she looked up at him with eyes that were bluer than glaciers, but colder. "After all of this time waiting to hear if you were living or dead, you really think I give a rat's ass if you're mad at me?"

"No, I guess you wouldn't have a reason to."

"Then what happens when you do come back? You go running off into the same territory where daddy got killed. Then you almost get blown up by some goddamn maniac and his kid. And now you're running off to try and get yourself killed one *more* time. I don't love you anymore, Jem! I ran out of it when all you left me with was worry and anger."

"I understand," he said. He put his hand against the railing and looked out at the meadow. "You know, I had a dream about you last night. About the house, just like when we were little kids. He was in it too…if you know who I mean. You were just a little girl." He took a deep breath and looked down, trying to keep his voice steady, "Ever since the time I was too young to know better, death has been coming to this very door to snatch up the people I love most, Claire. First, it was the illness that took Ma. Then that native boy who I shot. Then that bastard Elijah Harpe came here and almost killed you and Frank. You want to know why I ran off when I did? Why I keep doing it? You'll laugh at this, trust me, it's a riot, but maybe if I keep running, death will follow me away. Maybe it won't come here looking for me anymore."

"That's the *stupidest* thing I ever heard," Claire said. She wiped her nose on her sleeve and said, "You always were stupid."

Jem smiled and nodded, "Yeah, now that I said it out loud, I guess it does sound kind of silly."

"Why are you going out there? Why does it have to be you?" Claire said. "Hasn't this family given enough already?"

"Jimmy McParlan's a good man, Claire. A lawman. The kind I ain't seen in a long, long time. Reminds me of someone."

Claire stood up out of her chair and wrapped her arms around him and buried her face in his chest. He kissed her on top of the head and said, "I'll be back soon. You'll see."

There was a pretty woman hanging laundry on a line between two trees in her front yard along Pioneer Way. She smiled at Jem when he rode past and he tipped his hat to her and said, "Hello, ma'am."

He had to navigate around a crowd of miners on Pioneer Way. They carried their lunch pails and laughed loudly as they chattered back and forth, talking about their lives and work. Farther ahead, Jem passed a second group heading in the opposite direction, going home after a long shift. Their faces and clothing were black with soot.

One of those men was going home to that pretty woman, Jem thought. She would draw him a bath and he would scrub while she made dinner. There would be children racing in and out of the wash room, excited to see him. He might have just busted his ass doing thankless work for twelve hours a day in the pits of hell, but at the end of it, he came home to his family, Jem thought, and I am jealous.

Workers were still shoveling out the blast site surrounding the Proud Lady. The bar itself was quiet, with some of the patrons leaning on the porch rails to chat with the workers. A few of the men said hello to Jem. He stopped at Anna Willow's office, but no lights were on, and he decided to keep going.

The front door to the Sheriff's Office was shut. There had been no trace of Walt Junger or Billy Jack Elliot since the day the Marshal left. There was a thin man standing near the security gate, smoking a hand-rolled cigar. Doctor Royce Halladay looked up at Jem from under his hat and said, "Well, well. I was beginning to think that you had a change of heart."

"What are you doing here, Doc?"

"I assumed that we were going to mount a rescue effort."

"Who told you that?"

"A gypsy woman read it for me in tea leaves and chicken innards."

Bart Masters led two destriers around the security gate while lugging a handheld mining device over his shoulder. "Don't listen to him, Jem. Anna told me when I went to pick this contraption up from Adam Wells."

"What the hell is that, Bart? You planning on drilling them to death?"

Bart unslung the laser's barrel and held it like a rifle. "That boy Adam is one mechanically inclined son of a gun, boy, I'll tell you. When it's time for me to show you what this puppy can do, just stand back and find something to hold onto." Bart looked over Jem's shoulder and said, "Didn't you bring anybody?"

"Claire's husband Frank wanted to come, but I told him he needed to stay and protect her. I think he's patrolling the front yard with a shotgun as we speak."

"Christ, we're gonna get crushed," Bart said.

"Jem and I have been through this type of thing before, young Bart, so look on the bright side," Halladay said. "You will probably be the first to go."

They set out into the wasteland. Halladay inventoried the ammunition in his belt and checked the spare battery packs in his vest. He removed the rifle from his saddle and worked the action several times then inspected both of his pistols by spinning the cylinders to make sure there was a bullet in each chamber. Halladay had a small Mantis revolver tucked into the front of his waistband, and when he showed it to Jem, Jem nodded approvingly and showed him the one hidden under his shirt.

Halladay drew a knife from his shoulder holster that was the length of his forearm and he held it up in the sunlight to inspect the edge. Jem shook his head at the sight of the weapon and said, "Guess we're covered in case a sword fight breaks out, then."

"I am a practitioner of the surgical arts, young man. One never knows when he will encounter a tumor that needs to be removed."

Both men looked over at Bart Masters. Bart confidently patted the mining laser's barrel lying across his lap.

"Is that really all you brought?" Halladay said.

"Just wait and see, old man. Just wait and see."

Halladay laughed out loud. "This is quite a crew indeed. A sick old man, a miner with a homemade space laser, and an outlaw with eyes as blue as the oceans of Luatica."

"Can't you be serious for just one moment?" Jem said. "There's at least four men down in that canyon aiming to kill us, one of who has some sort of unholy weapon powerful enough to make us shoot ourselves before we even get there."

"Forgive me, Jem," Halladay said. "I will try summon the appropriate dread at our imminent demise."

"Whatever," Jem said. "Just forget it."

They rode across the grey flatland in silence. The long row of mountains ahead seemed to reach high enough to scrape the sun. The first trail up the mountain was blockaded. "What the hell?" Bart said. "It was fine last week."

"Expect all of the other paths to be blocked off as well, save for the one at the far end of the canyon. It makes perfect sense to force us up that hill," Halladay said.

Bart Masters rode ahead of them and Royce Halladay waved for Jem to wait for a moment. "I do apologize if my attitude is distracting you."

"It's nothing, Doc. I'm just wired pretty tight right now. I don't like these odds."

"I have been a dead man walking this planet ever since that awful night so many years ago. Not a single day passes that I do not ask myself why the hell I'm still alive. This is my twenty-second year with a fatal disease, Jem. It is like God prefers to see me suffer." Halladay leaned close to Jem and said, "So forgive me if I do not pay much attention to the odds. And perhaps, as I ruminate on it a bit, I come to wonder if the Lord kept me alive all this time just so I could be at your side at this particular moment."

"That's a long way to come just to be outnumbered and outgunned, Doc."

Royce Halladay's eyebrows raised. "Pardon my correction, sir, but while there have been many occasions when I have been outnumbered, I have never once been outgunned."

Hank Raddiger lifted his binoculars to check the path, but all it did was give him a sharper view of the thick brush he was hidden under. He propped up on his elbows, keeping the assault rifle steady in one hand and the wireless remote device in his other.

He was alone on the overlook, the sole guardian of the beaten up wagon that the Customs Officers left in the center of the path. It was the only access road to the canyon that hadn't been blockaded, and whoever tried to get close around that wagon was in for a hell of a surprise, Hank though. The assault rifle was for whoever survived.

Except for Jem Clayton.

Clayton was not to be harmed under any circumstances. If Hank's first round hit Jem Clayton, the second round was going into his own mouth, Hank thought. To hell with trying to explain a screw-up to Elijah or Little Willy or whoever the hell he thought he was.

Hank heard something and froze, seeing a lone figure come walking up the path. The man was unarmed except for a large industrial device strapped over his shoulders with a long hose connected to it. Was it a flamethrower? Hank wondered. It looked like something farmers used to spray down their crops.

Bart Masters paused to look over the wagon and the rocky cliffs on either side of it. He even looked in the area where Hank was hidden, but gave no notice of seeing him. Hank raised the wireless remote and held his breath, counting the number of steps the man would have to take before he pressed the detonation button.

Bart flipped a switch on his backpack and it came alive with a growling, vibrating noise like an engine. He aimed down the length of the hose at the wagon and squeezed a trigger underneath it. There was a high-pitched whine and a red circle of light appeared on the surface of the carriage.

"What the hell?" Hank whispered. The red circle started to smoke and the side of the carriage melted and caught flame. The light painted the interior of the carriage, directly over the stacks of plastic explosives hidden within.

The explosive's sticky linings turned to ash and the fuses and wires connecting them sizzled as they melted. Hank tried to slam the button on the remote in time but nothing happened. He cursed and threw the remote aside, lifting the rifle to aim at the head of the idiot with the backpack. He was about to pull the trigger when the sole of a boot crushed his hand against the ground.

Hank lifted his head to scream but a large blade flashed in the sunlight and all he saw was a lean, ghostly looking man holding the knife. The ghost smiled cruelly and plunged the knife in as he whispered, "Ave atque vale."

Jimmy McParlan could not tell if it was dusk or if the clouds had just rolled over the sun momentarily. He wondered if his eyesight had weakened to the point that he could no longer tell day from night. He could only take small, shallow breaths and felt excruciating pressure on his chest from his suspended shoulders. Both shoulders had already popped out of their sockets, and his arms were numb to the point that he no longer felt the pain of the steel bolts driven through his wrists.

The steel bolts in his feet still hurt, especially when he moved and they ground against his bones. The buzzards had returned. Jimmy McParlan panted like a dog and waited for death. Death was slow in coming.

Something burned brightly, high above him. He managed to lift his head enough to see flames lighting the mountainside. Whatever was on fire creaked as it rocked back and forth until finally it tumbled over the side of the cliff and smashed against the rocky walls. It fell like a dead phoenix to the desert floor.

There were figures high above on the overlook, standing where the wagon had fallen from. McParlan grunted unintelligibly and closed his eyes, worried that now he was hallucinating.

The Customs Officer sprayed the edge of the cliff with bullets, and Bart Masters dove behind the ledge. He swung the laser barrel around and charged it, about to fire over the ledge when Jem shouted for him to wait.

"They've got McParlan down there, nailed to a goddamn cross or something. Hold your fire. That ship down there is full of fuel. If it ignites, you'll burn everything in that valley."

Bullets struck the cliff again and Halladay lifted his hand to shield his face from the rock spray. "What do you propose, then? Shall we hurl stones at them?"

A voice called out from the canyon below, "Jem Clayton! Can you hear me?"

Jem laid flat and inched close to the side enough to peer over. In the light of the burning carriage, Jem could see Little Willy Harpe standing next to a large metal contraption with McParlan crucified in the center of it. "You son of a bitch!" Jem shouted.

Harpe shrugged and said, "Don't be like that, Jem. I just want to talk to you."

"Send up the Marshal and you and me can talk all night."

"Well, I would but he doesn't seem to want to do much more than hang around down here. How about you come to me and we'll see what we can do?"

Jem tried to make out where the Customs Officers were firing from, but they were hidden in the shadows and smoke. "Set McParlan free and I'll come down."

"COME TO ME NOW!" Harpe's voice boomed.

Jem squeezed his eyes shut and braced himself, waiting to fight the irresistible command. Nothing happened. Jem opened his eyes and saw Bart Masters stand up and head down the path into the valley below. "Bart! What the hell are you doing?"

Masters ignored him and quickly began navigating the winding trail until Jem lost sight of him. "He's the next one going on the cross, Jem," Harpe said. "Unless you walk down here on your own like a man."

Royce Halladay stood up and started to follow Bart Masters. "Doc! Don't listen to him. Try and fight it."

Halladay stopped and turned around. "That is exactly what I intend to do," he said. "Now are you coming with me or not?"

They walked down into the canyon together, past the wagon's burning embers, past the rifles of the Customs Officers. As they got closer, Jem could see Jimmy McParlan's head hanging against his chest. The Marshal's head was hanging down so low that his hair covered his one eye. Firelight cast shadows across his naked, battered form, and Jem could not tell if the old man was breathing or not.

Bart Masters was standing next to Harpe with his arms stiff at his side, like a military man waiting to be inspected by a superior officer. Harpe waved for Jem and Halladay to keep coming closer.

Jem stopped in front of Harpe and said, "You must be the famous Little Willy."

"You think so?" Harpe said with a grin.

"Maybe there's something we can do to work this out?" Jem said.

"I don't think so--"

Jem pulled his pistol out so quickly that he nearly fired off a shot point blank at Little Willy's face before he could say, "STOP!" Jem's gun fired, but his hand stiffened around the gun's handle just as he pulled the trigger and bullet went wide, tearing Little Willy's left ear in half. Royce Halladay was frozen at Jem's side, his gun half-raised.

Harpe grimaced and pressed his hand to his ruined ear. He inspected the blood on his palm and looked at the stiffened faces of Jem and Doctor Halladay. "You are unbelievably fast, boy. That almost got me. Who do you two want to shoot first? The Marshal?"

Jem felt himself turning to aim his Defeater at McParlan's chest. "What about the one with the laser?" Harpe said. Jem tried to stop himself from drawing his second pistol but it was beyond his control. He raised his second gun and aimed it at the face of Bart Masters, who stood defenseless.

Harpe turned to Halladay. "How about you? Wouldn't you like to kill this moody little prick yet?"

Halladay stuck his gun against Jem's chest. Harpe rubbed his hands together and admired his handiwork. He pointed at Bart Masters and said, "Point that ray gun at the old man." Once Masters had done so, he said, "Oh my, but don't you boys look cinematic!"

Harpe circled around them, going from one man to the next. "I know you're all in there. I can feel you. I'd let you speak, but it would just be you talking tough or begging for mercy, and I simply don't have the patience for it." He stopped at Jem. "You know? I had all sorts of plans for you. We were going to have ourselves a little party after what you did to me. But since I've come back I've gained a whole new perspective and realized I have much bigger things on my plate. So, on the count of three, you're all going to fire and I will get on with the business of recreating the universe in my image. Ready?"

Harpe started to count. "One…two….what the hell?" He looked up and saw a figure standing high above them on the cliff. It was an old man, wearing a long robe with fringe dangling from the sleeves. His white hair blew in the swirl of wind that rose around him. The old man looked down at Harpe and clapped his hands together with such force that it echoed throughout the canyon.

Mahpiya of the Beothuk chanted into the winds and aimed his staff at the creature tucked beneath Harpe's arm. Clouds filled the sky and turned black as winds whipped through the trees overlooking the canyon, sending leaves and branches into the air. Mahpiya drew circles in the air with his staff and suddenly yanked back like he was dragging a fish from the sea with a rod and reel.

One of the creature's long tendrils ripped itself out of Harpe's belly. Its tendrils dripped blood as it shriveled. A second one ripped free of Harpe's neck and he gasped and clutched the open wound left there.

Mahpiya's chant filled the valley as two riders on destriers raced down into the canyon. Hooves beat the ground as the animal's enormous legs pivoted each impossible twist of the path. Bug was in the lead, using his knees to steer as he lifted his bow and sent an arrow sailing into Little Willy's leg.

One of the Customs Officers opened fire on Bug as the boy flew past. Bullets riddled the back of his destrier, sending blood and fur into the air. Haienwa'tha's destrier leapt from the trail onto the ground and the young warrior hurled an axe at the Officer. The Officer stared at the axe's long handle sticking out of his face before falling down dead.

Bug's destrier fell over mid-sprint, sending him skidding across the ground. The second Customs Officer tracked Bug's rolling form with his weapon, about to fire when an arrow whistled through the air at him from high above the canyon. Osceola watched his arrow puncture the Officer's right temple and raced across the dark ledge to get to Mahpiya's side.

The medicine man reached into the satchel around his waist for a handful of fluorescent powder. It crackled when he blew it from his palm, carrying through the air and raining on Harpe. Another tentacle unseated from Harpe and he dropped to one knee, screaming in pain.

Harpe reached up and snatched one of the creature's free tentacles and started to pull. "What are you doing?" he shouted.

"Give me back my body, you thief!" It was Little Willy's voice that came from his mouth. "Go back to the grave where you belong, Elijah!"

"Let me finish my work!" Elijah roared back. Little Willy had pulled the creature away so that it was only connected to him by its head. The head was sunk deep in his armpit with foot-long fangs, drinking from his heart endlessly.

Osceola drew his finest arrow and notched it in his bow, aiming at Harpe while he was bent over and wrestling to keep himself from ripping the creature off.

Mahpiya waved a fan of feathers in front of Osceola's arrow and stepped back, raising his hands to shout the last incantation. Osceola's arrow punctured the creature's bulbous head, making jets of green filth spew out of it. Harpe lifted his head back and gasped for breath. His hold on the men lessened for a moment, and Royce Halladay forced his pistol away from Jem's chest, straining to turn the weapon on Harpe.

Harpe hollered in outrage at Halladay, "No! No! Stop! I COMMAND YOU!"

Halladay's face turned purple and blood spilled out of his mouth. He started to cough but managed to take another step forward. Harpe shouted, "SUFFER! SUFFER!" making Halladay hunch over in pain, but still he took another step.

"Suffer," Harpe panted.

"Been doing that for as long as I can remember," Halladay said. He grabbed Harpe around the waist and spun him around to face Jem, shouting, "Shoot him!"

The creature made terrified high-pitched noises and was trying to re-attach itself to Harpe. Jem tried to turn and get one of his guns centered on the creature while Harpe struggled with Halladay even as the creature's tentacles lashed both of their faces. "Get the hell out of the way, Doc!" Jem shouted. "I don't have a clear shot!"

"If I let go, we're done for. Shoot now." Halladay looked at him and said, "As a friend, I am asking you, Jem. Shoot."

Jem cocked back the hammer of his Defeater and fired into the center of creature's head. The bullet passed through the creature's large mouth and punched through Little Willy's heart.

Royce Halladay let Harpe slide out of his hands and smiled at Jem, "Nice shot." Something burned in his chest and put his hand up to it just as a warm rush of blood spilled out of the hole from Jem's bullet. He looked at Jem and said, "Oh dear" before collapsing to the ground.

Jem ran to him and pressed both of his hands over the hole, trying to keep the blood inside. "Bart!" he shouted.

Bart Masters was bent over on his hands and knees, retching into the sand.

"Bart! We need help!"

Halladay coughed forcefully. "That truly was an admirable shot, Jem. Sam would be proud. I intend to discuss it with him in the next minute or so."

"Stop that. You aren't going to die. I'll get Anna and she'll fix you up. Just lay still."

Halladay coughed again, more fiercely this time and blood pumped into Jem's hands. "I have been dying for twenty years, my friend. I just needed the proper motivation to get it over with." Halladay's eyes searched the night sky above, peering at the limitless stars. He smiled gently and tears streamed down the sides of his face. He took one deep, final breath, and when he let it out he said, "There's my girl."

21. Snakes Trampled

Anna Willow stood waiting by the front gate with her medical bag ready. People had begun to crowd the town square as word about the rescue party spread. Bart's wife, Emma Masters, stood wrapped in a blanket. Her face was like a flood of full-blown despair held back by the last stitches of a torn suture. Emma's sister, Janet Walters, was at her side, and somehow, Janet managed to look even worse than Emma.

Adam Wells rocked back and forth, nervously touching the tip of each finger to his thumb over and over. Frank Miller sat in his wheelchair holding hands with his wife, drumming on the twelve-gauge shotgun sitting on his lap. Claire stood staring at the road beyond the security gate and did not look away.

When the sky darkened, candles were passed around to the people and their lights drew the customers out of the Proud Lady to come and see what was going on. Anna listened to people giving excited explanations, and leaned close to Claire to say, "What a bunch of gossip-hungry wretches too cowardly to go with them, but they'll stand here all night waiting to see some bloodshed."

A burst of automatic gunfire echoed from Coramide Canyon, and then another right behind it. As soon as the shooting stopped, one of the men said, "That's it. They're done for. Jem and Bart and Halladay are dead! Find every wagon you can and evacuate the town!"

Mothers scooped up their children and ran down Pioneer Way as men grabbed their wives by the arm and started dragging them away from the front gate.

Claire Miller picked up the shotgun from her husband's lap and fired it into the air.

Everyone stopped and turned to look at her standing there with the gun held high and smoke pouring out of the barrel. She lowered the gun and jacked the spent casing out and chambered another shell. Claire's face was still swollen and the salve on her bruises shined brightly in the candle's glare. "Marshal McParlan was the first one digging your sorry asses out of the rubble when the bomb went off, and then he gave himself over to his enemies to try and save a town full of people who didn't lift a finger when the time came to go rescue him. Royce Halladay ain't seen the inside of Seneca 6 since I was six years old, but he went. Bart Masters never got into a fight since the day I was born, but he went too."

People in the crowd said nothing and did not move except for the few that looked at the ground and scratched the back of their heads. "So now, if those brave men *are* dead, who is left to defend this place and these people?" She showed them the gun and said, "This gun belonged to Sheriff Sam Clayton, my daddy, the last lawman we ever had in this sorry excuse for a town. If he were here tonight you can bet your sweet ass he'd use it on the first son of a bitch who came through that gate to do us harm. Since he ain't, I'll do it for him. It's time somebody made a stand."

Janet Walker pointed behind Claire and screamed in panic.

"Not funny, Janet!" Claire barked, then as she turned to look, she saw a half-naked Beothuk warrior sitting on a destrier at the gate's entrance. Haienwa'tha was smeared with war paint across his face and torso, and he did not move when Claire lifted the gun at him and said, "Holy shit!"

"Hoka hey," Haienwa'tha said. He raised his empty hands in the air and said, "Hoka Hey! El-halcon kola owa sich!"

"Give me that gun, Claire," someone shouted. "Shoot him!"

"Shut your mouth, goddamn it," Claire shouted back, never taking her eyes off of Haienwa'tha. "You stay right there, boy, or I will blow a hole through you. Now, what the hell are you trying to say?"

"El-halcon." Haienwa'tha formed his hands into a pair of guns and made firing noises, saying, "Pow pow." Claire shook her head in confusion and Haienwa'tha sighed in exasperation. He struggled with himself for a moment before finally saying, "El-halcon, friend. Haienwa'tha, friend. Friends hurt. Need medicine."

"Medicine?" Anna said.

Haienwa'tha nodded quickly, "Medicine, yes. For friend."

"I have medicine!" Anna said, holding up her medical bag. She ran past Claire toward his destrier and said, "Take me to them."

Haienwa'tha looked at the crowd of angry-looking people and at Claire's gun, then nodded and held out his hand to her.

"Get away from him, Anna," Claire said. "It ain't safe!"

Anna looked back at her and said, "This is me making a stand, Claire."

Haienwa'tha grabbed Anna's hand and yanked her up onto the back of his destrier, and with a kick in the animal's side, they were gone.

McParlan's wrist had torn free of its bolt and was dangling at this side. Jem and Bart lifted the heavy beams out of the ground and lowered them so that the Marshal was lying flat. Bart went to look for the drill, and Jem tried to rouse McParlan. There was no response.

Masters came back with the drill and said, "Let's get him off that thing." They worked quickly to unscrew the bolts from McParlan's wrist and ankles. Once they had him freed, they lifted the old man off of the cross and carried him over to the soft dirt. "We need water," Jem said. He looked up and saw Bug nearby, leaning over the body of his dead destrier. The boy rubbed his hands over the creature's soft black fur and squeezed his eyes shut to keep tears from spilling out of them.

"Bug!" Jem shouted. "Hey! Quit that. I need you." The boy wiped his face and looked at Jem. Jem pointed into the ship and said, "Go in there and find me water. Understand?" He tipped his hand to his mouth like he drinking Bug jumped to his feet and took off running.

Mahpiya arrived at the base of the trail and starting digging in his bag, sifting through the powders and roots inside of it. The medicine man's expression was grave as he kneeled beside McParlan and muttered prayers, waving his hands over the Marshal's face and heart.

Bug returned with a bottle and Jem poured a small amount of water against McParlan's cracked lips. The old man stirred slightly.

Mahpiya lifted McParlan's wrist and inspected the hole. He gave a sharp command to Bug, who took off running again. Mahpiya aimed a crooked finger at Jem's gun and held out his hand for it. Jem put his hand over his weapon and said, "Hell no. We'll wait and see what Anna says."

Osceola squeezed Jem's shoulder and nodded.

Jem reluctantly removed one of his Defeaters and handed it to Mahpiya. "Don't shoot him. I mean it. He's old and ugly and meaner than a grizzly bear, but I like the old coot."

Mahpiya opened the gun and removed a bullet from the cylinder. He drew a long, curved knife from his belt and stuck the tip into the bullet's casing, prying until the bullet snapped open. He held the casing over McParlan's wrist and tapped until a small amount of gunpowder sprinkled into the wound there. Mahpiya did the same over the other injuries and waved for the men to stand back.

Bug raced toward them with a flaming torch of wagon wood. Its bright light flickered and left a long trail of smoke that spiraled up toward the high rock walls above. Mahpiya took the torch and waited for Bug to go stand with the others. He lowered the torch to the hole in McParlan's wrist and ignited the gunpowder. Flames shot through the wound and out of the hole on the other side of his wrist. Mahpiya set fire to the other wounds, and stepped back.

McParlan hollered and kicked when he realized there were flames erupting from his wrists and feet like rockets. He beat the ground until the flames went out and Jem grabbed him to hold him steady. "Help is on the way, Marshal. Just hold on."

"No more of your help, goddamn it! At least the other sons of bitches didn't set me on fire."

Jem carried a torch around the site, setting fire to any pieces of the creature he found. To his disgust, he saw the tiny mouths on each sucker still moved, and the severed tentacles writhed and curled up as he set them aflame. The main portion of the thing was still attached to Little Willy. Its swollen head pulsated, as if it were still clinging to life despite all of the damage inflicted on it. The bullet hole in the center had clotted with gray pus and Jem drove the flaming torch into the hole, making the creature squeal and shrivel.

Bart Masters walked along the canyon floor kicking any remaining pieces of the thing into the wagon fire. Jem helped him carry the Customs Officers over to the fire and pitch them in. They picked up Little Willy Harpe and were about to do the same when Bug ran over, waving his hands.

Bug bent over Little Willy's head and grabbed a handful of hair. He started to saw the scalp line with his blade. He worked until the black mass of hair came free in his hand and he held it up with a loud, Beothuk screech. He showed the others his trophy, and both Osceola and Mahpiya raised their fists and returned his call.

Bart and Jem heaved Little Willy into the flames. His body crashed into the boards and his clothing caught fire. Jem watched until his face turned black and there was no other reason to keep looking. Harpe was finished.

A destrier worked its way down the path and Jem saw Anna Willow sitting behind Squawk. Her hands clutched the young man's waist as the animal lumbered dangerously close to the edge of the steep trail. Squawk laughed at her nervousness and brought the destrier to a stop at the bottom. She took up her medical bag and walked around the fire, but started to run when she saw Jem.

He caught her in his arms, mid-stride. "I'm ok," he said. "I'm all right."

Anna stepped back and collected herself. "I thought you were hurt. Who needs me?"

Jem walked her over to where McParlan was lying on a Beothuk blanket. He described the injuries and how Mahpiya had cauterized the wounds. The Marshal looked up and said, "These fools didn't want to rescue me. They wanted to turn me into a barbeque."

"Where's Doctor Halladay?" Anna said. She looked around the canyon and saw a body rolled up tightly inside another Beothuk blanket. "Oh God. Oh no."

Jem held up his hand and said, "Not now. There's later for that."

They fashioned makeshift drag sleds from pieces of metal looted from the Customs ship, one for the Marshal and one for the body of Doctor Halladay. The younger Beothuk navigated the trail carefully to get the sleds up and out of the canyon. The Marshal's complaining got louder at each bump in the road, but no one minded.

Everyone else started up the trail on foot except Jem, who went into the Customs ship and emerged carrying a jug of fuel in each hand. He splashed fuel around the ship and covered the metal X. He soaked the ground where the rotting remains of Elijah Harpe lay. He formed a ring around the crash site with fuel until it was empty, then tossed both containers onto the ground.

Bart Masters was waiting at the edge of the cliff with his laser in hand. He waited until Jem was high enough on the trail to throw the switch that sent the backpack rumbling to life. Bart picked a spot on the ship and squeezed the trigger, shining a red dot on the fuel lines that sparked as it cut through the steel casing.

The fuel inside the tank ignited and set off waves of flame that engulfed the rear of the ship and shattered the observation windows. The fuel on the ground sparked and flames shot eight feet into the air, racing along the wet trails like fiery horses of the apocalypse. Jem had to shield his eyes from the intense heat. He looked for as long as he could while the valley below was cleansed by flames.

Two men waited in the darkness at the base of the mountain. They sat on their destriers without moving, watching the party descend. Anna Willow leaned past Jem and said, "That's Billy Jack and Walt. What the hell do they want?"

"We're not here for trouble," Billy Jack Elliot said. "Just to talk. It's time you learned the truth about a few things, Jem."

"You wouldn't know the truth if it bit you!" Anna shouted.

"That's enough out of the women-folk," Walt Junger said. "What we have to say is only for men. Not for women and not for savages."

Jem turned to Bart Masters and said, "Take Anna and the Marshal back to camp."

McParlan sat up in the back of his drag sled and said, "Don't be stupid, boy. This is a goddamn trap."

"I agree," Jem said. "Those two just don't know it yet." He walked his destrier over to the Beothuk and said, "You saved our lives back there. Whatever you thought you owed me, we're settled up now."

Osceola looked at Mahpiya, who spoke Beothuk to him and pointed at Jem, the canyon, and the werja fangs on Jem's neck. Osceola looked at Jem in confusion.

"We're square," Jem said. "I did something for you and you did something in return. We're even."

Osceola reached for the inside of Jem's wrist and grasped it firmly. He pointed at Jem's heart, then back at his own, and shook his head no.

Jem smiled with understanding and said, "I like that much better, to be honest."

They rode until the mountains ahead were silhouetted by the light of both moons. "I know you have hard feelings for us, Jem," Billy Jack Elliot said. "After we show you what's up here, you'll feel differently."

"Is that right?" Jem said. He stayed back while Elliot and Junger rode ahead of him, wanting to keep them both in his view.

"In fact, this looks to be about the right place," Walt Junger said. The road was dark and narrow from the thick, overgrown brush along either side. Jem recognized the path that led to the mountain pass where he'd seen Squawk for the first time.

Billy Jack Elliot turned his destrier to face Jem. His voice was smoother than a rattlesnake's hides when he said, "It is time you knew the truth about your father's death. He was not killed by the Beothuk. We lied to you, and we are so very sorry."

"Well, what happened then?"

"We would have told you sooner, if you hadn't run off like you did. We figured it would be best to let the dead rest," Junger said.

"You going to tell me or does this overture keep going for awhile?"

"Old Man Willow shot your daddy," Walt Junger said. "That crazy old bastard got angry with your father when he found out Sam wanted to marry his daughter Anna. I know it's hard to hear, but it's the Lord's solemn truth. It was probably on accident, but Old Man Willow shot him. I swear to God."

"It was an act of self defense, Jem," Elliot said. "Now, we both know that you idolize your father, but he was far from perfect. Just like the rest of us. He went to grab Old Man Willow and Willow's gun went off."

"We should have told you the truth a long time ago, and given Sam a proper burial," Junger said.

Elliot nodded, "We were afraid of the scandal it would cause both your families. You've already been through so much."

"We admit that we were wrong," Junger said.

Jem smiled at that. "Well, now we're getting somewhere."

Walt Junger tapped his heel against his destrier's side and started moving it forward. His voice flowed with honey and sugar when he said, "I know this might be a shock for you, but I've been thinking that you could be my Chief Deputy. What do you say? Another Clayton in the Sheriff's Office of Seneca 6 has a mighty nice ring to it. Your daddy was Chief Deputy for years before taking over. You could do the same."

Junger was blocking Jem's view of Billy Jack Elliot, and Jem stayed still, anticipating the moment to come. Junger yanked his reins to the side and Billy Jack Elliot came riding up behind him with a Winchester rifle ready to fire.

Jem kicked his destrier in the ribs and it ran forward, crashing into Junger's steed. Jem grabbed Junger by the collar and held him fast, keeping his body between himself and Elliot's rifle. Junger tried to push away, but Jem grabbed the Colt Defeater from his right hip and stuck the barrel into Junger's stomach. He fired twice as Elliot rode past, splattering the Mayor with Junger's blood.

Elliot's destrier stopped running and he turned around, wide eyed, still holding his rifle but too astonished to do anything with it. Jem pushed Walt Junger out of his saddle and watched him fall dead on the ground. He raised his pistol to Elliot and said, "When you see Old Man Willow, thank him for warning me about your little trick."

Billy Jack Elliot dropped his rifle and spun in his saddle, leaping to the ground and running down the road on foot. Jem spurred his destrier and holstered his gun. Within seconds, the horse was beside Elliot, and Jem reached out to snatch him by the back of his coat.

Jem pulled Elliot's collar against his knee and lifted until only the toes of Elliot's boots dragged on the ground. Jem yelled for his destrier to go faster, until the wind rushing through Jem's ears was even louder than the Mayor's screams.

Birds took flight along the road at their approach and animals scattered out of the road at the sounds of the stampede. Jem rode close to a thicket of vines and barbed branches dangling from the rock wall and kicked Elliot into them.

Elliot bounced and rolled into the vine's tangled lengths. He attempted to free himself and only snared his arms and legs more completely. Eliot's head hung low and he said, "Cut me loose, Jem."

"Nope."

"You can't leave me here."

"Sure I can."

"I didn't do anything wrong, Jem. I told you what happened...it was...Old Man..." A deep howl high up in the mountains silenced Elliot as he struggled to look for its source. "What the hell was that?"

"That's your company for this evening," Jem said. "I'll go so you can all get acquainted."

Billy Jack Elliot watched Jem ride off, and managed to get his head out of the vines enough to see the shapes of several large creatures coming down the mountainside.

22. Heroes

Seneca 6's main square was empty, except for Anna Willow and Claire Miller. Claire's husband, Frank, was curled up asleep on the Sheriff's front porch with his coat draped over him like a blanket. Claire had gotten tired of telling him to go home and being ignored. She finally told him he could stay if he laid down and stayed quiet.

Jem rode through the gate and got down from his destrier to hug both women. Anna said, "What did those two skunks want?"

"Just to discuss a few things. They decided not to come back once they heard what I had to say."

"Well, good riddance," Claire said. There were shouts of laughter from inside the Proud Lady, followed by applause. Someone yelled out, "Tell that part again!" Claire shook her head and said, "See what you did? All anyone saw was Bart Masters riding back with Anna in one arm and dragging that Marshal in the other like he was some kind of storybook hero. They threw him up on their shoulders and carried him into the Proud Lady and we ain't seen none of them since."

"He's had to tell the story so many times that the latest version is you killed a twenty-foot space monster with your bare hands and he blew up a fleet of space cruisers with a ray gun," Anna said.

"Maybe it wasn't twenty feet," Jem said with a wink. "It was hard to tell with the armada closing down on us."

"You should go in there, Jem," Claire said. "They'll want to fawn all over you too, I expect."

"How's the Marshal?"

"His wounds will take time, and he'll be pretty immobile for awhile, but he should walk normally again," Anna said. "As long as he listens to me and stays put and I can manage to keep Janet away from him."

Jem opened the Marshal's bedroom door and walked into the dim-lit room. Jimmy McParlan was sitting up in bed looking at him. "I thought that girl told you to be quiet."

"You must be feeling better," Jem said.

"I'm fine and dandy after the stuff she pumped into me. Before you got here I was watching little pink bunnies dance around my room." Both of McParlan's wrists were bandaged and there were thick casts wrapped around his legs from his kneecaps to the tips of his toes. "Still hurts though."

"Want me to stay with you?"

"Hell no, you damn fool. You think this is the first time I've been crucified and set on fire?" McParlan smiled and said, "I'll be fine. Now take that pretty doctor lady home and make sweet love to her, boy."

"I don't know about that," Jem said.

"Then send her in here and I'll give it a whirl. She needs to promise to be careful with me though. I'm in kind of a fragile state."

Anna and Jem walked together toward the Proud Lady. Men standing on the porch saw him coming and called out to the people inside, "Jem's back!"

People flooded onto the street and surrounded him. Someone passed a bottle of whiskey through the crowd until it landed in Jem's hand.

"Nothing like a sip of whiskey after killing a fifty foot space monster," he said, nodding his head at Bart Masters. He uncorked the bottle and lifted it to his lips when Bart Masters said, "Wait a second, Jem."

Bart raised a glass and said, "Welcome home, we missed you. Bout time you showed up."

They came to Anna's front door and Jem stopped, scraping his foot on the porch. "What is it?" Anna said.

He laughed to himself and said, "McParlan told me to take you home and make *'sweet love'* to you. Sounds kind of creepy to hear him say it."

Anna put her hand against her face and feigned blushing. "Would that be such a terrible thing to have to do?"

He looked at her in the twin moonlight. "No. In fact, I aim to do exactly that. But maybe not tonight, if that's okay."

"Tell you what," Anna said. "Let me draw you a hot bath and get you out of those godforsaken clothes. When you get out, my bedroom door will be open. You can do whatever you want after that."

Anna walked into the house and headed toward the wash room. The pipes clanged as she cranked the handles and jets of warm water opened up to fill the copper basin. Jem went inside and shut the door. He stood in the doorway as Anna unbuckled his gun belt. She bent to grab his boots, telling him, "Lift your foot."

"You don't need to do that."

"You might as well get used to it. In this house we leave our boots on the porch. If you're going to stay here, you need to learn the rules."

"Actually, I was thinking about taking up in the Halladay house. I thought you might go over there with me and take a look at it tomorrow."

She yanked on the toe and heel of his first boot and slid it off. There was a hint of disappointment when she said, "If that's what you want to do." She held the boots away from her like they were filled with sewage. "Get out of those clothes so I can boil them. You smell worse than an outhouse."

Jem stripped and climbed into the copper basin. He settled down into the hot water and let it soak into his muscles. Anna came back into the washroom and pressed a sponge against his neck and started to scrub him. Jem closed his eyes and rested.

Old Man Willow's map was not easy to follow, with its stick figures and pyramid mountains. Jem stood on the place that he thought resembled the map's "X" and looked around the road, not far from where Walt Junger had died.

Any evidence of that night was gone. The bodies of both Junger and Elliot were gone. It was hard country in the wasteland, and Jem kicked a rock into the ditch that ran alongside the road. There were piles of rocks and dirt scattered by two decades of violent dust storms and the occasional flood.

Jem walked along the ditch inspecting the rocks. He dug out a few with the shovel he borrowed from Claire and after a few minutes, became frustrated and moved on. He came to a large pile of rocks buried on top of one another, cemented together with dried mud. He shattered the pile with his pickaxe and started to pry up a round stone from the ground when he realized it was the ball joint of a human femur.

He bent down and dug out the rest of the bone with his hands and starting searching for more. There were various pieces of a skeleton within feet of each other and soon, Jem had enough to assemble large portions of the legs and spine. He dug deeper and the ground started to cave in over an animal's hole. He stuck his hand into the dirt and his fingers went through what felt like large holes in a bowling ball and he yanked a human skull out of the ground. He sat by the side of the road, turning the skull over in his hands and brushing the dirt away.

He found tattered fabrics and as he cleaned them off, recognized them as pieces of the shirt Sam Clayton was wearing the morning he left from the Willow house.

Jem set everything aside and sat on the road for a long while. After some time, he folded all of the bones inside a blanket and placed it on the back of his wagon. He went back to re-check the area and kept digging until his shovel hit something metal in the dirt.

Sam's leather gun belt was stiff as a rock and both Colt Defenders were still in the holsters. He had to force the guns out of the holsters and smack them against the ground to break open the cylinders. The guns were still loaded, but the bullets were corroded to the point that Jem had to dig the rounds out of the chambers with his knife.

He cocked one of the hammers back and dry fired the gun. The action still worked.

Jimmy McParlan was standing hunched over on a set of crutches at the security gate to Seneca 6. Pain was etched across his face and sweat ran down his forehead. "What the hell are you doing out here?" Jem said. "Anna will kill you if she catches you out of bed."

The Marshal rested on one of the crutches and took his hat off. He turned to face the casket and nodded, "I came to pay my respects. Heard a lawman was coming home."

"It's just a pile of bones, Marshal."

McParlan squinted at Jem and said, "Seems like all the elected officials in this town have run off. Got any ideas about what happened to them?"

"Only what I already said about the subject."

"Is that right? Well, being that I'm the closest thing to the government left in this town, it's my responsibility to appoint emergency persons who can keep everything from going to hell.

What do you think of that Bart Masters fella? He seems like the even-minded sort."

"I couldn't think of a more decent person, Marshal." Jem fished in his pocket for the Sheriff's badge and held it out, "My father would be proud to know Bart was wearing his badge."

McParlan looked at the worn badge without reaching for it and said, "You really are dense, boy. I meant as the *Mayor*, not the Sheriff. *You're* going to be the damn Sheriff."

Jem laughed and said, "I don't think so. I'm not exactly a law-abiding enough citizen to enforce it."

"I've seen a lot of men with badges in my day, Jem. Most weren't worth a squirt of piss when it came down to the important parts of the job. I think you've got the stuff."

"Can I have some time to think it over?"

"Hell no. The way you people treat visitors, I might not be around much longer. Besides, who are you kidding? We both know what you'll say. Now get going and take that man home. He earned some rest." McParlan propped himself against the security gate to stand upright and saluted Sam's remains. "Hurry up, damn it, before I pass out."

Jem headed toward Claire and Frank's home. He thought about what he would say to Claire, and whether she would want to see what was inside the blanket before Jem dug a hole beside their mother's grave and laid the blanket inside of it. He wondered if she'd say no and be angry at him for asking. He wondered if she'd say yes and regret it.

The badge stayed in his hand while he rode, and he ran his thumb over the letters spelling Sheriff over and over. He could still picture Sam leaning back in the rocking chair on Old Man Willow's porch saying, *"Someday when you're an attorney out on some big Metropolis-Class planet, you'll look back on all this with amazement, I bet. All this fighting and killing over what? A barren bunch of land with the misfortune of having some of the rarest stones in the galaxy buried underneath it."*

"What if I said I'm not going anywhere? Maybe I'll be a Sheriff just like you?" Jem said.

"Just like me?" Sam said.

Claire's home was in sight now. Jem tucked the badge into his left shirt pocket and felt it bounce against his chest as he rode. He put his hand over it and pressed it to his heart and said, "That's right."

About the Author

www.BernardSchaffer.com

Bernard Schaffer is an author, full-time police detective, and father of two.

His novel, THE THIEF OF ALL LIGHT, will be released by Kensington Publications in Summer 2018.

As a twenty-year law enforcement veteran, he is a decorated criminal investigator, narcotics expert and child forensic interviewer. Schaffer is the author of numerous independently published books and series. He lives and works in the suburbs of Philadelphia, PA. Visit him @BernardSchaffer or www.bernardschaffer.com

The Bernard Schaffer Author Facebook Fan Page

Email: Contact@BernardSchaffer.com
Twitter: @BernardSchaffer

QUALITY ASSURANCE

At Dia de los Toros Publications, our goal is to provide incredible literary value to our readers for extremely fair cost. Our commitment to professionalism extends beyond the sale of our books. Please email us if you have found any errors with this publication (must be current-gen), and upon their verification, we will send you a special gift.

WE LOVE READER REVIEWS

Thank You for Your Purchase. Please know how important reviews are to our publishing company, which dedicates itself to providing quality and innovation to its discerning readership. Your continued support means the world to us.

Available from Bernard Schaffer

THE THIEF OF ALL LIGHT

SUPERBIA

WAY OF THE WARRIOR

GUNS OF SENECA 6

GRENDEL UNIT

And Much More!

Bernard Schaffer

Published by Dia de los Toros Publications

91564351R00165

Made in the USA
Lexington, KY
23 June 2018